A
Perfect
Mistake

M.T. OUTLAW

(A Sequel to *Discovering Yesterday*)

PAGE PUBLISHING, INC.
Conneaut Lake, PA

First originally published by Page Publishing 2020

ISBN 978-1-6624-0494-8 (pbk)
ISBN 978-1-6624-0495-5 (digital)

Printed in the United States of America

For Blue and Dexter

CHAPTER 1

The Joys and Perils of Returning Home

For some reason not understood by Dag Peyton, his flight from San Francisco to Honolulu was not an altogether pleasant one. He had lived for many years on the island and was quite familiar with the length of the flights to and from the mainland. He was also familiar over the years with uncomfortable seats that never seemed to accommodate his tall frame. In addition, he was aware that, to many, airline food sometimes left something to be desired.

The only problem with all that was that his flight was incredibly smooth, his seat was very comfortable since he was in his beloved seat 6L on his favorite airline, and the food was delicious. In fact, Dag often enjoyed surprising his friends by telling them that he indeed loved airline food. They would look at him in disbelief, but when he was a young adult and had the opportunity to expand his horizons, everything was so new and so exciting, and he fell in love with adventure, even the adventure of a strange new dish served on an airline. Yes, things were in sync for Dag for the first time in a long time. He even drifted off to sleep a couple of times listening to Gordon Lightfoot's "Carefree Highway":

> Carefree highway, let me slip away...
> Slip away on you...

So Dag could not quite grasp why there was such a longing in his mood, such a hesitation to be happy. Was he just a backward kind of guy? Did he actually relish having a contemplative mood that was sometimes melancholy? Dag just decided he would think about all this later.

He was returning to the island after a few weeks in the Bay Area. In fact, there was every reason to be happy, even joyful. He had returned to San Francisco after a long absence. He began his adult life there and was planning on making the city his home, yet there was a set of unfortunate circumstances that made him leave in 1979, only to be called back by a mysterious letter from a long-lost friend. When he did return, he reconnected with dear friends and actually was instrumental in solving a mystery which not only brought closure to many people but also helped him to realize that his reason for leaving in the first place all those years ago was unnecessary. Still, as a result of the trip, he felt as if all the puzzle pieces were in place, and he had a huge burden lifted from his shoulders—hence the lack of clarity as to why he still sensed some inner turmoil. Dag wondered why he was so pensive during the flight. He wondered if all the excitement of his very productive trip to the Bay Area made him realize that with so many of his problems resolved, he might be returning to a lackluster life, one that prior to the trip he relished. *No,* Dag thought, *that doesn't ring true, either.* He loved his life. He decided that he was just going to have to learn to live with a contentment that had alluded him for many years. He laughed to himself, thinking, *Well, you know there are worse things than peace and contentment.*

Dag's temporary uneasiness was placed on the back burner for a time when he arrived at the airport and was met by his colleague and friend, DJ. They had worked at the university in the business department for quite a few years, and they shared great respect for one another. For this reason, Dag knew he owed DJ a long and detailed explanation for why he skipped town during their last break, interrupting a dinner in fact, and gave no explanation. He was aware that DJ was perhaps one of the most understanding people he'd ever met, which was all the more reason Dag wanted to cover with great clarity his sudden departure, as well as his silence for several weeks. Dag was a bit hesitant to see DJ. He was fully aware that he could at times be remote with people, but it was not what Dag intended. He realized in hindsight what it must have been like to DJ for Dag to abruptly jump up and leave the Cove, their favorite hangout, that evening, without so much as an explanation. While he had no intention of being rude, Dag was so focused at times that his sense of common courtesy was at times lacking.

As Dag walked out into the sunshine, he looked right and then left and caught a glimpse of DJ in his jeep pulling up to the curb. "You have impeccable timing," Dag said as he opened the passenger side door and dropped into the vehicle, hoisting his duffel bag into the back seat at the same time.

"Well, we aim to please," DJ offered in a friendly tone. Dag wondered why, a moment earlier, he'd had any trepidation at all about seeing DJ again. DJ was a solid guy, a true friend. He understood the deep sense of connection and subtle nuances that make a friendship a true relationship. Dag briefly thought to himself that he worried too much.

The two picked right up where they'd left off the evening Dag leaped off his barstool at the Cove, surprising the very few patrons who were there that evening and hurried out the door without explanation before dinner had even arrived. Surprisingly, DJ asked no questions and was the same caring and jovial friend that Dag had known since they met. This made Dag feel badly in a way, almost with a tinge of guilt. He could not wait to tell DJ the whole story to vindicate himself.

"DJ, I have not always been the most considerate friend," Dag admitted, "yet I believe when I explain to you what has happened over the past few weeks, you will see why I reacted the way I did and why I have been so closed-mouthed about the goings-on."

DJ responded, "Dag, I would start by stating that you do not owe me an explanation, and that is true, but I believe you want to explain, and I must admit that I want to know, so I am not going to go through the process of letting you off the hook. We would just be wasting our time." With those words, DJ smiled the way he often did when he was being lighthearted, which made Dag smile as well.

Dag remained silent, yet in his mind he was thinking that in his life, he must have done something right to have crossed paths with such a good friend. DJ was kind and loyal to a fault, and while he would tolerate many forms of discourteous and abrupt and rude behavior, he was no doormat. Dag admired him greatly.

As DJ dropped Dag off at his downtown efficiency apartment, Dag hopped out and said, "Well, want to meet at the Cove later this evening? You have my word that I will not skip out on you this time, and I think you deserve a long explanation."

"Sounds good, buddy," DJ said as he drove away.

So now the stage was set for a story, an exciting yet true tale that had an ending that was happy, sad, fulfilling, and lacking…all at once. Dag found himself anxious to tell the story.

CHAPTER 2

Making Things Right...
and a Surprise

Dag was happy as he made his way to the Cove that evening. It was that same old twenty-minute walk he'd taken many times in downtown Honolulu, yet he had missed it; and when he reached the door of the Cove, his favorite little bar and grill that was tucked into a side street near Alakea Street downtown, he felt as if he were at home again and getting back to his old life. He welcomed the walk, the familiarity, and the peace that washed over him from being in a place that as a boy he knew he'd one day be, a place of his own in a city of his own with a life experience that was unique, off the beaten path, and sometimes surreal.

Dag sauntered into the Cove that evening, made the brief trip to the back, and sat at one of those rickety bar stools that he knew would collapse one day but likely not without him in it. DJ had not made the scene yet, so Dag thought he might as well look for Sally, the server who always gave them grief during their outings at the Cove.

"Looking for someone?" he heard a voice say from close behind him. Dag swung around and found Sally, boisterous and direct as ever. Dag smiled, nodded, and awaited his first insult. "Listen, Goober," she began, "last time you were here several weeks ago, you ordered a cheeseburger but didn't take the time to wait to get it.

Guess you were busy…so I saved it for you." Just as Dag registered her words and his lip began to curl to demonstrate pure disgust, Sally broke out in a laugh that could be heard throughout the little dive. As Dag turned around to see who was now looking at them due to Sally's guffaw, he noticed DJ coming in through the door, smiling, as was his way.

"Guy," Dag pleaded, "please come and save me from the clutches of this woman. She's got it in for me." A smile crept across the right corner of Dag's mouth.

"Don't worry, I'll save you," DJ said, turning to Sally. Then DJ directed all his energy toward the loud yet delightful server they had known for years. "Say, Sally, could you get us a couple of cheeseburgers that are not made of leather for once?"

"I don't know. Could you get an attitude that doesn't tell everyone what an imbecile you are?" Sally shot back without blinking. Dag was convinced that Sally could have been a superb stand-up comedian.

The three of them laughed, and as Sally walked by, she whispered to Dag, "Glad to have you back." Dag had never been directly complimented by Sally in his life. It was one of those unexpected sweet moments when someone, out of nowhere, tells you what you mean to them. Dag would not forget the moment.

With all the pleasantries out of the way, Dag was happy to now be able to turn his attention to DJ.

"Well, buddy," Dag began, "you have a story coming your way, and I'd like to get it off my chest. I have been told that I can be aloof and detached, but I want you to know that I have never done anything to intentionally derail our friendship. It means so much to me. If anyone deserves an explanation for the goings-on of the past few weeks, it is you. So grab a drink and settle in…"

All DJ had to say was, "Shoot."

Dag then related the story of what happened since he had last sat at those very barstools with DJ several weeks earlier. "I left here abruptly last time we were here because a former life had rushed into my psyche all at once, and I had to get closure. I immediately went home that night and made reservations for San Francisco. I hopped a red eye on Sea Coast Airlines, and three hours after I was sitting here with you, I was in the air and headed northeast to the Bay Area.

"You see, DJ, I graduated with my bachelor's degree and immediately left the South and headed to San Francisco," Dag began.

"Yes, I know something about that," DJ joined in the conversation.

"Well," Dag continued, "my family and I had visited there several times when I was a kid, and I grew to love the city. I immediately made two great friends named Jack and Annie. Annie connected me with a community health organizer position at the clinic where she worked, and my life was off and running. Jack and Annie came over to my loft frequently, and we had the time of our lives. You would love them.

"Well, it was the end of August of 1979, Jack's birthday in fact, and I invited him and Annie over to my place for steaks. The elderly woman who owned my place had a grill situated between her loft and the one next door, and all were welcome to use it. Anyway, as it turned out, Annie was unable to come that evening, so Jack and I had steaks and wine and talked for hours. Jack was staying over at my place because his place was being renovated. Late that night, Jack asked if I wanted to go down to a neighborhood place for a nightcap. We went down there, had coffee instead, and then made our way back to my place to get some sleep. As we reached my place, we noticed firetrucks and a crowd. It finally dawned on us that the fire was at the loft of my new neighbors. As the events began to catch up to our thought processes, the possibility hit us that the grill could have caused the fire. You can imagine how the thought of causing the death of someone could mess with a person's mind.

"Being young and impetuous, I saw no way out of the situation but to leave the city, as if leaving would mean leaving the memory and the guilt behind me. Of course, that didn't happen, and I spent the last forty years with the idea in the back of my mind that I likely caused a fire that ended the lives of the young couple and their son who lived in the next loft. There were times when I would forget about it, but then out of nowhere it would invade my thoughts, and it surprised me every single time—that pain, that worry, that sadness.

"To make a long story a bit shorter, I discovered through my new reconnection with Jack as a result of the letter you brought to me here that I was not the one who caused the fire. Still, I recalled some things that night that set my old friends and myself on a track to solve this mystery of who started the fire and why. It turns out that I had actually seen two of the characters in this drama on the street that night. They were hurriedly walking away from the fire."

"Well," DJ prompted, "what happened? Did you find out who did it?"

"Yes, we did, my friend. As it turned out, there were connections of the couple in the loft next door to the syndicate in Brazil as well as to the richest people in town, and as is my luck, I happened to move next door to this hotbed of activity in 1979."

"Are you kidding?" DJ offered excitedly. "Your lucky day!"

"Indeed," Dag said sarcastically. They both laughed. "Since I had moved next door to this activity, a rich shipping magnate in town who was in the middle of the controversy, and whom I might add was one of the kindest and most generous people I've ever met, needed at the time to discover whether or not I was involved, since I had moved in right in the middle of these events, so he secretly set up a position at the clinic, since he knew the director of the clinic, so that he could interact with me and watch me at the same time."

"This sounds like something out of a crime story on television," DJ said, more interested with each passing moment.

Dag continued the story. "Anyway, Jack's place was being renovated, and so he came over to my place to stay for a few days. As I mentioned, it turned out it was his birthday, and he and Annie and I were going to celebrate. Annie couldn't come, so Jack and I grilled steaks and then went down to a local café for some coffee. As we made our way back home, there were firetrucks everywhere with people running here and there. That is the part of the story I mentioned before.

"We thought that since the bodies of the couple were found that it would be just a matter of time before the body of the little boy would be found. Well, that night here at the Cove you gave me that letter, I took off for the mainland, and I learned that there was a body of another adult male found, but they never found the body of the little boy."

"And you went back because you knew you had some info that could help?" DJ inquired.

"No, buddy," Dag replied, "I went back to see if Jack had more info about who or what caused the fire, yet in doing so, I discovered that I had some information about the goings-on that evening that helped to solve the case. As a result, I became embroiled in a process that took all my attention for the last few weeks. That is why I was so scarce recently, and I do apologize."

"Listen, Dag," DJ said, "you can be remote and quiet and unresponsive, but you do not have a cruel or duplicitous bone in your body. I knew you were not intending to shun me or freeze me out. We were just worried. That's all."

Dag realized once again how blessed he felt for having the friends he had. "That's very understanding of you, my friend," he said.

The remainder of the evening was a happy memory for Dag. He and DJ talked about other things that had been happening for the past several weeks. DJ spent his break from academia reading a couple of mystery novels, and he also let Dag in on a little secret.

"Say, guy," DJ began, "how long have we known one another?"

"Who knows, man," Dag replied. "We had met here one evening over twenty years ago, and then you came to work at the university about seven years ago, I guess. Remember all those years you were working on your doctorate? We spent hours upon hours talking about it here at the Cove."

"Yeah, I do," DJ added. "We were so tired of talking about it that we eventually made a vow to never talk about work or research when we were here at the Cove. I think that was a pretty wise move, if you ask me."

"Indeed, my friend. You can love your work, but talking about nothing but work can make a person weary," Dag offered. "So why is it that I think you want to talk about work?"

"Well my friend, I don't want to talk as much about work as I do about leaving work," DJ confessed.

Dag was surprised. "What?" was all he had to say.

As DJ began to speak, Dag suddenly found his words and began to let them out before DJ could utter a sound. "I thought we both decided we loved work and that we never wanted to retire. I thought we were going to stick it out there for many more years. I thought…" Dag began before DJ interrupted.

"You thought it was going to last forever. So did I. But you know that old saying that says that life is what happens when you are busy making plans? Well, that's what's happening here. I know you wanted this to continue for a long time to come, and I know how you feel," DJ completed Dag's thought.

"Well, I wasn't going to say that, but come to think of it, that was exactly what I was thinking," Dag admitted.

"It's not set in stone yet, guy, but I have been offered an adjunct position back in Davenport, my parents aren't getting any younger, and I have family there," DJ said.

"Wait a minute! You are going to leave the island and move to Iowa?" Dag almost shouted. Dag had some very good friends in several parts of the island, but he felt a tinge of loneliness that, for some reason, hit him hard. In his mind, he knew that DJ was from Iowa and that hearing this news would not really be a stretch for anyone else, but he was just surprised.

"Well, I will know something this coming week, not because I am waiting for them to respond but because they need an answer by then, and I told them I would comply," DJ said.

The topic of DJ leaving continued for about another half hour, and then, realizing that no decision had been made and that there was no more information forthcoming since DJ had not made up his mind, they spent the rest of the time talking about their lives and the fun they had at the Cove, speaking as if the little run-down pub and grill had been created out of nothing just for them. There were some endings that Dag did not enjoy, and this was one of them, but he vowed to not end the evening on a down note. Whatever occurred, he wanted to support DJ the way DJ had supported him for so many years.

When they parted that evening, DJ hopped into his jeep and scooted down the road, while Dag walked back to his apartment, sensing more than ever that another chapter was closing in his life and feeling sad yet thankful for DJ. DJ offered to drop him off at his place, but Dag opted for the walk that he'd taken so many times before, and having been absent recently, he wanted to take in the downtown areas in the evening again, as it was so quiet and so peaceful. He spent some time reflecting upon how different the downtown area of Honolulu was from Waikiki, and he enjoyed the stroll. Yet on this evening, he thought about DJ and, perhaps a bit more selfishly, thought about how much he'd miss DJ when he came down to the Cove without him.

While he hoped DJ would decide not to go, he had a sense that DJ was further along in his deliberations than even he himself realized.

On his walk home, he thought about the joy that DJ had brought to life. He recalled when DJ had that student who was just convinced that socialism was the fairest and most efficient economic system on earth, and he had several in the class agreeing with him. With the full support of the class, DJ tried that old experiment with the class in which he agreed that he would run the class as a socialist experiment. He gave an exam, and after the exam he said, "Okay, I am now going to average the grades in the class and give everyone that average as their grade on the exam." Interestingly, the ones who were so pro-socialism were also exceptional students who made good grades, and they started an uproar, telling DJ how unfair he was being. DJ simply said, "This is socialism. Are you in or are you out? Decide."

Yes, DJ had a way with students. He could make them his friends and still command respect. A true educator he was, and he was in it for the right reasons. At any rate, Dag had a few days before he would hear DJ's decision about leaving, and this of course would cause his life to change as well, yet Dag had no idea of the degree to which his life would change...no idea.

CHAPTER 3

A Change of Seasons

Dag marched into his office the following week, refreshed and ready for what might come his way, and he was thrilled to be back in class. He had to finish out this semester before he began his totally online teaching career. Yes, nine more weeks and he would be working from home...or wherever he happened to be at the time. Dag realized anew what a blessing it was to love one's work and have the freedom he experienced. Still, the joy, for that day at least, was short-lived.

"I'm leaving, my friend," DJ stated matter-of-factly as he strode into Dag's office that morning. Apparently, he had pondered the idea all evening and night, and while he realized all the good things about staying, there were some real reasons why he *needed* to go. His departure would not be until the end of the semester, which was still nine weeks away, and that would give Dag some time to wrap his head around his best friend's leaving. It would also give some time for true acceptance. At this point, however, Dag could not conceive of ever being accepting of this change.

DJ was doing what many people do at this point in their lives. He was considering the end of his career and other opportunities as well as responsibilities that were out there. DJ, like Dag, felt as if this were the richest and most fulfilling time of his life, yet there were things to do, events to attend to, promises to keep. He felt as if he were being called back to his hometown. That happens with many people.

He closed the door to his office and for a moment thought of ways to get DJ to change his mind, yet in the back of Dag's mind, he knew he would never do that. He was wise in that regard. He had always had friends who knew what they wanted and needed to do, and he was also good at supporting them in their decisions, no matter how much he disliked those decisions. He knew that DJ was a good man and an intelligent one, and he also knew that he had never seen DJ make a decision that would not result in the optimal outcome for all concerned, as much as was possible.

Dag tried to tell himself that with all the types of instant communication that was available today, he would remain in contact with DJ and visit him often, yet he knew how way leads on to way and how time and distance can still strain even the strongest of relationships. Dag thought to himself, *This must be the denial part of the grieving process.* He was nowhere near an anger stage, and he in fact did not anticipate ever being in that stage. In the back of his mind, Dag knew that he was quite accepting of change in time. It didn't take him long to realize that he was simply going to do everything he could to make these last few weeks with DJ memorable ones. His goal was to be as supportive as possible.

As the time progressed, both Dag and DJ, as well as their other friends, recognized the inevitability of this decision of DJ's, and the transition mindset began. As Dag was in a particularly sad mood one day, he received a text message from someone who completely brightened his day. The text said, "Hey, island guy, the guys and I are planning our trip and want to know what dates work out for you to host three clowns from the Bay Area." It was Annie…his dear friend Annie. While he was thrilled to hear from her, every bit as important as the call was the subtle unspoken message that accompanied it— the realization that people do maintain connections and that all was not lost with DJ's move.

"Well, you guys just feel free to come any time. I have a very small place, but we will all work together, and some of us codgers will have to sleep on the floor," Dag offered.

"No problem here, guy," Annie said. "This will be part of the adventure." After talking for about fifteen more minutes, Annie hung up with the promise to call Dag back soon concerning date of arrival and departure of the trio. Dag was really looking forward to introducing his past to his present, as if to finally make his life appear to have flowed in one steady stream. It was one of those puzzle pieces that Dag just realized he had yet to place.

In what seemed to be a matter of minutes, Dag's phone rang again, and again, it was Annie saying, "Okay, dude, headed your way next Wednesday and staying for a week. Can you handle us that long?"

"One week? That's it?" Dag blurted out.

"Well, guy, we don't really have a mystery to solve this time, so we didn't want to be those guests who tend to stay too long, you know what I mean?" Annie stated.

"Ok, then," Dag began, "I will make a deal with you. If the three of you can steal away from the Bay Area for an unspecified time and not yet set the time of departure to go home, I promise I will tell you when enough is enough. What do you say?"

"You're on, my friend, but I will still need to check with the guys on that. I can guarantee you they will be on board, but I will check anyway. You know how courteous I am," Annie said, tongue in cheek.

"Deal," Dag responded, and with that the conversation ended, and he was excited anew about his reconnection with his dear friends and their impending visit. Dag also realized that this would give Dag an opportunity to introduce his island friends to the friends of his young adulthood.

In preparation for the visit from the trio from San Francisco, Dag went shopping for an extra-large stock of coffee and other staples. He knew they would spend most of the time eating out, yet he also knew that occasionally they would want to kick back at Dag's place, pop open some wine, listen to 1970s music, and relax. One definite plan he made was for all of them to meet DJ at the Cove on Friday to make the introductions and enjoy an unforgettable evening with four of the best friends he'd ever had.

Dag bought all the supplies he needed for his visitors and informed DJ of their visit. DJ was excited to meet them as well, mainly because, while Dag had no issue mentioning his past life or his old friends, he never went into great detail. DJ commented at one time to Dag how he'd never in his life met someone who lived in the present as much as Dag did. Dag and his friends on the island could have a wonderful time at some fun event, and they would all talk in subsequent conversations about how memorable it was, and Dag would contribute very little to the discussion that centered around fond memories. *Perhaps Dag's disconnection with the past was a result of the events that had occurred in the Bay Area so long ago. Makes good sense,* DJ thought. DJ was happy to have the upcoming opportunity to connect to Dag's past.

The first of the week sped quickly by, and Dag found himself at the airport welcoming his friends. The three from the Bay Area rolled into Dag's Subaru without stopping the conversation, and most of the conversation was the endless banter between Jack and Annie.

"Told you he'd be here on time," Jack said to Annie.

Annie responded, "Yeah, but you know how out there those professors can be." She couldn't hide her smile.

Gates made a brief appearance into the conversation by stating, "Yeah, he's so out there that he gave us a free trip to the islands. Dag, you feel free to stay 'out there' as long and as often as you like." The laughter ensued.

"Yeah, and speaking of 'out there,' this one forgot that today was the day to head to the airport for the trip! He thought it was tomorrow," Annie said, tilting her head toward John Gates. Gates just looked sheepishly down at his shoes.

It was as if they were family. The bickering, the laughter, the joy, the support, and it was all surrounded by a bond that seemed unbreakable.

CHAPTER 4

When Worlds Collide

Dag set up the Friday get together with everyone, and he was excited, as he felt for the first time that this group getting together was a true gift to him. His experiences with each of these individuals were so varied, and yet he felt as if their presence in his life was something that was meant to be. He had met Jack by chance immediately after moving to the Bay Area in 1979, and he had met Annie immediately after that. He met DJ in 2003 as a neighbor when Dag was working at the university and DJ was completing his doctorate, and then they became even closer as Dag introduced him to the administrators at the university upon completion of DJ's degree, and they became not only good friends but colleagues as well. Finally, in 2018, he met John Gates, the detective, as a result of his investigations that occurred in response to the reopening of the case in 1979, which indirectly compelled Dag to leave the Bay Area and come to the islands.

So for Dag, having this group together would be fun as well as meaningful. It would indeed be bittersweet, however, as DJ was moving and the trio from the Bay Area would not be staying forever. For a moment, Dag sensed that aloneness, yet he immediately stored it away in his mind as his thoughts came back to the impending joy that was going to occur at the Cove on Friday. Yes, any issues concerning where life would go from here could easily be placed on hold while Dag entertained his dearest friends. He was curious as well as excited about what this gathering would bring.

Friday came very quickly, and Dag anticipated all day the inter-action between DJ and his friends from the Bay Area. He had done a couple of the tourist events with Jack, and Annie, and Gates, and he was ready to show them how a regular day unfolds in the islands.

As the three of them walked with Dag from his place to the Cove in the downtown area, Dag thought about how much he loved his life and the people who had made it worthwhile, and four of them were going to spend the evening with him. It was strange that his friends from another life were walking with him on a path that was such a part of his new life, and it brought a sense of excitement as well as a sense of closure, of a melding together of the circles in the journey his life had taken. As they entered the Cove, that neigh-borhood bar and grill that Dag had called his second home for years, Annie was resolute to pick DJ out of the crowd. Of course, as usual, there was no crowd, but there were about five people, and Annie did walk directly up to DJ immediately and said, "Are you DJ?"

DJ, looking surprised, said, "Yes. How did you know?"

Annie responded, "Because you have a pained look on your face that can only come from having spent too many years hanging around Dag Peyton."

They both laughed. Jack and Gates were warm and friendly with DJ as well, and DJ returned the pleasantries with great ease. Of course, they had to find a common topic other than the weather, and besides the weather, the only thing they had in common was Dag. As a result, he became the focus for about an hour, and the laughter again ensued. Dag, for no reason he could fathom, nudged Jack and told him that he was sitting in the very chair he was sitting in when he read his letter weeks before. Dag was anxious to share all facets of his life with his friends.

"Now how did you and Dag meet?" Jack asked DJ.

"Well, if I remember correctly, I had moved to the island in 1996. I lived down here in the downtown area, and I happened upon this place, the Cove, in my wanderings one day. I was going to grad-uate school at the time. After spending almost an entire career with an MBA, I thought it might be a good time to alter my career path and work on the PhD. One night, after a particularly difficult week of school and work, I dropped in here, and there was one, yes one, other individual in here, and it was Dag. We sat at the bar and talked for what became several hours. He was working at the university, and after a time, he encouraged me to apply there once I finished my degree. I did apply about seven years ago, we became colleagues as well as friends, and the rest is history," DJ stated in a melancholy way, perhaps thinking about his impending departure.

"And DJ…may I tell them, DJ?" Dag asked.

"Sure," DJ said sadly.

"DJ is retiring and moving back to Davenport, Iowa, at the end of this term. Thankfully, I am going online full time then as well, so I don't have to sit around the office and miss that big lug," Dag said, wanting to be funny but feeling sad as well. "But on a more pleasant note, we are all here now, and that is what is important. I feel as if my life is coming together, as if I had lived in two different worlds that are now joined, and it is a good feeling."

DJ commented after only a brief period of introductions that he wished he'd been connected to this group in the 1970s. "Man, that would have been a trip," he exclaimed.

"In many ways, I do too," Gates said, "but if we had, all the things that occurred might not have occurred, and we might not be in this very place right now, so I am just going to be happy that life brought us here."

"Hear, hear!" DJ replied, raising his glass as if to toast the occasion. The rest joined in the toast, and DJ hung on every reminiscence shared by the crowd, adding his own memories of Dag to add to the tapestry of this unforgettable evening.

DJ was a tall and stocky man of Scandinavian descent, and he was also patient to a fault. When Dag mentioned this to the group, Annie blurted, "Well, to be around you for all these years, he would have to be. Dag, you can be kind of remote sometimes."

Dag looked around the group and noticed all heads nodding in agreement, so he felt no compulsion to debate the topic. Instead he opted for humor and said, "Well, okay, but if you really get to know me and look just under the surface…you will find an even deeper remoteness."

The four friends laughed, and then Jack added, "Not true, my friend. You can be quite connected…when you want to be."

"Yes," Annie added, "when he wants to be. Dag, when do you think that's going to happen?" The group erupted in laughter.

At once, the five of them became a quite cohesive group. Dag was pleased when his friends met one another and were subsequently good friends to one another. It just felt as if he were bringing the world a bit closer together—his world, at any rate. As the merriment continued, Dag realized that he had experienced yet another event that he could add to his collection of wonderful memories.

The adventure at the Cove was so much fun for the group that they decided to do it twice more before the trio of Bay Area visitors headed back to the mainland. During those get-togethers, the group of now five friends recounted how they had met Dag, his little idiosyncrasies, yet most importantly for Dag, they also confirmed how much they loved him, even if those particular words were never spoken.

After a week of island treks by walking, driving, or hiking, in addition to an exceptional evening at Diamond Head Theater, it was time for Jack and Annie and Gates to head back home. John Gates in particular hated to leave, not because he feared a separation of friends again but because he had become enamored with the island. He was especially drawn to conversations about the hiking, the snorkeling, and the surfing that was ever available on island. He even said to Dag, "Say, don't be surprised if I pop in more frequently. I love this place." He stated that to Dag several times.

"Sounds just fine, John," Dag replied.

"Great," Gates added. "Sometimes I just need to clear my head."

Dag was, of course, pleased that any of these visitors would want to return. In fact, he stated rather emphatically, "I want you guys to return as many times as you possibly can, and you will stay with me. Please do not be concerned about overstaying your welcome. It is not possible for you to do that."

CHAPTER 5

A Valiant Attempt at Normalcy

With heavy hearts, the trio from San Francisco boarded their plane, and this time they were the ones to surprise Dag and DJ, leaving plane tickets for the two of them under Dag's coffee cup at his apartment. Dag called DJ to tell him the news.

"Say, guy," Dag began, "those crazy visitors we had left tickets for you and me to visit California. You in?"

"Are you kidding?" DJ exclaimed. "Count on it! But when are they wanting us to come? I am trying to tie things up here on island, and I need to plan."

"I have an idea," Dag offered. "These are actually vouchers for a trip, so why don't you get your act together, prep to leave, and then you and I can fly together to the Bay Area, spend some time, and then you can move on to Davenport from there? Saves you some cash for flights."

"That is an amazing idea, man!" DJ said excitedly.

And with that, Dag called the trio on the mainland, thanked them for their generosity, and said that he and DJ would be there to visit them in about seven short weeks. All were thrilled that the cadre of friends was growing and that the contact was as free-flowing as if they lived next door to one another.

In later days, DJ had to regretfully pull out of the Bay Area trip, as his father was ill. DJ felt the need to move on from Honolulu directly to Davenport as soon as the semester came to a close.

CHAPTER 6

How Change Begets Change

As if several weeks away on the mainland and DJ's impending departure were not enough change for the present time, Dag spoke to DJ one day about making another change himself.

"Buddy," he announced, "since I am not going to have you to kick around anymore, I am thinking about making a move myself. I think I am going to pack up, slip this little neighborhood I have known for so long, and head out to the ewa side of the island. They have some condos out there that are cheap. They have an 897 square foot one for only $450,000. That is a steal for the island. With such a shortage of housing, I have been talking to a realtor and think I will take the plunge. What do you think?"

DJ wasted no time in responding. "Well," he began, "I only have two comments. First, I think it's a great idea, and second, you will have to drop back into downtown and pop in on the Cove every so often to keep Sally on her toes. One of the reasons I hate to leave the island is that I have saved up so much banter for her that I won't get to use, and it's killing me inside!"

"Oh, absolutely," Dag said, and the two burst into laughter.

"Even though it is a minor change compared to the one you are making, my friend, it is still quite a difference in terms of my everyday life. The good news is that out there in Makakilo, there are some peaceful places, and it is really growing," Dag offered.

"Oh…Makakilo?" DJ countered. "You are really going up into the hills then."

"Yes, I think so," Dag responded. "Just kind of ready for a change of my own. In fact, I am going to look at the place this afternoon if you want to tag along."

"Sounds good," DJ said. "Besides, I need a break from packing. Gets to be exciting one minute and then depressing the next."

"Totally understandable. Besides, I need you to see the place so you will know where you're going to stay when you come for extended visits," Dag said resolutely.

For a brief moment, Dag wondered intensely about how he was going to fill the void that the absence of his best friend would leave. Little did he know that voids are often filled, whether we want them to be or not.

That afternoon, Dag and DJ made the trek out to the ewa, or west, side of the island. They enjoyed the drive, stopped for an early lunch, and then made their way up into the Makakilo hills. It was a partly sunny day, and yet as they ascended, the clouds enveloped them. By the time they reached Makakilo Heights, it was a cloudy day that became about ten degrees cooler.

"Wow," exclaimed DJ, "I hope you like cold weather." Of course, it was still seventy degrees, but that was considered cold to islanders, and there was a breeze.

"In fact, I do, guy," Dag retorted.

The pair made their way onto the doorstep of the small condominium. The units were made four to a unit, and they were connected, though there was a breezeway from unit to unit as well. They were small, yet still twice as large as the small efficiency Dag had called home for many years.

They spent about half an hour looking at the cozy little place. Dag had exhausted his list of questions for the realtor, and in as much time as it took to make himself one of his famous cheese sandwiches and a pot of coffee, Dag exclaimed, "I'll take it," and the deal was sealed. At least, it was on Dag's end.

"As you likely know," the realtor said, "there are so few building permits and so little space that homes are at a premium, so if I contact the office and there have been no higher offers made this morning, I will close the deal for you, pending all the financial checks of course. If you like, I can call them now to confirm."

Dag nodded at him anxiously, and the realtor called his office. After about twenty seconds of "uh-huh, uh-huh," he closed out the call and turned to Dag saying, "If all your financial matters fall into place, it's yours."

Dag and DJ looked at one another, and Dag said, "Great!" Still Dag knew that this step was a further separation from the life he knew. He felt sadness and at the same time a measure of peace in knowing that perhaps this new venture would bring him a sense of renewal and adventure as well.

As they walked away from the little bungalow that would become Dag's new home, he noticed his new neighbors standing in the breezeway between their condo and Dag's. The woman was looking at the man with her hands on her hips, and the man was standing with an expressionless look. She turned and scampered into the house quickly, and the man then turned to Dag, nodded, and went back to sweeping the breezeway.

It was strange to Dag how powerful first impressions can be. He immediately thought that the woman was abrasive and the man was tolerant. His reasoning made him realize that this might not be anywhere near the truth of the situation. If he learned anything through his research methods classes, it was that we cannot take a snapshot in time, generalize it, and make any kind of accurate or warranted conclusion. The reflection of this occurrence immediately left his mind.

Now, it seemed, Dag's life was all abuzz about imminent change. He was happy about that in a way, since it allowed him less time to lament DJ's upcoming departure. The two hung out almost continually during the last few weeks of DJ's time on island, and Dag would not have it any other way. Dag even asked DJ if he wanted to go with him one Saturday to look at furniture for Dag's new place, to which DJ replied, "Well, I'd almost rather have my fingernails extracted than spend a day looking at furniture, but throw in a free lunch and you have a deal."

"Deal," Dag said, laughing aloud.

The two spent a fun and relaxing day, and DJ even appeared to enjoy the process of selecting furniture. Dag perceived that DJ enjoyed it so much because Dag was not into it either, and Dag was also not picky about furniture. So Dag quickly took DJ's recommendations regarding furniture, and off they went to enjoy a long lunch at Monkeypod Kitchen, one of Dag's favorite hangouts.

Dag used to take the long trek out to the west side to go to Monkeypod for a relaxing drink near the lagoons, but now that he was going to live on the west side, he'd be able to be a regular at the wonderful hideaway that reminded him so much of the Cove downtown.

It was yet another memorable afternoon, and the two made their way back into town. As Dag dropped DJ off at his place, he thought about how few opportunities they were going to have to do this, and he felt a brief sense of sadness that was overcome quickly by what was accomplished during the day. *Besides,* Dag thought, *I am really not losing anything. DJ and I will remain friends. All will be well.*

In time, Dag wondered how he could give DJ the proper send-off. Having reached a decision, he began to take photos and create a book of events in DJ's life on island. He even had a photo of their first meeting at the Cove so many years earlier, as Sally and others at the Cove took photos of their customers and posted them on the wall. Dag borrowed it to make a copy. All these snapshots in time Dag would piece together with appropriate sayings, clippings, and ticket stubs of events they had attended, and he would send it ahead of DJ so it would arrive at his new home in Davenport, where he could look at it and reminisce.

Dag was particularly proud of how he pieced together the last page of the gift. It was a photo of DJ as he was walking out of Dag's office one day. Dag had asked him a question, and DJ had turned around, looking over his shoulder at Dag, with that kind half-smile that made people like DJ immediately. The photo looked as if DJ were leaving, and Dag placed this poem by Robert Frost under the photo:

> Nothing Gold Can Stay
> Nature's first green is gold,
> Her hardest hue to hold.
> Her early leaf's a flower;
> But only so an hour.
> Then leaf subsides to leaf.
> So Eden sank to grief,
> So dawn goes down to day.
> Nothing gold can stay.

CHAPTER 7

The Art of Saying Goodbye

The remaining days on island for DJ flew by, and the day of his departure arrived.

Getting DJ to the airport was not easy. There was a traffic mishap on the H1 freeway, and it was not an easy one to fix. When there was a serious traffic entanglement on the island, it often meant that traffic was at a standstill, since the off-freeway options were few and far between. Still, they arrived at the airport, allowing DJ enough time to get checked in and then relax for a time before takeoff. Dag parked his car in the parking garage and walked with DJ to the security entrance.

"I guess all this is hitting me, and I cannot believe it," DJ said wistfully, as if his mind were elsewhere. "I don't live here anymore."

"Yes, my friend, and whatever sadness you feel, just remember that I have to see all the old places we used to hang out over and over again—constant reminders of how things have changed," Dag returned. "Of course, it's all about me," Dag said, laughing.

DJ's laugh at Dag's comment turned to a blank expression and then to sadness. Unable to speak, he gave Dag a long hug and, without looking him in the eyes, turned and walked away. In the last clasp of hands in friendship, DJ slipped Dag a note. As DJ disappeared through the doorway to the terminal, Dag opened the note. It read as follows:

> Dag, there are no words I can think of on my own,
> so I can only offer the words of Shel Silverstein:
> "There are no happy endings.
> Endings are the saddest part,
> So just give me a happy middle
> And a very happy start."
> Thank you, Dag, for a very happy middle.

Dag had not felt such a sense of loss in a very long time. He found himself being thankful that he was older, as he knew now more than ever that endings were a part of life and that he would survive. Still, the sense of sadness remained.

And so a new chapter had begun for both of them.

Dag knew that this would not be an easy time for him, missing his dear friend, but there were now no barriers to his being able to travel to Davenport for an extended stay. DJ would be thrilled, they could make new memories there, and all would be well.

Dag resolved that on the ride back home and in fact for the rest of the evening, he would try to think of something to make him happy. He drove down to the Cove downtown and walked through the entry and back to the old wooden bar that he and DJ had called their second home for at least two decades.

In no time, there appeared Sally, the old server, acting as if life were too much, bantering with the few people who made appearances, and seemingly disliking everything and everyone, yet Dag knew she loved every minute of it.

"Well, I'll be," Sally exclaimed as she finally laid eyes on Dag. "Where's your sidekick?"

"He's gone, Sally," Dag said sadly, trying to keep a stiff upper lip. "I just dropped him off at the airport. He said that his main regret was that he had stored up so many insults for you, and it was killing him that he wouldn't be able to deliver."

"Probably best for him," she replied. "He never won a sparring match with me, anyway."

"Truth is," Dag said, "he just couldn't come down to say good-bye. It would have been a bit more than my stoic old friend could've handled." He looked at Sally with a warmth that she happily returned.

As she turned to go back to the kitchen, Dag noticed the slightest sign of a tear in her eye. Dag, resolved to keep the night upbeat, bantered with Sally more than usual, and then he left the Cove for new environs.

CHAPTER 8

Turning a Page

The end of the semester had come, DJ had moved back to Iowa, and Dag was settling into his new home in the high hills of Makakilo Heights. In addition, he was fully online with his teaching now as this new semester was set to begin in a week, and he felt strange, as if he should relax and get excited all at once. It was Saturday, and he decided that he was going to take unpacking as he took everything in his life…one step at a time. He could drive some crazy with his sloth-like processes, but after years of having to please others, he decided to take things more slowly, enjoying life and doing the things he loved. He also learned that most any task can be done if one does not become overwhelmed and simply sticks to it.

Dag often worked on Saturdays—slowly, methodically—yet worked just the same, and he quickly realized that this new online job would be the same for him. He had a schedule that allowed for Sundays off, yet Dag had to finally stop to analyze himself and realize that he in fact loved working. So many people he knew were retiring right and left, yet Dag could not conceive of retirement.

He set his unpacking aside once again and strolled around the grounds of his new place. Just steps outside his bungalow was a panoramic view of the city below, Diamond Head in the distance and the endless Pacific Ocean, ever reminding him how small he was in this vast universe. Dag found peace in that thought. Still he was pleased with the frequent cloud cover and fog that enveloped him and his new home, as if he were in the clouds and removed from the confines of earth.

He resolved that the next day, Sunday, he would go to church, stop by the farmers' market for some fresh vegetables, drive home, and spend the day slow cooking a stew that he would eat early in the evening while watching the clouds go by. He would mix those vegetables with some delicious Chinese food, which he would pick up from a local eatery tucked into a side street in Kapolei, and take in the peace and quiet of the day.

Yes, Dag was at peace with life and with himself. The only problem at this point was that for Dag, time did not slow down at his new home either. He attributed this to his contentment with his life, and that was likely true, yet every day was brief, and every precious evening was the blink of an eye.

Perhaps I need some chaos in my life to make the time go more slowly, Dag thought jokingly.

CHAPTER 9

Calm in the Midst of a Storm

Sunday came quickly, as did all days recently, and Dag made his trek down the hill to a small church at the base of the hill and then to the farmers' market. There was always great locally grown food to select, and Dag wanted it all. There were so many farms with great produce, and the rich red soil of the islands made for a quite fertile and tasty harvest. He stopped at one point to see a young woman at a small stand, seeming to be out in the middle of the grounds by itself. As Dag walked by, the woman said loudly, somehow breaking the peace and quiet that had been Dag's day up to this point, "Uh, sir...sir... may I have a moment of your time?" Dag turned to the right and to the left, almost certain that he was not the one whose attention she was seeking. She pointed directly at him, smiled, and said, "Yes, sir, may I speak with you for a moment?"

Why Dag was the focus of this woman's attention was a mystery to him. Still, opting to be courteous, Dag turned and said, "Yes, did you need something from me?"

"Why, yes," the woman said, in a quieter and more delicate tone. "I work for the development department of the city, and as you know, the west side of the island is growing by leaps and bounds. It would grow even more if we could get more of our residents to support initiatives to build and expand our commercial area beyond what is presently being offered. There is so much potential here that we hate to see it go to waste by those who seem to want to live in the past. If you could just sign this petition…"

"Well, ma'am, if by living in the past, you mean keeping the waters and land pristine and beautiful as they are now versus being covered with buildings and roads, I am afraid I am not going to be on your side here," Dag offered quite directly. "Still, I would be happy to hear what you have to say. Perhaps you can change my mind." Dag doubted seriously that she could, but he decided long ago that it never hurts to hear another point of view.

The woman's tone and facial expression changed, and she responded, "I am not sure I am going to be able to change your mind. You seem pretty fixed on your present point of view."

"Well," Dag added, "many people have a fixed set of ideas in their minds until someone or something convinces them to change, wouldn't you agree?"

"Perhaps," the woman replied, still not as engaged as she was when she blurted out Dag's name from across the field.

Dag surmised quite quickly that the woman was not in a mind-changing frame of mind when she solicited signatures from passers-by. She wanted a clean and quick signature so she could fill her quota and be on her way. Dag was not a proponent of that line of thinking. Still, she tried.

"Sir, these islands are in the dead center of two continents, the most remote islands in the world, yet a critical stopping point for China-US relations, or for any Asian nation for that matter. We cannot progress unless we are willing to grow our cities and develop our businesses so we can better contribute to the world economy as well as to local jobs. Everybody wins," the woman began.

Dag responded, "While I appreciate that point of view and can indeed see your point, there are losers in that scenario. The losers are the people who want to keep their island home pristine, and there are definite losers among the wildlife that will be displaced from their homes altogether. We have already done enough of that."

The conversation continued for about ten more minutes, and Dag concluded that the woman was right. He really had no intention of changing his mind, and he liked for nature to stay the way it was.

Yet even with this less than optimal exchange, Dag felt good. He gathered his fresh produce, paid for it, and went to his car.

What a beautiful Sunday, thought Dag as he pulled into his parking stall at his tiny bungalow on the hilltop. Dag had no plans for his Sunday afternoon except to have a nice, leisurely lunch, watch the basketball playoffs, and take a highly coveted nap. His afternoon of peace and rest each Sunday was a reward that he had given himself for working during the week and even on Saturdays as well.

Dag had been born on the mainland. He had family there, and he missed them, yet his move to the islands all those years ago was something he was proud of, something he treasured. He loved the remoteness, the serenity, all the modern conveniences yet at a slower pace, tranquility. He saw it as a chance to begin again, to see what else life had to offer.

Meanwhile, there was unpacking to do. He grabbed a box to unpack and put it beside his recliner and opened it up, only then realizing that he could unpack and eat at the same time.

After giving himself that pep talk yet one more time, Dag fumbled around the kitchen for the leftover chow mein from his dinner from the Chinese restaurant the evening before, added some fresh vegetables to it, placed it in the slow cooker, found the remote that had strategically hidden itself under the cushion on his recliner, and settled in for the pregame show that would allow all the experts to tell Dag why one team was going to win and the other was not. Yes, Sunday afternoon was shaping up to be an enjoyable one indeed.

The final game of the playoffs turned out to be less than exciting. The series was 3–0 going into this game, and they were playing best out of seven. Dag was hoping for some last-minute firepower from the underdog just so there would be something to keep him from slipping into that Sunday afternoon nap prematurely. Halfway through the fourth quarter, the favorite had about a 25-point lead, and Dag's eyelids could no longer fight the temptation. He drifted off to sleep just as the announcers themselves seemed to settle for a monotone resignation that the outcome of the game was inevitable.

Suddenly, Dag awakened with a start after hearing a blood-curdling scream from next door. The tiny bungalows were connected, four to a cluster, with only a small breezeway in between each of them, and the breezeway only served to trap and amplify the scream he heard. He quickly surmised that it was a disagreement between his new neighbors. While he didn't sense any signs of physical abuse, the argument was intense, the angry words relentless, the unease palpable.

"You are cruel! You need to be taught a lesson!" yelled the woman of the house. It was interesting to Dag that he never heard the husband say a word—only the wife. Since he had moved to Makakilo Heights, he had seen the husband daily, walking past on the sidewalk in front of their bungalows, carrying an empty basket, never anything else. He would walk by at about 5:00 a.m., and Dag would observe him from his kitchen window as Dag made his pot of coffee for the day. Then, like clockwork, at about 8:00 p.m., the man would return looking tired and drawn, with the same empty basket.

In the brief time he had been in his new place, Dag had never heard the man speak, and Dag surmised that this man was not one seeking many friendships. The only two things Dag knew was that the man's wife seemed to be upset with him constantly, yelling at the top of her lungs, and that his name was Kimo. During her tirades, she would scream the name "Kimo."

Kimo appeared to be about sixty years old, about five feet ten and slender, with salt-and-pepper hair that had once been jet black and dark skin that seemed to have spent many years in the sun. He never looked up as he ambled by, and he never seemed distraught from the many tongue-lashings his wife threw his way. Dag couldn't put his finger on it, but the man seemed to have an unspoken inner peace, and he appeared to have found his peace in silence.

Or he could be the devil in disguise, Dag thought.

On this particular Sunday, however, life changed for Kimo, as his wife heralded that she was leaving. "You will never see my face again, you worthless old fool!" she exclaimed, and with that, she was out the door with a ferocity that made Dag wonder what could have been done that made this woman so bitter. He thought of all the possibilities:

1. Perhaps he beat her. No, he seemed way too mild-mannered for that.
2. Perhaps he was not a good provider. No, if that were the case, surely she would be working some to make ends meet, and she never left the house as far as Dag could tell.
3. Perhaps she just hated her life with him. Could be, but this would all be speculation.

Oh well, Dag decided that he'd invested too much time in pondering the mysterious life of Kimo and his disgruntled wife, so being newly awake, he fumbled yet again for that remote and watched the highlights of the boring game that ended a half hour earlier, while pulling some pictures out of a box so he could hang them at some point.

An hour later, Dag took to his daily tasks, which included planning to plant a makeshift garden, which was the size of a square of cement on the sidewalk, making some cornbread, and slowly heating the vegetables he'd purchased at the farmers' market along with some of his black pepper chicken and chow mein from the Chinese restaurant. He smiled as he thought of how boring his life would appear to many, but he loved his life of peace. The only threats to his tranquil life involved Kimo next door, and actually not so much Kimo as his wife. Other than that, almost every morning came with a soothing cloudiness that made the living seem slower, a cool and welcomed breeze that heralded tranquility, and quietness that helped Dag to center himself each day.

With the mayhem having died down a bit, Dag grabbed a couple of teabags, dropped them in a quart-sized jar, and set the jar outside for some sun tea. As he placed the tea on his lanai, he heard the faint sound of humming. Since the only sounds he usually heard were from the less-than-placid home of Kimo and his wife, he could only assume that the humming was coming from Kimo's house as well. Dag realized in an instant that this was the first time he'd ever heard humming from that neighboring bungalow.

Had she really done it this time? Had she really left him? Dag felt ashamed, as his first thought was about the potential for quiet instead of the potential demise of a marriage. Hearing Kimo's humming, he wondered if Kimo simply did not care that she was gone. Perhaps he was indifferent.

As they say, you can love someone or hate someone, but both of them involve strong feelings. Indifference is when you really don't care, and indifference is what Dag felt about quite a few things. If he were engaged in something and truly believed in it, he went all out to support it. If he didn't have that exuberance, he couldn't force himself to have it. As Dag always was fond of saying, "It is what it is." He wasn't proud of his indifference, nor was he ashamed of it. He laughed to himself as he realized he was even indifferent about indifference.

And so it was that Dag would rise to do his work day after day, Monday through Saturday, see Kimo every morning at 5:00 a.m. walking in front of his bungalow, and watch Kimo return with that empty basket about about 8:00 p.m. Then Dag had an opportunity to interact one day with Kimo when Kimo's door was jammed shut, and for some reason, he could not open it. Then and only then, after their brief time as neighbors, did Dag hear Kimo trying to enter his own home and ask if he could be of assistance.

"Can I help you out, neighbor?" Dag asked, trying to make it seem as if they had been cordial to one another in the past.

"Don't think so, my brother," Kimo said softly as he pushed the door open mid-sentence.

"Oh, okay then," Dag said. He was very surprised at the next sound he heard.

"Want to come in for some tea?" Kimo said, again quite softly.

Dag was taken aback just a bit, and before he could decide what to say he heard himself saying, "Sure." He followed Kimo into his place with an air of trepidation and curiosity. *Hmmm,* thought Dag, *this is where all the abuse had occurred.* Then he felt guilty for making a judgment before knowing the facts. He didn't even know if there was anything to consider. Kimo then broke the silence.

"How do you take your tea, sir?" Kimo asked politely.

"Well, is the tea going to be hot or cold? And please call me Dag," Dag said, happy to be getting the pleasantries out of the way.

"Hot, my friend," Kimo said, again very politely.

"Just honey and lemon if you have it," Dag offered.

"Same here," Kimo said, slowly gathering the honey and the lemon and pouring the tea as if it were a solemn ritual. Dag watched as the man cautiously and deliberately went about the task of making the tea, and he was struck by the attention to detail he showed in getting it just as Dag requested.

"This tea is perfect," Dag said. "I noticed the attention you paid to the task, and I thank you for that."

"Well, I offered you something. I wanted to give my best," Kimo said, totally having Dag's attention. Dag was in full admiration of this man, even though they just met. It seemed to Dag that Kimo appreciated life and was going to make every moment full of quality and richness. *What an approach to life,* Dag said to himself.

Dag could not explain it, but he seemed to be pulled into Kimo's life that day. He was entranced to some degree by Kimo's calmness, by his kindness, by his unobtrusive nature. The quiet grace of the man made Dag want to know his secret to serenity, and Dag, though having seen him for several days, had only met him an hour earlier. Dag wondered if Kimo had something to hide, perhaps being one of those people who does something horrific, and then on the news you see a neighbor the next day saying, "He was a quiet person—kept to himself…" *No,* Dag thought, *I am not going to let myself go there.*

Dag enjoyed the tea, made polite conversation with Kimo for about thirty more minutes, and then exited to his own place, happy for having finally met his calm, peaceful, friendly, yet mysterious neighbor.

CHAPTER 10

The Peace to be
Found in Chaos

From that day forward, Dag and Kimo seemed to connect more often. There was the occasional nod of greeting when they would pass one another. Once, Kimo even smiled when he passed by Dag's place one evening, carrying that same empty basket. In the two weeks since they first met, Dag had tea with Kimo three times, and it was interesting to Dag that when he was with Kimo there was a feeling of peace, of serenity. Dag always felt as if any worries he had were not that important, and that the important items on his calendar could wait. He found Kimo to be soft spoken and kind. For that reason, he was taken aback when one day he heard the police come to Kimo's door in the breezeway between their homes. Not getting an answer from Kimo, the police knocked on Dag's door.

"Good evening, sir," one of the officers said abruptly. "Do you know the gentleman who lives next door?"

"Yes, I have interacted with him a few times," Dag replied.

"How long have you lived here, sir?" the other officer interjected with a curt air similar to the other officer.

"About four weeks," came Dag's reply, mimicking the officers' abruptness.

"Do you know how long your neighbor has lived on these premises?" the first officer asked.

"Not exactly," Dag offered.

"Well, sir, give us a timeframe in which you know he has lived here," the second officer stated.

"He was here when I got here, sir," Dag stated coolly.

"So you are telling us that you have lived next to this guy for these several weeks and you haven't interacted with him more than a couple of times?" the second offer continued.

"That is exactly what I am telling you," Dag responded.

"All right. Well, if you see him, please give him this card and have him contact us," the second officer said, clearly unhappy with the lack of information Dag had to offer.

"Will do, officers," Dag said and quietly yet swiftly closed his screen door.

The officers departed, and Dag placed the card of the officer on his coffee table. Later that evening, he saw Kimo returning home. He decided he would get this perceived unpleasant task out of the way.

"Hey guy, this is a card a police officer gave me and asked me to give to you. They want you to call them. I didn't give them any info. Truth is, I don't know any info, so that made not giving any that much easier," Dag said with a smile, trying to make light of the situation.

"Okay, my friend. Say," Kimo offered politely, "want some tea?"

"Sure," Dag responded cheerily, certain he was going to get some info concerning the police and their visit.

The two visited for about an hour, with Kimo telling him about when Kapolei, with the adjoining Makakilo in the hills, was a small town instead of the thriving "Second City" it had become. He spoke of the open fields, which had now given way to a university, thriving malls, loft apartments, restaurants, and the rail currently under construction that could potentially transport people into Honolulu and back efficiently. The old Makakilo that Kimo talked about sounded as peaceful as Kimo's placid demeanor. Once again, Dag forgot about the police visit and was enthralled in the quiet serenity of a conversation with a man whom Dag thought of as an old friend, even though their acquaintance was quite new. At the end of the conversation, Kimo was as polite as ever, saying, "Stay well, my friend."

"And you as well, Kimo," Dag offered. Then as if to once again try to stoke his own curiosity, he said, "I hope all works out okay with the police."

Kimo only responded with, "It always does, my friend."

Now Dag exited Kimo's bungalow with a renewed curiosity. *It always does?* Dag asked himself. *So he has had run-ins with the police before, and he somehow gets out of it every time. Perhaps he is some master manipulator and just knows how to persuade people because of his passive comportment.* Now Dag was really confused. He wondered if he happened to know the kindest man on earth or if he was now connected to a man who was quite schooled in the art of deception. The mystery surrounding his new friend was ever broadening and ever interesting. Dag was quite perceptive. While he never had a driving curiosity about many things, he could pick up on subtle nuances quite well. Still, he could see no reason why Kimo would have this shroud of mystery over him. Dag thought that perhaps he was simply misunderstood. That is what Dag wanted to think.

Days passed, and Dag did not see Kimo early in the morning nor late in the evening. It was strange to Dag that he was concerned about the well-being of a man he'd only met a matter of weeks earlier, yet he was indeed concerned. Then, on one calm Friday evening, Kimo passed by, unshaven, unkempt in general, carrying that same empty basket. Dag intentionally walked out to his breezeway to appear to accidentally bump into Kimo.

"Hey, buddy. How are you?" Dag asked.

"Oh, a bit tired, I suppose, but being tired makes for welcomed sleep," Kimo offered, always at peace.

"Well, my friend," Dag said, "I was going to offer you some tea, but I see you are tired. We can do this some other time."

"No, not at all, Dag," Kimo said cheerfully, "I'll be over right after I shower, if that's okay with you."

"Well sure," Dag said quickly. "I'll steep a couple bags and see you in a few." He was glad to make this reconnection. He had a desire to help Kimo in some way, to make his life easier, though Kimo appeared to be at peace in this most troubling of circumstances.

Kimo appeared about twenty minutes later with a fresh mango to offer to Dag, who sliced it and added some cheese to a plate, and the two of them talked about finding peace in life. Kimo came up with some hard and fast rules—simple rules—that to Dag were true pearls of wisdom. If anyone else had said them Dag would not have been as invested as he became, yet Kimo seemed to live them, and they seemed to work. Dag wanted to call them pieces of advice, yet Kimo said that one of the secondary rules was to never give advice. The primary rules were as follows:

1. Be part of the solution in other people's lives.
2. Live simply.
3. Love selflessly.
4. Don't keep score.
5. Forgive constantly.
6. Live your beliefs.
7. Don't let your ego take over. Remember the prophet Isaiah, who said, "Woe to the man who is wise in his own eyes."
8. Remember that the little things in life are actually the big things.
9. Focus on the other person.
10. Let go of duplicitous people. Their intrusiveness is a reflection of their own lack of self-worth.

Dag reflected upon how simple these rules for living were. Kimo even said that life is simple, but people make it complicated. Refuse to complicate life. All it does is shorten it. Kimo related a story to Dag in which he said that scientists now project that there could be as many as 350 million galaxies in the universe. Of those 350 million, we are in one of them, and in that galaxy are many solar systems, and in our solar system there are several planets, and we are a tiny speck on one little planet in the entire universe. And Kimo's entire point was that if all this is true, why in the world would we worry about anything? Dag reflected on this, and while some might be left feeling insignificant and small in the scheme of things, Dag felt immensely better, for in his life he'd been a worrier, an organizer, a handler, a statistician, a monitor, a record keeper, and a budgeter, and while those characteristics were admirable to some, they are the very traits that can take the joy of living away. Dag was happy that in the past few years, he recognized this and was happy to think he was doing better. Kimo's demeanor helped him immensely.

At his own home that evening, Dag found himself wishing he could be more like Kimo. He was happy to have found such a friend, who had lived next door all this time. He was pleased that they had both reached out.

CHAPTER 11

When Life Hands You Lemons

Dag found himself overwhelmed with work for the next few weeks. During that time, he rarely saw or spoke to Kimo, and it seemed as if he had fallen back into that same old grind. Finally, one day, Dag was driving up Makakilo Drive to his little home. Working from home now, he had spent too much time indoors and decided to take a drive. He went to the North Shore, ate at a roadside fish taco stand, dropped by the Dole Plantation for a pineapple ice cream cone, and now he was headed back home.

As he was nearing his home, he saw Kimo, sitting at a bus stop waiting for the downtown bus. Though Dag was tired, he pulled off the road, emerged from his car, and yelled across the street to Kimo, "Hey, buddy, you need a ride somewhere?"

Kimo waved his hand as if to say "no," so Dag hopped back into his car and headed home. *I wonder why Kimo would be going downtown at this time of day,* Dag pondered. Then realizing how tired he was, he pulled into his driveway and exited his car. Having seen Kimo at the bus stop made him realize for the first time that his wife must have taken the car when she left. At their next encounter, he would tell Kimo that he was always available to drive him wherever he needed to go. He was sorry that he had not thought to check into this before. He vowed to pay more attention, but it seemed that Dag was chastising himself more and more about this lately. He wondered how many things in life he'd missed by not paying attention. Then he smiled as he realized he was losing interest in this train of thought. It took no time for Dag to enter his bungalow, turn on some music, and join in with the Doobie Brothers...

> Ohh ohhhhh...listen to the music...
> Ohh ohhhhh...listen to the music...
> Ohh ohhhhh...listen to the music...
> All the tiiiime...

When a middle-aged woman walking by his place looked over, smiled, and began to dance and sing along, Dag decided he'd better tone it down a bit. Dag had no idea why, but he always seemed to love life, and he always felt blessed. He saw too many people in life who were busy, serious, with no apparent light in their lives. Dag knew how they became that way, and he could see it happening to him as well if he didn't take care to not let it happen, so he made a conscious effort to be happy, even silly sometimes, simply enjoying life. He viewed his occasional day trips around the island as adventures, and he stopped when he felt like stopping, connected with new people when the mood struck him, and relished in the fact that he was in a world of his own making his own rules. He was proud of that.

That next encounter with Kimo took place two days later. The weekend was finally upon them, and Dag ran into Kimo as Kimo was opening his front door. "Hey, neighbor," was all Dag said. He never wanted to intrude, but he felt that their few discussions had warranted acknowledging Kimo when they saw one another.

"Want some tea, my friend?" Kimo asked politely.

"Sure, be over in a second," Dag said, feeling a bit like an anxious child when he said it. "You need some time to get settled in?"

"No, Dag, come on in and make yourself comfortable. I'll be back in a moment," Kimo offered calmly.

Dag yelled into the next room as Kimo disappeared, "I will be happy to give you a ride anytime you need one. I saw you at the bus stop and thought you might be without transportation."

"Indeed, I am," Kimo responded. "Indeed, I am, but you know what I have discovered? The bus is quite efficient and gets me there in good time. I just needed to go to a county meeting the other evening. I just have an interest in county affairs sometimes. I find the city planning to be fascinating at times. I also am surprised at the lack of planning that occurs at times. I mean, they brought the Superferry out here to take people and vehicles from one island to another, which I think is great, yet they failed to do an environmental impact study first. Why would they not want to see how this move would affect marine life as well as life on the islands themselves? I am for progress, but this is not good stewardship in my view."

"Well," Dag posited, "I am glad all is well. I mean, someone needs to have an interest in those things, right? It keeps our county moving ahead."

"Yes, it does, and sometimes they need encouragement to keep things moving in the right direction," Kimo said softly.

The discussion over tea this evening centered around the rapid growth of Makakilo and its history. Makakilo City was situation in the hills above Kapolei with a population, Dag guessed, at about eighteen thousand. With the elevation of their bungalows being at about the same elevation as the top of Diamondhead Crater on the opposite side of the island, they enjoyed cool evenings and days that were often about ten degrees cooler than the temperature down the hill in Kapolei. Businesses were booming, and everything Dag wanted or needed was in the Kapolei area. He would make the trek into Honolulu every week to hike to the top of Diamondhead and then into town for the occasional evening of theater or a fine dinner, yet most of Dag's life was about living in Makakilo. Dag was happy to learn about the area from Kimo, a native Hawaiian who seemed to exude the Aloha spirit.

Since the next day was Saturday and Dag had a rare Saturday off, he asked Kimo, "Say, I was wondering if you'd like to go to the farmer's market down the hill with me tomorrow. I have no plans, and I was trying to schedule a slow relaxing day." While Dag had known Kimo for a bit now, he was unsure as to what Kimo's response would be, since he thought it likely that Kimo was not a real mixer in terms of social engagement.

"Love to," Kimo said shyly, and they made plans to leave early to get the best the market had to offer and perhaps to drop by a few arts and crafts stands in the same vicinity. Dag then said good night, and they went their separate ways in anticipation of a relaxing Saturday morning.

Dag prepared for bed in a slow yet deliberate manner, taking in the breeze slowly coming through the window, enjoying the smell of plumeria from the trees that were in full bloom outside his bedroom window, and absorbing the peacefulness that was present in every Makakilo evening. He drank a cup of chamomile tea to drop off to sleep, enjoying a catalog from the Vermont Country Store during his slip into the world of slumber. Dag had just enough time to finish his last sip of tea, circle a box of goodies he wanted to purchase from the catalog, and switch off the light before sleep overtook him. He felt a contentment that had not been available to him for the last several decades. He welcomed it.

Saturday came quickly for Dag, and he rolled out of bed, showered, and was planning to have a leisurely cup of coffee before knocking on Kimo's door, when he looked out the window and saw Kimo sitting on his stoop with his famous empty basket and two empty boxes. Dag stuck his head out the window and said, "Hey, guy, you want some coffee for the road?"

"Sounds good, Dag. Black is fine," Kimo said in response.

After the coffee was made, they piled into Dag's car and scooted down the hill, ready for a nice day of getting fresh organic food and seeing a few of the sites of the bustling village where they lived. They both seemed to be prepared to enjoy a very productive day of enjoying life to the fullest yet at their own pace, and they seemed to be completely in sync.

Just as Kimo exited Dag's car, a man who appeared to be in his fifties walked up to Kimo and said, "You know, you've got some nerve. I am trying my best to help this community grow, and you have been nothing but a thorn in my side for years. You're what's wrong with this town!"

Dag said instinctively, "Now hold on buddy...you have no right...."

Kimo stopped him. "Dag, please let him go. He doesn't bother me one bit." Once again, Kimo had that peaceful look on his face that defied understanding for Dag. He smiled and said, "Would you look at those papayas!" Dag sensed that Kimo clearly did not want to talk about this episode nor the mystery behind it, and he was not going to ruin this day or their friendship by badgering him about it, so Dag dropped the subject for now.

As Kimo walked away, Dag worked to keep up with him, vowing someday to solve the mystery of the kindest man in the world who appeared to be on the outs with more than one person. He had never before sensed such a disconnect between the man Dag knew and the clear and apparent discord that surrounded him. Dag was anxious to learn more. He decided to wait it out, knowing that he was patient enough to allow this mystery to reveal itself.

CHAPTER 12

Getting to Know a
Truly Rich Friend

Several days passed, and the summer wore on. Dag again became engrossed in his work and his routine. As he arrived home one evening after going to the farmer's market and began to realize he was doing the exact same things he did every day for weeks, he shook himself out of his complacency and decided to knock on Kimo's door to see if he had any more words of wisdom for a friend who was anxious to experience a bit of variety in his life. Dag slowly entered the breezeway and was about to knock on Kimo's door when he heard the most beautiful soft ukulele music he'd ever heard. Kimo was not just playing an instrument. That instrument was coming to life as Kimo was gently strumming. The gentle evening breeze, the fresh smell of the salty ocean, and the soft light of the candles in Kimo's home drew Dag into the room like a siren song. Without knocking, he gently opened the screen door and seated himself on the floor by the front door. Kimo turned to acknowledge him without interrupting his playing, and for the next five minutes, Dag felt incredible peace.

As Kimo's song came to an end, Dag spoke in a soft whisper as if to recognize that any sound would break the aura of peace. "May I ask you a question?" Dag asked in such a mellow tone that even he could barely hear what he was asking.

"Of course, my friend," Kimo responded to Dag, also very quietly.

"I need to know your secret," Dag queried, as if Kimo would pull out a written set of instructions for perfect inner peace.

"My secret for what, my friend?" Kimo said.

Dag replied, "Your secret for being so at peace."

Kimo slowly put the ukulele aside and said, "My brother, we are meant to be at peace. We are meant to enjoy our lives. We weren't created so that we could have difficulty. We did that to ourselves. We were supposed to enjoy this beautiful earth and the beautiful people from everywhere who make up this earth. Just remember that when you surrender to peace, you are doing what man was originally meant to do. Instead of asking my secret to a life of peace, you might also ask why you do not feel that peace. It is about introspection."

Dag might have been seeking an easier answer than what Kimo provided, but he felt uplifted in a way because he now knew someone who found peace in his life, and as a result he knew it was possible to find it. Still, there were some hard facts that Dag also knew. While he knew that Kimo was a centered and confident individual, he also was aware of the conflict in his life, and he simply had to ask Kimo about those challenges to the peace he'd clearly found.

"But if I may be so bold, Kimo, your wife was not happy and she left you. She seemed to be so close to your peaceful nature all the time and did not feel it. I cannot understand that," Dag said with trepidation.

Kimo smiled, which immediately put Dag at ease, since he was not sure that he had not perhaps gone a step too far. "Dag, my happiness was not my wife's happiness. I could try my entire life to make her happy, but if she was not happy within, nothing I could do could make her truly happy. I loved her, and so I was glad she left, because she needed to find her happiness. If I truly loved her, I should be happy that she is now hopefully on a journey that brings her true happiness. I do not know if she is closer to it now, but I do know that she was not going to find it here, so I must accept that she was with me for a season and that the season is ended."

Dag once again knew that the tranquility that Kimo felt came from within. It was not about how you addressed people and how they reacted to you. It was more about how an individual allows himself to feel, how he chooses to view life. If that is addressed well, the conflict in life is just noise. This, Dag realized, was the lesson for today.

The conversation continued with pleasantries as usual until it was time at last to bid farewell until the next time. Kimo was one of the few people Dag had met with whom he preferred to talk about the small things that made life richer. Every time Dag left Kimo, he felt as if a piece of his life had come together. Dag felt at peace with this new friend. He seemed to think of frustration that had beset him in his life, and when he was around Kimo, he would always tend to let the frustration go. What joy Dag felt in letting that go.

As the days moved on, Dag felt a desire to really get to know Kimo. He looked at him as a mentor of sorts, though he would not have told that to Kimo, and he assumed they were actually approximately the same age. He was unsure as to whether or not Kimo would be amenable to that distinction.

The real mystery for Dag lay in the juxtaposition of how he felt about Kimo to how apparently countless others felt. Dag felt as if it were Kimo, and now Kimo and Dag, against the world. Kimo seemed quite meek and nondescript to the outside world, yet he had apparently engaged enough of the outside world to be at odds with many of them. He was at odds with his wife, he was visited by the police apparently several times according to Kimo himself, some of the neighbors had mentioned the "strange man living next to Dag," he was involved in county meetings, and then there was the man who approached Kimo at the farmers' market. *What is going on?* Dag found himself thinking time after time after time. Then he recalled that he always saw Kimo with that mysterious basket, empty every morning and empty every night. Soon, Dag told himself that he was going to have to discover the mystery of the empty basket.

Still, Dag was more than pleased to have met Kimo, and if Dag's interaction with Kimo was any indicator, Kimo was one of the finest people he'd ever met.

Time passed, and again Dag went several days without seeing Kimo, except for the routine glimpse early in the mornings and late in the evenings, with Kimo forever carrying his mysterious basket. Little did Dag realize that he was about to at least discover what the basket held.

One evening, as Kimo returned home from one of his daily journeys to the unknown, he once again had trouble getting into his own front door. Once again Dag saw him, jutted his head out the door and offered, "Hey, Kimo, anything I can do to help?"

"No, my friend," Kimo said without turning around. "Want to come in for some tea?"

Dag accepted graciously, as he was beginning to enjoy their not-so-regular tea sessions.

"Just made some banana bread, Kimo. Would you like a piece?" Dag asked. He'd had a couple of bananas that were not going to make it one more day, and they were of a rich sweetness that made for a perfect bread. *There's another lesson,* Dag thought. *Nature tells us that things are supposed to get sweeter with age.*

"Sounds good, Dag," Kimo stated in his quiet and unassuming manner. As Dag ducked back into his place to retrieve the bread, Kimo went into his place to open it up to take advantage of those trade winds that had been around now for about a week. As Dag emerged and crossed the breezeway, he noticed Kimo's mysterious basket on the breezeway by his door. He must have placed it there to try to pry open that stubborn front door of his. As Dag walked by, he glanced in the basket and noticed what appeared to be pellets of pet food at the bottom of the basket. "Seems innocent enough," Dag whispered to himself as he opened Kimo's door to announce his presence. He was going to tell Kimo that he had left his basket out in the breezeway, but then thought better of it. Dag did not want to interfere nor give the appearance of interfering.

Kimo came around the corner of the living room door and said, "Please come in." Dag entered, and there began yet another fascinating conversation in which Dag learned of the philosophy of life of a man who seemed to have captured such inner peace. In fact, Dag was surprised when Kimo mentioned the basket.

"Have you seen a small basket, Dag?" Kimo queried as he looked around the room.

"Why yes, Kimo," Dag offered quickly. "I saw it out on the breezeway. I wasn't sure whether or not you intended to leave it there. Looked as if there was some leftover food in it."

"It is cat food, Dag," Kimo said placidly. "I take it to the park every day to feed the feral cats. There must be dozens of them. It is sad that they are there and no one gives them a home. I am glad they are here on island so they never have to deal with extreme temperature changes, especially if they have to stay outside all the time. You know, we as humans are responsible for the welfare of animals, and the most horrific atrocities happen to them. We as people should be ashamed."

"I agree," Dag posited. "You know, I heard a man talking about animals on a radio show the other day, and he commented out of nowhere that animals were placed here solely for us to do with them as we please. I couldn't believe how callous he was."

"It is sad and maddening what people will say about anything really," Kimo added. "You know, the Lord created animals before he created man. I heard a minister one day say that animals don't go to Heaven because they don't have souls. I thought, 'What arrogance.'"

"Strange," Dag said. "Does he think there is something written that affirms that point of view?"

"Don't know. There are some who say that they don't go to heaven because they didn't receive grace the way people did. My response to that is they didn't *have* to receive grace the way we did because they didn't *fall* from grace the way we did," Kimo said with a tone that was a bit more adamant than his usual mild-mannered speech. "Also," he continued, "King Solomon in the Bible could possibly be the wisest man who ever lived, since the Lord gifted him with great wisdom, and he posed the question as to whether our spirits go upward and the spirits of the animals go into the earth. His response was that we *do not know*. If he didn't know, I am not going to let a fellow traveler on earth with me today convince me differently. Animals are here, and we are supposed to take care of them."

"Know what I heard just today?" Dag offered. "I heard that the Senate just passed a law that made animal cruelty a federal felony."

"Now that is a step in the right direction," Kimo concluded, "but the sad part for mankind is that we have to have a law like that at all. Loving and taking care of animals is a privilege, and we should see it as such."

Once again, within the span of half an hour, Dag found something else to respect and admire about Kimo.

"So you go down to feed the feral cats every morning?" Dag inquired.

"Yes, and every evening, but it is a more complicated process than that. The local animal shelter has assigned some people to each of the island parks. My assignment is right down the hill. When we can, we catch the cats, spay and neuter them, and then return them to the wild. That way they can have a better quality of life. Many of them have become quite tame, at least around me. My only problem is that, since my wife took the car, I have no way to take the containers or to get the cats to the shelter for attention," Kimo said. "More tea?" he added.

"Yes, please," Dag responded. "Well, look, why don't I help you out? I can take you down the hill in the mornings and then bring you home. Then you can do whatever work you need to do at home and I can take you back down in the evenings. Then on Saturday morning, we can get whatever cats we can to the shelter for the spaying and neutering and then return them to the wild when the time is right."

"My friend," Kimo replied, "I am very grateful, but this is quite a time commitment for you, and I cannot ask you to do this."

"Kimo, you are not asking. I am offering. It would be my pleasure to help you out," Dag countered.

Kimo then, in a few short words, accepted and taught Dag a new lesson when he said, "Well, one should never turn down a blessing. I accept your kind offer."

After another cup of tea, Dag left Kimo's home with a renewed sense of purpose and a joy that he seemed to feel nowhere else as he felt it in the presence of his new friend.

CHAPTER 13

Makakilo Mornings

The next day, after his life-affirming talk with Kimo the night before, Dag awakened with a sense of calm that he rarely felt. If the benefits of having a stabilizing influence in his life were ever apparent, it was on this morning.

Mornings in Makakilo were usually quite a bit cooler than Kapolei, which was situated just down the hill, and on some mornings, the fog would sit atop Makakilo that would make someone down the hill look up and see a little town covered in clouds. Dag loved those mornings. It was the life he dreamt of…he was on an island, on a hilltop, in a bungalow, at his kitchen table, surrounded by clouds…and peace. *How could anyone not love this life?* he thought. Then he realized that part of that peace could be attributed to Kimo, his mysterious and incredibly wise new friend.

Dag's phone rang, breaking the silence.

"Hello?" Dag said.

"This is your buddy Gates from the city, Dag. What's up?" John Gates asked cheerfully.

"Hey, guy, not much. I have moved to a peaceful place in the hills west of town, and I am hoping that you three slugs from the Bay Area would come and keep me company," Dag said jokingly.

"Well, my friend, that is why I have called," Gates said. "Annie and Jack want to come out there in about a month, and I want to as well, but I don't want to wait that long. I was wondering if you care if I come out solo a bit earlier."

"Mind? I would be glad to have the company. I have moved and have met a great new neighbor, but other than that, I work from home and am ready to rock and roll. When can you get here?" Dag asked excitedly.

"Well, to be honest, I can come at any time. I have a whole bunch of news for you, but I will just tell you in person. I talked to Jack and Annie, who said they can come later but that I should call you and come on out there, since there is really nothing holding me back." Gates didn't seem to want to offer more at that time.

"Then all I have to say is *get on that plane,*" Dag said more loudly than usual.

"I can be there in two days, guy," Gates offered.

"Excellent. Just call when your plane lands, and by the time you get your luggage, I can drive up to pick you up," Dag posited.

"Sweet! Talk to you soon," Gates said and hung up before Dag could even say goodbye.

Well, Dag thought, *this is a great turn of events.*

CHAPTER 14

Living and Loving Life

The only problem with life going well at any particular point in time was that, when it was going well, it also went quite rapidly. Dag went about his business in the same old way he always had, and before he knew it, two days had passed.

Dag loved his job. There is that old saying that if you love what you do, you never work a day in your life. Well, this was the way Dag felt about teaching in general but particularly about teaching online. The students were accessible, and he could spend countless hours at peace in his home doing better quality research that he could share with the students. He loved it so much that he ate it up, never tiring of the interaction and the enjoyment he took out of clarifying something for a student and helping that student to see a process better than before. He especially loved when a student told him how he or she would be able to utilize what had been learned. In addition, Dag was learning so much himself.

For many, it would appear as if the student would state these things to simply ingratiate himself or herself to the professor, but research methods was a very straightforward course—there are very real and practical ways it can be used, and Dag knew when a student truly saw its usefulness and applicability.

The courses were going well; he was able to collaborate with some other online professors who were conducting research, and Dag stopped in his tracks one day to reflect on the fact that he had all he wanted in life. What a blessed man he was. Just when he thought it couldn't get any better, Dag's phone rang.

"Hey guy," said a familiar voice, "I just landed at the airport and need a ride. I can do Uber if I need to if you are in the middle of your day."

"No, I am on my way," Dag said immediately, recognizing the voice of his new yet trustworthy friend, John Gates. Dag quickly grabbed his keys and headed out the door for the forty-five-minute drive to the airport.

Dag would arise at three-thirty each morning. He would walk five miles for exercise, do some light resistance exercises, and then eat breakfast, shower, and start his workday by 7:00 a.m. He also worked a couple of hours every evening and altogether put in about ten hours per day, so he didn't mind taking a quick break to grab a friend at the airport. He might normally have a slight concern about someone coming to stay with him while he was in the middle of a semester, but one thing he learned quickly about John Gates was that he believed in getting the job done first, and he would clearly be respectful of what Dag needed to do for his work. Dag too was serious about work, fulfilling an obligation, being dependable. Dag grabbed his keys and headed for the airport.

The drive to the airport seemed brief for Dag, and just as he pulled up to the curb, Gates was walking out the door, having received his luggage.

"Hey guy, how's it going?" Gates asked in his direct and casual way. Dag was surprised at how quickly he and Gates became friends. Of course, Gates was the detective who questioned him about all the goings-on in the Bay Area in 1979, so John Gates had an eye and an ear for truthfulness and genuine discussion. He picked up quickly that Dag had no agenda.

Dag never saw Gates frustrated, except on one occasion during the investigation, when he and Gates went to eat at Gates's restaurant called Paul's. A woman who knew the restaurant business well and was perplexed that a beat detective had procured enough funding to create such a wildly popular hideaway for the rich in the city of San Francisco came up to their table, turned to Gates, and said condescendingly, "And just how did *you* come upon enough money to make this place a go?"

Gates calmly placed his fork down, looked up slowly, folded his hands together, and quietly asked, "And exactly why do you want to know?" At that moment, Dag's admiration for Gates grew exponentially. The woman walked away briskly, and Dag realized that it wasn't that he admired Gates because of his quick wit and his ability to defend himself. Rather, it was because he could use that wit to eviscerate someone if he so desired, but he never wanted to resort to that. He was a better man than that. One thing that Dag appreciated about himself was that he picked up on very subtle life lessons, thought about how he could apply them to his life, and if possible, made every effort to do so.

"Going great," Dag said, responding to Gates's question. "Glad to have you here. Now a warning for you—my new place is really kind of old, and while there is more room than I had downtown, it is still small. That said, you stay as long as you like, forever if you want. I have no other plans. Also, when are we going to get a visit from the other two of the Bay Area trio?"

"Thanks, man," Gates said, replying to Dag's generous offer. "On the other matter, not sure when they are coming. I expect within a couple of weeks. Maybe three." The small talk continued for the entire trip, with Dag and Gates having a comfort level with one another that was appreciated by each of them.

"Perfect," Dag replied. "You know, John, I am really glad we are all keeping the connection going. I was a little worried, but in hindsight, especially at this time in our lives, I didn't see why we couldn't keep the connection." Dag was now pulling into his parking space in Makakilo Heights.

"Yeah, in fact," Gates offered quietly, "that's one of the things I want to talk to you about after I get my things in and unpacked. Wow, it's cooler up here...and cloudier."

"Yeah," Dag replied, "I love it to be honest with you."

"Amen," Gates said. "Kind of like home back in the city."

The conversation stopped until they were in Dag's place and Gates had settled in his room. All the unpacking took about thirty minutes, and Gates appeared to take Dag at his offer to make himself at home. As Gates entered the living room and sat down, Dag brought him a drink and sat down himself, anxiously awaiting whatever news Gates had for him. It turned out that he was surprised yet happy with the news that Gates had to share with him.

CHAPTER 15

Going My Way?

"I've made some changes in my life," Gates began, as he told Dag his story, "and I wanted to see what you think."

"Shoot," Dag offered with all his attention focused on the now-quite-serious John Gates.

"Well," Gates began, "I had such a good time when I was last here, and it made me begin to think about what I was going to do with the rest of my life. The only thing keeping me in the Bay Area was that it was a fantastic place to be, and then there was my job and the restaurant. That place became an unexpected cash cow for me.

"Anyway," he continued, "I have been in law enforcement for about thirty-five years, and I realized recently that, while I love working, I do not want to work for anyone else anymore. So I retired from the agency."

"John, I have not known you for long, but it is a surprise to me nonetheless because you were so engaged in what you were doing," Dag said in a flustered fashion.

"I know, Dag, I know," Gates offered, "but there's more to life."

"True," Dag said, "but did you sell the restaurant too?"

"No," Gates said quickly, "but why would I? The managers run it now, and I have stopped making any decisions at all about its operations. I just get the profits." Gates laughed as if he himself could not believe his good fortune.

"So, my friend, does this mean you can stay awhile?" Dag asked, realizing that Gates had more to tell.

"Sure does. In fact, I was wondering if I could impose upon you until I find my own place," Gates said shyly, which was a side of Gates not often seen.

"Of course," Dag responded, "but I just have a couple of questions. Why are you looking for another place? Are you wanting to rent or buy?"

"Definitely rent. I am finally unencumbered and intend to stay that way, unless I can get a great deal in a good location," Gates replied, "and I want another place to get out of your hair."

"Let me make this easy on you, guy," Dag said. "Just stay here permanently. I have second room you can stay in, and there is easy access to anything island-wide here. What do you say?"

"This is amazing!" Gates almost shouted. "Are you sure? If it helps, I can fix almost anything in a house, I enjoy doing repairs and updating things, and I will share expenses and pay rent."

"You don't have to sell me, my friend! Get your address changed to this one, and welcome home!" Dag said, smiling.

This certainly was a nice surprise that Dag had not expected, but *sometimes*, he thought, *things just work out.*

CHAPTER 16

The Process of Settling In

Gates was having some things shipped out to the island, and he said he had to make a quick weekend trip back to San Francisco to tie up some loose ends. Dag said, "Well say, if it's just for a weekend, mind if I tag along? Then we can catch up with Annie and Jack for dinner and let them know they will now have two reasons to visit the islands."

Gates said, "Works for me. Here's what I have to do: I have to inform all the staff at the restaurant where I am and how I can be contacted. I need to stop by and say goodbye to some friends, and I need to close out a few accounts. I know that sounds pretty dramatic since it all is happening so quickly, but when I do something big, I am all in. What I am thinking is that all this can be accomplished and leave time for a long evening with Jack and Annie on Saturday night. Sound good?"

"Sure, but when do you want to do this?" Dag questioned. "Truth is, I need to wrap up some things with school here, and I would prefer to go between semesters if you don't mind, but that's not for two more weeks."

"That will actually be perfect. I can get settled in here and relax, handle much of this over the phone, and that will make the face-to-face transactions quicker and easier once I get to the Bay Area," Gates said.

"Sounds perfect!" Dag said with true excitement. He was very glad Gates was making the move southwest to the islands. "I will call them and tell them to plan on dinner on that Saturday for the four of us when we get there, and I will bum around with them while you get things wrapped up. Of course, I will let you tell them the news about your move on that Saturday night."

And with that, the stage was set for another great weekend with the four friends.

CHAPTER 17

Meeting Kimo

No sooner had this pleasant yet unexpected announcement been made by Gates than Dag ran into Kimo in the breezeway one evening. Dag opened up with his usual, "How are you, my friend?"

Kimo then opened with his usual line of, "Fine, my brother. Want some tea?"

"Sounds great, Kimo, but I have something to tell you first. A friend of mine from the Bay Area came to visit the islands, and he made a quick yet well-considered decision to move out here, and he is staying with me, so I now have company," Dag said, hoping Kimo would invite Gates over for tea as well.

"He is welcome to join us," Kimo said immediately, as calm and genuine as ever. Dag was quite pleased at Kimo's welcoming nature.

"Great, and thanks," Dag responded.

Dag hurried back into this place and went into Gates's room, where he was putting some clothes away, and said, "Say, guy, I have this amazing neighbor I want you to meet. He is low key, friendly, and so wise. Anyway, he has just invited us over for some tea. Want to come along?"

Gates, who never turned down an invitation for a new adventure, replied, "Absolutely," literally dropping all the contents in his hands in a box and heading with Dag out the door.

Dag was surprised that Gates and Kimo got along so well, not because he expected them to be at odds with one another but rather that he didn't perceive that they had that much in common. Kimo was an introverted, retrospective person who pondered life and was the definition of calm, while Gates, though measured and thoughtful with his words and actions, was a man of action, outgoing, engaged, energized. Still, while Dag was pleasantly surprised at first, he realized quickly that the two appeared to have a similar type of inner spirit that served them both well, and it seemed that Gates had more than a passing interest in Kimo's life that made him yet another student of Kimo, whom Dag began to call the Wise Man in the Clouds, since he was such a sage and because the days in the Makakilo hills were often covered in fog. The first conversation Gates had with Kimo seemed like it was the hundredth. Gates was poised to listen to everything Kimo said, at times actually appearing to be in another world. Dag had never met someone who seemed to be as fascinated with another individual as Gates was with Kimo.

Gates, a detective, asked Kimo questions, to which Kimo was happy to respond. Gates at one point asked, "I hear that you read people well. How do you do it?" Gates asked the question with intense interest.

"Well," Kimo replied, "I don't force them into what my first impression of them is, and I realize that, given time, people are going to tell you what they are all about, even if they do not consciously want you to know. The key is not talking but listening and observing."

"Makes very good sense to me," Gates offered. "So since that is the case, can you tell me who I am?" Gates smiled as he posed this challenge to Kimo.

"As I mentioned, I do not rely on first impressions, but we have been here about twenty minutes now, and I think you are engaged with life, likely do not know a stranger, are very measured with your words, are very kind when the world allows for it, and you do not suffer fools well. You would give them the shirt off your back if they truly needed it, but you do not mix with those who choose to remain ignorant. You have much joy but do not laugh aloud much. Could be a cultural thing or even a work-related self-imposed requirement. You are thinking that you are missing something in life, from your own perspective, if you don't mind my saying," Kimo said, waiting for Gates's response. Since Gates appeared a bit bewildered, before he could respond, Dag jumped into the conversation.

"Wow, did he peg you or what?" Dag said, smiling.

Gates was amazed, stating, "Yes, I think you are pretty much on the mark, but how did you pick up on this after such a brief time?"

"Well, my new friend, I saw you bringing some things into Dag's place, and while I did not want to interfere, this breezeway does not allow for much privacy. I saw you interact with a couple of people who passed by, I saw you pet a neighbor's dog, and I heard you talking to someone on the phone. I didn't hear the conversation and would not want to eavesdrop, but from a distance, I could hear your tone, and as a result, I could sense your mindset was one of problem-solving, helping, attention to the other person, yet your tone suggests an unresolved need. In certain matters, you have to be in control of the situation to a degree that I believe suggests chaos within. Most controlling people I have met have an internal chaos. They seek to control the external because there is internal conflict," Kimo offered, to the further amazement of Gates as well as Dag. Gates was uncharacteristically silent after Kimo's full analysis. He appeared to Dag to be soaking in all he'd heard.

Yes, Kimo was not of this world. Dag was of this world, yet conversations with Gates and Kimo made him realize how grateful he was that he could recognize truly deeply rooted people when he saw them.

CHAPTER 18

The Neighbor Sage

As the weeks passed by, Dag was happy that he and Gates began to have tea with Kimo regularly, and Kimo seemed to thoroughly enjoy the exchange. In fact, while Dag was content to watch the exchange between Kimo and a very respectful, sometimes overly respectful Gates, Dag realized that he was wrong when he conjectured earlier that they were different. Taking Kimo's advice and simply listening and observing helped Dag to realize that these two men were quite the same, only wrapped in different packages. Gates's outward appearance was one of action, excitement, and business, while Kimo's was one of calm, quiet, and peace. Still, they were two men who had the same motives yet had two very different approaches. It was as if they were destined to meet, and Dag enjoyed being a witness to it all. As Dag realized this, the old saying "You can't judge a book by its cover" rang true. As Dag grew older, he realized that all these old sayings he'd heard throughout his life were truly wise… "Everything in moderation" was another one that seemed silly and boring to Dag in his youth, yet it turned out to be a recipe for peace and good health.

One day, Dag returned home from running some errands, and Kimo was out in a chair in the breezeway talking to Gates. Dag appreciated this. He always liked for his friends to know and interact with one another. As Gates said goodbye to Kimo and followed Dag back into their bungalow, Gates had some questions for Dag concerning Kimo.

Gates began innocently with, "I cannot imagine that this guy is not respected far and wide. He is so wise. He just seems to have the right mindset, almost as if it is what it is supposed to be. Does that make any sense?"

"It makes perfect sense," Dag countered, "yet I have seen him in direct conflict with several different people in the brief time I have known him, and still he handled every negative encounter with tact and a peaceful approach. The ones confronting him, however, did not."

"What do you mean?" Gates queried. "Do you think there is a side of Kimo that we do not see, a more sinister side? I mean, we all have flaws, right?"

"Well, I had barely moved in when I heard his wife screaming at the top of her lungs, and the police came by asking me about him one day. Neighbors think he is strange, and when we went to the farmer's market one day, he was approached by a man who was very angry with him. I cannot tell you the reasons, and the only reason I am telling you this is because I would completely believe Kimo, no matter what the story turns out to be. I have seen his kindnesses and his day-to-day actions, and I can only chalk the whole thing up to his being wildly misunderstood by many people. The idea that there would be any ulterior motives or underhanded behavior on the part of Kimo is unconscionable to me," Dag conjectured.

"Well, I guess time will tell, guy," Gates responded. "Of course, as it stands now, I can certainly see why you would have the mindset you do concerning Kimo."

"Yes, it is a true mystery to me," Dag said.

"You know, the day I moved in, before I even met Kimo, I saw him out by that big ficus tree on the grounds here, talking to someone who did not seem very pleased with Kimo at all," Gates added.

"And let me guess…Kimo was standing there, not saying a word…just taking the heat," Dag offered.

Gates responded, "As far as I could tell, yes."

"I wonder if there is a way to get to the bottom of this, just in an effort to help Kimo," Dag said.

"Don't know, but I would only want to do it if we truly think it is something Kimo would want for us to do. One thing I have learned about him in this brief period of time is that he minds his own business and does not seem to need too much help in the world," Gates asserted.

"You are right about that," Dag said.

In the coming weeks, Dag and Gates and Kimo began to spend several evenings a week together, talking about life in general, with Dag and Gates stating that they wished that they had known Kimo for a long time. They both perceived that life would have been much easier had they approached life the way Kimo did.

Kimo's personality was an attractive one, not because he was engaging or handsome or had a way with words. There was simply a knowing look he had about him. He never tried too hard to make an impression, and every statement he made, every look he gave, and every decision he made was genuine, honest, and with good intention. How odd it seemed to Dag that anyone could see him any other way. Yet there were others who saw him in a different light, and Dag just knew they had to be wrong. *Perhaps bad fortune just seems to find Kimo,* Dag thought. *Bad things do happen to good people.*

CHAPTER 19

The Search for Answers

As was the new ritual for Kimo, Dag, and Gates, they were sitting in Kimo's kitchen one evening, listening to one another, pondering life, finding peace and joy through quiet and well-spoken words. Gates mentioned recently to Dag that it was as if he had been in another world every time he left Kimo's presence, and Dag, after reflection, said he felt the same way.

This evening, in particular, was a good one, because Dag was finally and subtly able to bring up once more the conflict that seemed to arise between Kimo and others. Kimo even seemed to welcome the conversation.

The discussion of neighbors came up, Kimo mentioned that he knew several of the neighbors, to which Dag responded, "That's great, but I never see you interact with them."

Kimo replied, "Well, many of them knew my wife, and she likely spoke with them on an almost daily basis when I was down the hill. Others believe that I am anti-progress for the Makakilo area, and still others have shied away, perhaps because they have heard things and choose to be standoffish. It's all fine, though. They don't bother me."

Gates said, "It requires great inner peace for a person to have others think these things and not wish to respond. I admire you for that."

"Well," Kimo replied, "I cannot control what others think. I can only control my truth and how I interact. No one can say I have belittled them, or raised my voice to them, or spoken ill of them. If I do not do these things, then whatever it is they have against me is their issue, not mine. You have heard the expression 'What others think of me is none of my business.' Well, I embrace that saying wholeheartedly."

It took very little time for Kimo to move on to something more pleasant, yet before he did, he mysteriously added, "I think that most of the people who are upset with me have reasons that come from the non-personal realm, and these individuals up here at home have what they perceive to be personal reasons. I don't know why. I truly don't know why."

At that point, Kimo began to strum his ukulele, which was the well-received cue for Dag and Gates to sit back and enjoy the music rather than pursue a topic that was clearly not weighing on the mind of their wise friend in the least. The remainder of the evening was pleasant. Then the clouds moved in.

CHAPTER 20

An Unwelcomed Reality

Dag and Gates retreated to their place, and Gates said, "Want a nightcap before you go to bed?"

"Sure," Dag said, and he sat down while Gates poured two drinks and handed him one of them.

"Dag, I have a bit of a problem," Gates said, "and I think you deserve to hear about it."

"Shoot," Dag replied.

"Well, okay. You know," Gates began, "that I loved my work in law enforcement, and I had a particularly good feeling about being a detective. I had dreamed of it for many years as a young man, and when my dream became a reality, I was very excited."

"I can see why, John," Dag added. "Adventure, intrigue, doing so much good, having to figure out complex cases."

"And that is the issue," Gates responded.

"What?" Dag said.

"Figuring out complex cases. That requires intense and often exhausting hours of research, logic, almost reading people's minds sometimes," Gates said, almost sadly.

"John, what's up," Dag said, wanting to know what the problem was.

"I am beginning to suffer memory loss," Gates said. "My mother had dementia, and my father had full-blown Alzheimer's. I did the

DNA test and was found to carry the variant that causes late-onset Alzheimer's, and of late, I have begun to have memory lapses."

"John, I think at times we all have battles with memory," Dag offered, trying to make the situation lighter than he knew it was going to be.

"Dag, I was asked to resign as a detective because I was beginning to show signs of memory loss that go well beyond what would be considered normal," Gates admitted. "I came here because I truly love it here, but I had to get away. You are the only one who knows about this. It is going to get worse. Have you noticed that lately I have been forgetful?"

"Just a few times, but nothing that appeared to me to be out of the ordinary," Dag said. "Oh yeah, and then there was the time when you and the others came out here the first time and you had forgotten the day of departure. Was that part of the memory loss as well?"

"Uh, yes…sure was. I just wanted you to know before things got worse, Dag, and they are going to get worse. I hope you don't regret your offer for me to stay here," Gates said apologetically.

"John, you don't sign on for a friendship by saying I will be around until the going gets tough," Dag replied quickly. "You can count on me."

Gates rubbed his forehead, hiding his eyes as if he didn't want to think about what the future would hold.

CHAPTER 21

The Long, Long Weekend

Dag's semester ended, and the time came for Gates's trip to wrap up his life in San Francisco. He was happy that Dag was tagging along. They were both looking forward to seeing Jack and Annie. For Gates, it was a weekend of big events, leaving a lifelong home for new environs. Sometimes, as Gates soon discovered, the logistics of moving is never as difficult as saying goodbye to friends you will now engage by text and the random visit, friends who will tell you to keep in touch when you both know neither of you will, and passing acquaintances who deserve a nod because they were a part of the mechanics of daily life. The most difficult goodbyes for Gates were the ones whom he could tell would genuinely miss him when up to that time he had no idea they gave him a second thought. Still, closing the chapter was exactly what he planned to do.

As Dag grabbed his bag to head out the door with Gates, Gates stopped him. "What's going on?" Dag asked innocently.

"Before we go a step further, Dag, I need to tell you something," Gates said, a look of fear in his eyes that Dag had not seen in him before.

"Sure. What is it?" Dag asked curiously.

"Well, I am scared. What I told you about last night scares me. It scares me that I could lose my memory. Some might say that if you lose your memory, at least you might not know that you have a problem. That's nonsense. Seeing your life fade away…in many cases, you know it's happening, and you are powerless. I don't want to have this problem. At least, I think it will eventually be a problem," Gates said in a whisper.

"Nothing we can't work out," Dag said. Gates shook his head.

"I grew up with a father who gradually lost his memory. Dementia set in with him when I was relatively young, and we later learned it was full-blown Alzheimer's Disease," Gates began. "I didn't think it could happen to me, but I am clearly having longer and longer periods of forgetfulness that concern me. I can only imagine the things I am forgetting that I never recall again or that people are too kind to mention to me.

"You might not have noticed it yet, but you will. I have contacted a doctor to have some tests run. While some might think it to be silly, I took that DNA test that's on the market today, and it actually said that I carry a variant for early-onset Alzheimer's," Gates said, beleaguered.

"Yes," Dag said, "you have mentioned that to me."

"See?" Gates said, "I cannot even remember having told you that. I don't see immediate and drastic changes that need to be made. I just need for you to be aware of it and tip me off if something goes wrong or if I am not grasping something," Gates added.

"Of course, you can count on me, John," Dag said. "In all honesty, I cannot recall an incident in which you have forgotten something major, but I will do anything I can to help you in the future. Who's the doc you are going to see?"

"Oh, it'll be a long-term thing, but I will fill you in on all that after we get back from the Bay Area. Is it ok with you if we drop it for now and talk again when we get back here?" Gates added.

"Of course," Dag said. "I just want to say goodbye to Kimo."

"You can try, but I just looked over there and it is totally dark. I think he's out somewhere. Check it out," Gates said.

Dag walked over to his doorway and, seeing total darkness at Kimo's place, decided to leave him a note instead. He quickly scribbled a note to tell him where he and Gates were going and when they planned on returning, and then he stuck the note inside the cracks on Kimo's door.

After going back into Dag's place and grabbing duffel bags, itin-
eraries, and laptops, Dag and Gates headed out the door and hopped
into Dag's car. It was a beautiful early Saturday evening, and the
twilight was peaceful, like so many Hawaiian nights. The ride to the
airport was brief and uneventful, and then about two miles from the
airport, Gates's silence turned into frustration. "Damn it! I left my
wallet at the drugstore at the bottom of the hill. See what I mean?"
he said, clearly upset with himself.

"That is absolutely no problem, guy," Dag said. "Let me whip
the car around and we will pick it up."

"Well, I left it there when I went down the hill early this morning to get some toiletries for the trip. I need to call to see if they still
have it," Gates said. Ten seconds later, they confirmed that they had
the wallet and that he could swing by at any time.

"Okay, they have it. I cannot believe I went the entire day and
didn't remember this. It's not like me at all," Gates offered, still frustrated with himself. As they approached the exit to turn around, a
thought hit Dag. "Look," Dag offered, "why don't we head on to the
airport, and we can unload the luggage, I can have a drink, and you
can take my car back to pick up the wallet. Besides, lately the agri-
cultural check that we have to send our bags through has a line like
you wouldn't believe."

"That actually makes good sense. I mean, we are nearly at the
airport anyway," Gates admitted. "Cool. I can be back in two shakes.
Time me," Gates said, finally showing a hint of a smile now that the
situation was going to be resolved. Gates did not like inconvenience
or forgetfulness on his part, so the smile was a good sign.

"Besides, and I want you to remember this," Dag said having
stuck his head back into the door before Gates departed, "forgetting
this is something that could happen to anyone. I am here to help you
when you slip up, as promised, but along with that, I am going to tell
you when I think you might be overly concerned about an incident."

"Fair enough," Gates said. "Fair enough."

"Oh, and that is one of the only stores around that continually
has Haribo Peaches. Pick up a bag for me, okay?" Dag asked.

"You betcha," Gates said, and he sped away.

In no time, it seemed, Gates was back and all was well, Haribo Peaches in hand.

They boarded the plane, they had a pleasant flight, Gates handled all his pressing business in the city, and before long it was Saturday night in San Francisco, and Dag, Annie, and Jack were waiting for Gates at the Blues Trip with open arms. Dag decided that if anything were going to be mentioned about Gates's problems with his memory or about his move to the islands, Gates was going to have to be the one to address it. Dag just thought that seemed like the right approach.

"Why are you down?" Annie said to him immediately as he approached the table.

"And what makes you think he's down?" Jack conjectured.

"Because he has a sparkle in his eye almost all the time, and it is not there." Turning to Gates again, she said, "What gives, John?"

"As you can see, my friend, I didn't tell them," Dag offered.

The look Annie and Jack gave to Dag was brief, and then they fixed their eyes on Gates, who said, "Look, this is a really good thing. It is only briefly sad. I have closed up my business here in the city and am moving to the islands, where Dag is putting me up for the foreseeable future."

Dag was always quite impressed that Annie and Jack could pick up on a cue and do and say the right thing immediately. Jack began with, "That is great!" Annie followed with the same sentiment.

"You know," Annie said, "I like it because it's another reason to go to the islands. There are now two of us on each side of the Pacific to make sure we keep the trips going, and we will likely see you more if you're there than if you stay in the city. I think this is great!"

Thanks to incredible intuition from Dag's dear friends Jack and Annie, the gleam in Gates's eye returned somewhat, and the weekend was turning out to be a positive one once again.

It took no time for Dag and Gates to decide to stay in the Bay Area for another couple of days. It also took no time for "another couple of days" to turn into a full week.

CHAPTER 22

Living Large

The four friends had more fun than could be had it seemed. They visited all the old haunts, with Annie's loft being ground central. Each of them went off on their own, with plans always being made for where to meet up for a fun lunch or long, long dinner to celebrate the simple yet profound joy to be found in the richness of life.

The foursome went to Bart's for nightcaps, to Harry's for a quick lunch, to Joe's down the street from Annie's for a cup of coffee and to the Blues Trip Lodge for late-night jazz, as well as to Dexter's for sushi. Dag watched the others eat sushi, as he was not a fan of the dish. He loved seafood but not raw.

One day, the group packed a lunch and spent the entire day in the park, listening to 1960s folk rock and kicking back in general. At the end of that day, they retreated once more to Bart's for a nightcap, vintage music, and the sharing of memories that never seemed to get old. There were moments when Dag wondered yet again how his life would have been had he never left the city. He loved it so, and he could see why Jack and Annie loved it as well. Still, this did not stop him from trying to convince Jack and Annie to relocate to the islands as well.

Jack's response was an understandable one. He said, "There is every good reason for me to state that at this point in my life relocation would be ideal, but whether it is a good thing or a bad thing, I would have this constant gnawing need to be back here in the city I love. Every fiber of my being tells me to go, but I cannot. It is as if I was made to be here in the city. It is part of me. It is all of me."

Annie's head was nodding the entire time Jack was speaking. "Yeah, I cannot believe that this knucklehead is reading my mind, but I have to admit that I could not have said it better myself. Were I to leave, in some strange way, it would seem like a betrayal. So strange." This time, it was Jack nodding in agreement.

"Well," Dag replied, "the good news is that now we have equal forces on each end prodding us to keep in touch. This way, it will really seem as if we each have two homes."

"Right you are," Annie said.

To highlight the end of the week of fun, the group took a boat ride to Alcatraz, toured it as if they were visitors, and then ended the fun at Annie's for some coffee and a very serious discussion about when and where the next meeting would be.

At once, Dag's phone rang, and as he heard the message from the other end of the line, his joy evaporated into thin air.

CHAPTER 23

A Stolen Goodbye

"But how? What happened?" Dag was heard asking the person on the other end of the line. The three friends could tell something was dreadfully wrong, as they witnessed Dag turn pale. He now had all their attention, yet they were polite and did not disturb him in the middle of his call. Still, they were more than anxious to discover what could have shaken Dag so. After a long silence, Dag softly asked the person on the other end, "I am in San Francisco and am headed back tomorrow. Do you need me to leave tonight?" At this, the trio with him assumed the worst. But what could have made Dag so sullen all of a sudden? After what seemed like an eternity for Dag's friends, he finally hung up the phone and sat with a despondent look, as if he did not know where to begin.

"Dag," Annie said with an uncharacteristic gentleness in her voice, "what's wrong?"

"Kimo is dead," Dag said as if he were unable to comprehend it himself.

"What? Who's Kimo?" Annie said without thinking. She and Jack looked at one another with a questioning look.

"What?" said Gates. "What happened?"

"Well, of course, they don't know all the details yet," Dag offered, "but he was definitely murdered, and here's the rub…" Dag's words trailed off.

"And what's that?" Jack interjected.

"They found him dead in my place," Dag said.

"Kimo was an older local man whom I befriended when I moved to Makakilo on the west side of the island," Dag began. "That is, I say I befriended him as if he were in need of my friendship. Turns out I was in need of his. He became, in a very short period, one of the kindest and wisest men I ever knew. He had an approach to life that was to be envied, and he loved life and was a clean and gentle spirit. John has met him. John, am I right?" Dag asked, hoping someone else would speak for a moment.

"You certainly are, Dag," Gates said, taking over the conversation for a bit. "Kimo had words of wisdom that were so simple that he made you continually wonder why you did not adopt his way of thinking earlier. Sounds strange, but he was two steps ahead of the thoughts of others, yet with that advantage, he still never used it to his advantage. He was approachable, soft-hearted, and strong, all at the same time. The idea that he would be murdered is something I cannot wrap my thoughts around right now."

"So what are you guys gonna do?" Jack queried. "You know there is going to be a lot of action around your place now, and still you know you have to get back to answer questions and try to discover what happened. The idea that this happened in your place is kind of creepy."

"Yes, it is, Jack, but I think we have to get back as soon as we can to answer questions and to try to discover for ourselves how this could have happened and why. I am involved in this for several reasons. I knew Kimo and interacted more with him than probably anyone else at the present time, I lived next door, and he was murdered at my place. I just realized how difficult that was for me to say. One thing I will say is that I bet that whoever did this, if they knew Kimo at all, knew also that he was a wise man, and that alone had to be a bit frightening to them. They have a couple of suspects seen jumping over the lanai railing and running into the hills."

Gates chimed in, "And now you are thinking like a detective, my friend. I think what we have to do is to research the people known to have a conflict with Kimo, identify potential motives, and scour your place ourselves to discover why this would have occurred at your place. Yes, it is imperative that we get back to your place as soon as possible. Wait," Gates added, "I am acting as if I am still on the job and that we are all interested in working on this. Sorry if I am overstepping."

"Are you kidding?" Annie said. "I am just jealous that we are not over there right now working on this! I mean, we all know we are good at solving cases." The guys all laughed a bit, reflecting on the case they recently worked on there in the Bay Area.

CHAPTER 24

Westward Ho

"Well, I have the solution, my friends," Dag offered. "Why don't we *all* go back to the islands tomorrow morning? Of course, that is going to require that we get busy immediately to make that happen."

Without blinking, Jack spoke up and was more decisive than any of the other three had ever seen him. "Okay everyone, let's do this. I will see what flight these two are on tomorrow and see if we can get on it. Then we all go home to pack."

Annie added, "Great, and when you get everything together, all of you come over to my place to stay the night. Guys, what time is your flight tomorrow?"

"One-twenty p.m.," Gates said. "Or was it four-twenty? I can't..."

Seeing Gates struggle with this detail, Dag said, "Oh yeah, we were going to leave at four-twenty but decided on one-twenty." Gates looked at him with appreciation, knowing they'd never discussed an alternate time. Gates had just forgotten the time. Annie and Jack apparently failed to notice.

"Okay, I will set up for a car to pick us up at my place at 11:00 a.m.," Annie responded. "If Jack cannot get us on the same flight, he can get us on a later one, and we can go to the airport early with you guys anyway."

"Great," Dag said, "and since Gates and I are living out of our suitcases, packing is no big deal, and we will pick up some wine and snacks for this evening and some breakfast for in the morning."

"Great planning," Gates said, "and I for one am anxious to get back to the island." The other three looked at one another with a knowing glance of agreement, and the team disbanded briefly, to meet later at Annie's loft on Lost Mission Street.

Despite the tragedy that was Kimo's demise on Oahu, and despite all it was going to take to get back there in a timely fashion, the four made the best of the evening at Annie's place, and during that evening, the four reminisced about the case they recently worked on there in the city and how the outcome was a good one that kept the group together and helped them to make a new friend in Detective John Gates.

As the group talked about old times, the conversation went from the old case involving Max Verdon to the new case, now hitting very close to home, especially for Dag. As they discussed the new case involving the death of Kimo, Dag shared some of Kimo's wisdom with the group. Where possible, Gates supported Dag's comments.

"It sounds strange, but I am convinced that if Kimo were here, he would tell us not to complicate or overthink this case. He would tell us to first look for the obvious. He told me on numerous occasions that he could tell so much about people by just listening, and he also said that if you listen closely, people tell you in subtle ways what they are all about and what their motives are. Maybe we should listen to Kimo to help us solve his case," Dag said, happy to be using Kimo's wisdom to apply to his approach to this crime.

"That makes quite a bit of sense, Dag," Gates said. "Kimo was not a complex man, and from the look of it, he did not have a particularly complicated life. So it is wise to begin with the simple approach: get a list of people who might have had an issue with him, find out what we can, and see if anything leads us to the murder."

Turning to Jack and Annie, Dag said, "You guys would have loved Kimo. Heart of gold, a peaceful man, a giving man…and yet a misunderstood man from what I can tell. He had some people who were not kind to him, as if he had done something to them, and yet it simply was not in Kimo's nature to be unkind. He seemed to be a very strong man, and yet he never appeared to use his strength to gain advantage over anyone. He reasoned with people. He did not strongarm them."

"Then how could this have happened?" Annie posited. "It just doesn't make sense. Your friend Kimo had some enemies, that is unless it was a random burglary attempt gone wrong because they knew you weren't home, and Kimo happened in at just the wrong time."

"No," Dag said, "the police said based upon the conditions, it appeared that nothing was amiss in my place and the target appeared to be Kimo. I am just not sure why he was in my place. Keep in mind that I had given him a key, and I had no problem with Kimo being in my place, yet he never came over without an invitation, though he'd have been welcomed at any time. I am confident that he knew that."

"Perhaps he was hiding from someone," Gates offered.

"Now that is intriguing," Dag replied. "I never thought about that idea. That must be why you got the big bucks as a detective all those years." Gates laughed.

Gates added, "If he were hiding, that means that he was expecting some unpleasant company and likely someone who would have no trouble coming up to his place. That is, the individual might have not been concerned about being seen."

"An assailant who was known to Kimo and perhaps others in the complex...hmmm," Dag said, even more intrigued than before. "Well, as we have said before, it's a place to start."

The evening flew by. The four friends were all able to get on the same flight the next afternoon, and they arrived at the airport in plenty of time to do so. They also wrangled their way to getting four center bulkhead seats. There were five to a row, with the fifth seat being taken by a gentleman named Cary. Cary was a man originally from rural Virginia, stocky, ever smiling, and worldly wise, and he actually made a comment to Dag, by whom he was seated, that turned out to be very helpful in the case.

Of course, the four friends discussed the murder at length during the flight, and their new acquaintance Cary couldn't help but overhear. At one point, he said, "I do not mean to intrude, but the two of you who knew the man who was killed keep saying that it doesn't make sense that this man was so disliked by someone that they would want to murder him, but the fact is that based on the evidence someone did dislike him that much. As much as it hurts to hear this, don't exclude research to see if your friend Kimo was doing something that was directly responsible for someone disliking him. That is, what activities was he involved in and who wouldn't like his involvement? If all these people he ran into had an issue with him, it wasn't an isolated incident that he was on the bad side of people only once."

Armed with this new information from their new friend Cary, they arrived on the island, and Dag even exchanged contact information with Cary in case they ever decided that their paths would need to cross again. It appeared that Cary had lived on the west side of the island for years and was quite familiar with the goings-on in the town of Kapolei, even to the point of knowing many elected officials and businesspeople in the area. Jack is the one who recommended that Dag get Cary's contact info, in case Cary could be of help to them down the road with the investigation.

The four found Dag's Subaru in the parking garage. Of course, the parking charge was a few hundred dollars since they had overstayed in the Bay Area. Dag had forgotten about the car at the airport and gulped when the booth attendant said, "Eight days, $335." After absorbing the shock of that, Dag and his friends motored to the ewa side of the island to Dag's new digs. While they knew what had occurred and that there would be people wanting to question Dag and perhaps even Gates, they were surprised to arrive at Dag's bungalow and find it open with the police inside.

Dag wanted to be certain that he was doing everything right in his interaction with the police, so he immediately told them who he was and that they were, in fact, in his living room. The police were quite courteous and began to immediately ask questions.

"Sir," asked the first detective, "just how well did you know the deceased?"

"I have only recently moved out here to the ewa side of the island, but he and I became acquainted soon after that and have spent quite a few hours together over the past several weeks," Dag offered.

The second detective chimed in, "Any idea why anyone would want to kill him?"

Dag was about to tell the detectives all he knew about Kimo appearing to have several people who did not like him, but he caught himself in midsentence, looked at Gates, and altered his approach.

"Well," Dag said, "I know that…uh…I wish that I could tell you something specific that would help you out, officers, but I do not know of a single thing that would make someone want to kill this fine man. He was a gentleman, very wise, and I never heard him raise his voice to anyone. One could reason with him if in disagreement, and in fact, it is baffling to both of us that this could occur as some kind of vengeance." Dag turned to Gates, nodding as if seeking Gates's approval of what he had just stated.

Gates picked up the cue, nodded, and added, "Yes, I haven't known him for long, but Dag's description seems right on point to me." Then Gates turned to Dag and whispered, "What was Kimo's last name again?"

"Akamai," Dag said softly.

"Right, right," Gates responded. Dag was surprised at Gates's failure to recall Kimo's last name, but then he recalled their conversation of the week before. Dag had yet another concern that perhaps Gates's retention of facts was in question.

Dag asked, "Is there anyone who has taken care of funeral arrangements or a memorial service of any kind?"

The first detective turned to the second detective, who had walked across the room and was about to ask him Dag's question, but the second detective had heard the question and responded, "Last I heard, no one had claimed the body." This surprised Dag. He decided that, if that were the case, he had some tasks to do to help to give Kimo the kind of service that in Dag's mind he so richly deserved.

CHAPTER 25

The Strangest Farewell

Dag realized he had not known Kimo for long, but with no one having claimed the body, Dag was determined to give Kimo a proper service of farewell. He contacted the mortuary, had Kimo cremated after checking with the police to get approval, and set a date for his ashes to be scattered in the Pacific Ocean at Kaena Point on the west side of the island. Since he had no real way of knowing who Kimo's friends or acquaintances were, he decided to create an obituary to make sure that more than just a notice was published concerning Kimo's death. The problem was that describing Kimo was going to be a challenge since he had not known him a long time. He didn't even know his age. Still, with fingers on the keyboard, Dag wrote from the heart:

Recently, the island of Oahu lost a true treasure. Kimo Akamai of Makakilo lost his life, a life that was energized by his spirit, a spirit of giving, a spirit of oneness with the land, a spirit of wisdom that gave him and those around him great peace....

As Dag wrote the rest of the tribute, he became very sad, almost despondent, finally reflecting upon what a tragedy it was that Kimo lost his life. Through the sadness, though, Dag had a sense that, even though Kimo would not have wanted to die the way he did, he would somehow be one with the peace that death and heaven would bring.

Focusing upon Kimo's calmness and acceptance of things he could not control, Dag continued with the preparations for Kimo's farewell, not knowing what to expect. Little did he know that he and his friends were in for a big surprise.

As the day approached for the memorial service, Dag prepared a singer to sing some of Kimo's favorite songs, some faith-based and some secular. With the help of Jack, Annie, and Gates, he pieced together a program of sorts, and they drove out to Kaena Point with the ashes of Dag's dear friend. When they reached the end of the road, which was the beginning of the hike up to Kaena Point, Gates exclaimed in a way uncharacteristic of him, "What the...?"

As the four friends got their bearings and surveyed the landscape, they saw at least five hundred people making their way up to the place where Kimo would be laid to rest. Feeling daunted by the entire experience, Dag stammered, "I...I don't know what to do."

"Well guy," Jack responded, "these people saw your announcement, many of them likely have heard the circumstances surrounding Kimo's death, and so this crowd could be filled, with mourners, gawkers, or perhaps even murderers."

Dag, with much trepidation, made his way up to the top of Kaena Point with his friends, still perplexed at what appeared to be an outpouring of interest at the passing of this man whom, Dag assumed, had very few friends. At the top of the point, there stood a rock that could easily serve as a platform of sorts, and the crowd gathered around it as if awaiting the keynote speaker. Dag reluctantly strode to the platform and, as he was about to begin, looked briefly at the crowd. He thought his mind must have been playing tricks on him.

He saw Kimo's ex-wife, many police officers, several elected officials he recognized from television and on many posters around town, and to top it all off, Cary, the man who sat beside Dag on the plane coming from San Francisco! Why would these people have an interest in giving a sendoff to a man whom Dag was almost certain had never been visited by any of them? He felt as if his entire life were running rings around itself and culminating at this particular day and time.

As Dag gathered his wits about him, and with looks of total support from Annie, Jack, and Gates, he focused on his eulogy and, for a brief moment, wondered where to begin. He was confused in his own mind because there was everything to say and nothing he could think of—all at once. Still, he knew he had to do Kimo justice, and this resolute mindset finally set him on a path to deliver the address of a lifetime.

"Ladies and gentlemen," Dag began, "we are here today to pay our respects to someone whom I met by chance…at least it seems that way. You have heard that saying that life is what happens when you are busy making plans. Well, Kimo Akamai entered my life one day, as I just happened to move into the bungalow next to his up in Makakilo.

"If I were to tell you that I know all there is to know about Kimo, that would not be true, yet what I knew of him astounded me. When someone passes, I know that many kind things are often said, but rest assured that the things I say to you today are my truth. The world is a lesser world today because Kimo is not in it, yet in a different way, he *is* still in it. He is in us, in everyone who knew him. The poet Robert Frost once stated in one of his poems that you cannot touch a flower without troubling a star, and I look at Kimo as a flower who was in our lives for a reason. He was the epitome of calm in the midst of a storm, a refuge that could only be appreciated if we, in our hurried lives, stopped to listen to him and to think about what is important.

"I often sat on the floor of his living room, enjoying the silence, and then calmly hearing him speaking wisdom through the silence that left an indelible mark on my mind and soul in the most positive way possible."

Dag glanced up briefly to see Kimo's ex-wife exit the crowd abruptly. He somehow was able to continue speaking as he kept an eye on her descent, which wasn't that difficult since the entire trail back to the cars was clearly visible from where Dag was standing. He noticed briefly that the cars were parked askew, as if they were a rag-tag group of horses half-tied in front of a saloon in the Old West. Dag continued the eulogy.

"Kimo once told me that a person will only listen to you to the degree that you listen to them. Part of his success as a person was also that, when talking with a person, he always turned the positive attention to the person with whom he was speaking, asking how they were, what makes them joyful, and what their goals were in life. That kind of selfless attention comes from one who is focused on others for their benefit, as well as from one who is self-assured. Yes, Kimo Akamai was happy in his own skin. Many of us could aspire to be like Kimo, and if we are not that way, we should strive to find out why.

"I recall taking Kimo to eat pancakes at the local pancake house down the street early one morning. He held the door open for an elderly man with a walker who was moving ever so slowly. Half apologizing for making us wait, the old man looked at Kimo, who was still patiently holding the door, and he said to Kimo, 'I think you must be an angel,' to which Kimo replied without hesitation, 'Or maybe you are.'

"He always sought and easily found the goodness in others, and he was ever so hesitant to criticize someone," Dag said. Yet in finishing, Dag added words that might have sounded rather pointed. He concluded by saying, "There is such an outpouring of support for Kimo here today. I hope he found in living the same support he has found at his passing."

As Dag turned to release Kimo's ashes, a strong wind seized the ashes that were quickly dropping from the urn and caught them up and miraculously carried them, as if they were never meant to touch the earth. Where the ashes finally rested, no one will ever know. With that, Dag turned to his friends and became part of the group of four that was the last to descend from Kaena Point. That is, all except for one individual, and that lone remaining mourner was Cary, the man Dag and his friends met on the plane from San Francisco to Honolulu.

Noticing Cary still at the top of the point, Dag told his friends to go on to the car while he turned back around and went up, meeting Cary on his way down. The two stopped, and Dag began the conversation.

"Hi. It's Cary, right?" Dag offered as a conversation starter.

"That's right. I guess you are wondering how I ended up here," Cary replied with a half-smile.

"You can understand why I am quite surprised to see you here," Dag said softly yet pointedly.

"Certainly," Cary admitted, not in the least bit defensive. "After I heard you guys talking on the plane, I was quite intrigued by the whole mystery of how this gentleman died and what the possible motives could be. So I set out to see what the newspapers said about the incident to see if there was perhaps any rapid closure that would settle my curiosity. Seeing nothing, I then thought that at least I could find something in the obituaries, and that is when I ran across your notice about the service being held out here."

"Well, that certainly ties things together," Dag said, once again in his old friendly manner.

"Yes," Cary said, "I guess it does, but there is more to the story that I haven't told you."

"Oh?" Dag responded.

"Yes," Cary said, "and I really came today to talk to you."

"So what information could you possibly have for me?" Dag said more intently.

"I am a police consultant," Cary said, "and I have some tips that I think might help you in this case. I was hoping that perhaps we could grab some coffee at some point and discuss how I could perhaps be involved in helping you to solve this case."

Dag stood speechless and perplexed, thinking one more time about how life bears so many surprises.

CHAPTER 26

A New Colleague

"I am all ears," Dag said, slightly skeptical and not caring if it showed.

"Well," Cary said, "this island is a small place. It is not a good place to commit a murder, so I am thinking that the mindset of many criminals on this island would be to stay close to the goings-on that occur with respect to the case, because he or she is going to have to be able to react and move in an instant."

"Makes good sense," Dag offered, warming up a bit to this new person having such a vested interest in the life and death of his friend. "So, what might this actually mean?"

"One thing it could mean is that the perpetrator was actually at the memorial service," Cary said, waiting for a subtle glimmer of interest from Dag, and then continuing. "I have found that in all my research, when the sphere of influence is tight, as it is here, the perpetrator is often highly involved in the events that occur post-murder. You have heard that old saying about keeping your friends close and your enemies closer? Same principle."

"So what you are suggesting is that we investigate attendees at the service first to see if there is a possible connection?" Dag asked.

"Indeed, my friend," Cary said.

Dag then said quickly, "If only we'd taken a picture of the crowd. I could kick myself!"

"No need," Cary offered, smiling. And with that, Cary handed Dag his phone, having pulled up several pics of the service with all the attendees visible. "At your service," Cary said, smiling even more broadly.

Dag decided that Cary was worth keeping around.

As Dag's conversation with Cary ended, he made his way back down the mountain to his three friends, who were waiting outside Dag's car. "Oops," Dag said. "Forgot to unlock for you."

"No worries," Annie said, "but you owe me a drink now."

"And how is that?" Dag said, smiling.

"You left me outside the car to melt in the sun, and I became parched," Annie said too dramatically.

"Disgustingly contrived, but okay," Dag said, as Annie smiled and hopped into the car.

On the drive over to the Monkeypod Restaurant, Dag introduced Cary's comments to the group, and they were all quite interested.

"You know," Gates commented, "we often hired police consultants who helped the detectives. They are specialized in different aspects of law enforcement. The ones connected to solving cold cases were quite good at sharing good advice. This isn't a cold case, but he could very well be worth his salt, but I have a question for you. Will he have to tell the police here every move we make concerning this case? In my professional role as a former detective, I would have to say yes."

"That is an excellent question, John," Jack said. "Why don't we invite Cary over to your place for dinner and see what we can find out?"

The other three agreed that this would be an excellent idea. Having given Dag his contact information, Cary clearly would likely welcome a call from Dag, and they could certainly use his help. Dag called Cary immediately upon their return to Dag's bungalow.

"Hello, Cary?" Dag said as someone picked up the line on the other end. "Dag Peyton here. I guess you were not expecting to hear from me this quickly."

"Oh, I don't know," Cary said politely. "I have almost learned to never be surprised at anyone's behavior, and I must say I am really glad you called. I am interested in what you know about this case."

"Well," Dag replied, "I do not want to get ahead of myself, but I think we could use your help. Still, I hope you understand that, not knowing you very well, we were wondering if you'd like to come over to my place and shoot the breeze sometime with my friends and me. You see, we have worked on a case before and have developed an interest in solving cases."

"Sounds perfect. Here on the island, I am a police consultant. I essentially teach classes in criminal justice to current police officers who want to brush up on their skills," Cary began, "and I don't really get into the weeds with them concerning real cases. Having been around real cases but rarely being involved in them anymore, it kind of gets in your blood, and I miss it. When do you want me over? I am free any time after about 7:00 p.m. on any given day."

"Well, how about tomorrow night at about 8:00 p.m.?" Dag offered.

"Excellent. You still live up there on Makakilo Drive?" Cary said.

"Now how did you know that?" Dag asked quizzically.

"Homework," Cary said as he hung up the phone.

CHAPTER 27

Making Sense of It All

Dag didn't know whether to be flattered, impressed, or violated. He had no idea why Cary would have already sought Dag's address, but when he mentioned it to his three friends as he hung up the phone, they did not seem concerned at all.

"Well, Dag," Jack began, "he heard us talking on the plane about the murder. He heard that it happened in your condo, and the news was not silent about the crime nor the location of its occurrence."

"Well, of course," Dag responded, seemingly happy about that solution. As a result, they turned their thoughts from that concern, and it didn't take long for the conversation to come around to more details about the murder. They were deep in conversation when there was a knock at the door. It was a police detective.

"Hello," he said stoically, "are you Dag Peyton?"

"Yes, I am," Dag offered hesitantly. "Are you here about the murder case?"

"Right," said the detective. "The name's Augafa. James Augafa."

"Come in, sir," Gates offered over Dag's shoulder. Gates having been a detective himself, Dag was glad Gates was taking the lead.

Detective Augafa was a husky man of Samoan descent. He was as tall as Dag yet about two hundred eighty pounds. There did not appear to be an ounce of fat on him. Dag imagined he could find it easy to intimidate many people, yet with the group, he had a professional yet courteous demeanor.

The detective began, "I am here to ask a few follow-up questions, since the murder occurred here and since we had a couple of concerns post autopsy."

"Shoot," Gates said.

The detective turned to Dag and said, "Sir, are you ok with having these individuals with you while I question you?"

"Certainly," Dag responded quickly. "In fact, detective, this gentleman was a detective with the San Francisco Police Department for thirty-five years," Dag said, pointing toward Gates.

"Excellent," Detective Augafa said, seemingly fine with the presence of each of the parties. "Just needed to ask if you were aware that there were two separate substances found under Kimo Akamai's fingernails. Under the fingernails of his right hand were two kinds of paint, one of them yellow, and the other kind appears to be from paint used in artwork, and under a left fingernail was just the one kind of paint that paint appears to be from a painting or some other type of artwork. Does any of this make sense to you?"

"No, it doesn't," Dag said. "Do you think that the paint would have come from something in my place here? If so, please have anyone feel free to look around."

Detective Augafa responded as if he had hoped that Dag would make that statement. He said quickly, "We might need to do just that, sir. Of course, we had a preliminary investigation and had forensics come in, yet things can be missed, and now that we have something additional to focus on, perhaps we can uncover something new."

"Sounds great," Gates chimed in. "Where do we go from here?"

"I will take this info to the chief, and he can take it from here," Augafa offered, and with that, he exited with a brief half-smile while stating over his shoulder, "We will be in touch very soon."

"Thank you, detective," Dag called back.

As the detective exited Dag's home, Dag immediately turned to Gates for a reaction to the visit. Without waiting for a comment from Dag, Gates said, "It might be a good thing that Cary has come into our lives. He might be able to assist us as much as we assist him."

Annie, Jack, and Dag looked at one another, wondering what Gates could have meant. It appeared that Gates had an idea.

CHAPTER 28

The Wonders of Clear Thinking

Before the group plunged too deeply into this new information, Gates suggested that they take a break. He said that too often in law enforcement, they would get so bogged down in the minutiae that their thinking became clouded and they actually had trouble reasoning. He said they needed to do some activity that would take their minds off things for a while.

He started by having Dag's Echo play a song, and then the group went around the room requesting their favorite songs as well. The selections were surprising, touching, funny, and a bit scary. Annie began with her favorite song, which was "White Rabbit" by Jefferson Airplane. When she said the name, the room erupted in laughter.

"Now I *know* you're yanking my chain! There is no way," Jack said almost gleefully.

"Get over it, bub," Annie retorted. "This is a song about drugs. I never was into drugs, but it was very popular when I was young, and I always liked the song, so deal with it." Annie sang along until the end, and Cary concurred that the song was very good and had a deeper meaning as well:

> One pill makes you larger
> And one pill makes you small

And the ones that Mother gives you
Don't do anything at all…

As the conversation continued, the four guys became better acquainted with a very contemplative and thoughtful Annie, who was much more emotionally intelligent than any of the others would have imagined.

When it was Jack's turn, he asked Alexa to play "IGY" by Donald Fagan of the group Steely Dan. The group was mesmerized as Jack sang along:

On that train of graphite and glitter
Undersea by rail
Ninety minutes from New York to Paris…

The entire group agreed that the song was a good one indeed, as it put all of them in a more mellow mood. Jack just said that, to him, the song had a great tempo and was also a song of hope for the future. Not having considered that before, the rest of Jack's friends experienced a learning moment and concurred.

Dag came next, who immediately offered up "What You Won't Do for Love" by Bobby Caldwell, and he too, sang along word for word:

Guess you wonder where I've been
I searched to find a love within
I came back to let you know
Got a thing for you
And I can't let go…

After the song ended, Cary asked Dag why he had picked that song, and while Dag indicated that he liked it more for the instrumental portion of the song, it was also a superb song to get lost in…an escape in the mind to a faraway city that was foggy and chilly, where no one knew your name, with a hot tea at a sidewalk café.

"Dag, that was deep," Annie said, half joking, half serious.

"Why do you say that?" Dag responded.

"Because it was oddly specific," she replied, smiling. "You've been thinking about that song for a long time."

Dag just snickered and dropped it.

Gates then pointed to Cary, who was quick to respond. The group was once again surprised when Cary requested "Lord, Be Thou Near to Me" by Selah and Jim Brickman:

> Oh, Lord, I come with heart here open
> For in my hour of darkness I may be
> Seeking the joy of love unspoken
> Oh, Lord, be thou near to me...

Everyone was touched at this song and at the depth of their new friend who requested it. They listened to it again.

Gates was the final contestant for this fun time of mirth, and his friends could not decide whether his selection was a surprise or not. Still, his choice was *Seasons in the Sun* by Terry Jacks:

> We had joy, we had fun
> We had seasons in the sun
> But the hills that we climbed
> Were just seasons out of time...

What followed was a fascinating interlude of quiet contemplation, as each of the five friends tried to discern the meaning behind the selections of their friends. For a moment, the friends were quiet, yet it was interesting that, in the minds of each of them, they were seeking the positive meanings of the songs. That mindset spoke directly to the mutual love and admiration they had for one another yet would likely never address.

After what amounted to about two hours of relaxation and further discussion about the songs and what they really meant, it was time to focus on the case yet again.

"Okay, gang, let's get back on this case," Gates said. "Does everyone feel a bit refreshed?"

"Surprisingly, yes," Dag said, as heads around the room were nodding.

CHAPTER 29

Back to Work

Cary had to duck out for a time to take care of some business at the police station, and so the rest of the crew spent that time talking about what a quality fellow Cary was.

"You know, he's got a goodness about him," Jack said.

"Yeah," Annie said, "and it's beginning to bug me."

"No, it isn't," Dag said, smiling at Annie. She was not happy about the fact that Dag could see through her. She smiled.

Gates explained that he was impressed with Cary's comments about the case and that he thought that Cary's insights were spot on. As a result, they were all excited when Cary showed up again at Dag's bungalow at 8:00 p.m.

They were all glad to get to know Cary, who had an interesting past in law enforcement. To many, he might have appeared to be quiet, yet behind that calm exterior, Dag and the rest of the team discovered a fascinating man who would serve to make the case an interesting one indeed.

Cary was from back east, and his last home was in Virginia prior to moving to Hawaii. He worked as an intelligence consultant for the military around the Pacific Rim before doing essentially the same work for the police force in the Hawaiian Islands. He now worked as a private consultant, but he still was sometimes contracted to work for the police, and he did pro bono work on the side. He also occasionally went back east to remain connected to the police department in Clifton Forge, Virginia, about forty-five minutes from Roanoke.

Jack began the conversation with Cary that evening. "So, Cary, here's what the police detective said when he came by yesterday. Apparently, there were two different kinds of paint under Kimo's fingernails. Any idea what that's about?" Jack and Annie were fascinated when people were so good at what they did that they appeared to have extrasensory perception. While they didn't know Cary that well yet, he appeared to possibly be one of those people.

"Well," Cary said immediately, "there are several things that this could mean. It could mean that it was just a coincidence, but often it means that the deceased didn't die immediately and was trying to struggle with the killer. It could also mean one more thing." Then Cary sat silent.

"And what's that?" Annie offered impatiently, as was sometimes her way.

"It could mean that the deceased was trying to leave a clue as to the identity of his killer," Cary said slowly and emphatically, as if it was what he believed.

"Agreed," Gates said. "I mean, what other reasons would there be for having two different types of paint under one person's fingernails at one time?"

Dag added, "Now wait. Is there a chance that perhaps the two types of paint ended up there at two different times, and maybe a shower or handwashing would not wash them off so that they appeared to be left there at the same time?"

"It's a possibility," Cary said, "but not likely that the amount of paint that was there would be left there over time and have survived washing or showering. If Kimo Akamai was as you describe him, I would think he'd be quite meticulous about his appearance. I am not suggesting a vain focus on looks but rather a concern about cleanliness, and anyway, who wouldn't notice and try to remove paint from under one's fingernails?"

Cary was a kind man, a straightforward man, and wise. That was a combination that was hard to beat.

Jack and Annie discussed the tinge of sadness they would feel if the time came to part from Cary's company. Cary had become an integral part, not only of this case but of this cadre of friends. Dag was the first to mention it.

"Yeah, that Cary is a great guy, and I wish there were a way to bring him into our world more often to spend more time with the gang," Dag, said, clearly stating what everyone else was thinking.

CHAPTER 30

The Power of Alliances

With this new information in their minds, the seemingly ever-growing group of friends embarked on a search for clues as to why Kimo Akamai had two separate kinds of paint under his fingernails. Since one of the paints was suggested to have been from a painting, and since the murder appeared to have occurred in Dag's bungalow, it only made sense to search Dag's place for similar types of paint. An initial search produced nothing of significance.

"Okay, help me out here," Annie said. "What types of things could have that kind of paint on them other than paintings on the wall? I mean, we have looked at the few paintings Dag has, and the list is short. You must admit, Dag, you are not an art collector." She looked at Dag and smiled.

"When you're right, you're right, sister," Dag said, no longer surprised nor offended by Annie's direct nature. "Wait," he added. "Kimo painted on the side. I wonder if he had anything sitting out that would give us a clue. I have a key to his place."

"Well, what are we waiting for?" Jack said, walking out the door of Dag's place and heading to Kimo's.

"Hold on, guys," Gates said, I will call and check to see if the police are through with Kimo's place. We don't want to overstep."

"Here," Dag said, handing Gates a card that provided Cary's number. "Call Cary and ask him to check. As a consultant, he would not be able to give the okay on his own, but he is closer to the police here and could check for us."

"Great idea," Gates said, dialing his phone as he spoke. In what seemed to be only a moment, he was off the phone and gave the all-clear to go into Kimo's place.

The group of four friends entered Kimo's home with a trepidation that even they did not understand. As they looked around the small and well-kept home, they took care to look and not disturb anything. Having looked for about an hour, they were beginning to think they had reached a dead end. Jack, seeming a bit more exasperated than anyone thought Jack was capable of, plopped down in a wicker chair that had about a two-inch wide platform on the bottom of each foot. When he landed in the chair, it slid about five inches from its original resting place, revealing a small dark spot on the floor that stood out on the quite clean light-colored bamboo floor that surrounded it.

"I want this to go faster than it is going," Jack said.

"Well, the last case we worked on took thirty-eight years," Annie said in her snarky manner, referring to the loft fire that involved Dag and Jack in 1979. "What is it about this case that you find to be slow?"

"Okay, if you place it in that perspective, I guess I can go a little longer," Jack responded, trying to hide a half-smile.

Gates was the first to notice the spot on the floor. "What's that, Jack?" he said, pointing to the spot that had been revealed under the front left foot of the wicker chair.

Dag walked over to where Jack was sitting and peered down at the spot. "Hmmm. Maybe it was just a dirty place where it has not been cleaned," Dag said, not believing it himself. Kimo, while not to the extreme of being fastidious, was certainly too into cleanliness to have missed the spot.

Gates took one glance, and his experience told him what it was. "Looks like dried blood," he offered, "and I think we should call Cary and see if he will contact the police and have them come over as soon as they can." Everyone nodded, as this new knowledge brought some new excitement into the case.

It took about a half hour, but a police forensics officer appeared at Dag's door with Cary in tow. The spot was examined, and the officer took a scraping from the spot and said he would be in touch. Cary turned to Dag and said, "I'll follow him and see what information I can get for you guys."

"What would a drop of blood be doing *under* the foot of a chair?" Annie said. "Now I can see it being *around* the foot of the chair, but under it?"

Gates jumped in immediately. "Yes," he said, "and what are the odds that the spot was not noticed and the foot of a chair placed exactly on top of that spot? Of course, if someone were intentionally trying to hide the spot, why not just remove the spot all together?"

"That is easy," Dag said, happy to contribute. "Do you see the spot where the drop of blood landed? Well, right there is a crack in the floor. Just under the shiny finish of the floor is a layer of very porous wood. The blood has likely soaked through much deeper than the surface and has become indelibly connected to the floor. In order to remove that, a giant chip would have to be taken out of the floor, which might be quite noticeable. It would be easier just to cover up the spot of blood."

Jack jumped in with, "But why would there be a drop of blood in Kimo's place anyway?"

Gates looked around at his friends, as he commented, "Perhaps the murder did not occur in Dag's place after all. The group sat silent for a moment. This small cadre of friends was becoming serious about this case, indeed.

That evening was one of diversion for the group of friends. They took a walk along the lagoons at Ko Olina and then decided to just grab a bite at the Monkeypod Kitchen nearby. It was a night of fond memories and relief that the first case in San Francisco had turned out so well. It began with the usual banter between Jack and Annie.

"So, Jack," Annie began, "did you ever think that life would lead us here, to Hawaii, with a renewed connection to Dag and an opportunity to hang around with a seasoned police detective?" Annie pointed to Dag and Gates, respectively.

"No. In fact, I want to instinctively run away from Gates," Jack offered with a smile. "Thankfully," he added, "I don't have a reason to hide from him."

Gates responded, "Now this is intriguing, Jack. I guess my question would be…what made you bring that up unless there was some point in time when you *needed* to run away from the law?"

"See what I mean, Annie?" Jack said. "They are too smart…too smart."

The group then burst into laughter as Dag said, "Sounds as if we need to let sleeping dogs lie."

Dag's phone rang to momentarily break the levity. It was Cary.

"Hello?" Dag said, as if he didn't already know who it was. Dag thought for a moment about those little formalities that people use or phrases from the past that have become idioms. He recalled his young great nephew who one day innocently asked why we say "roll down a window" and "hang up a phone." The little one had no frame of reference for understanding these phrases.

"Dag," Cary said, "the blood in Kimo's place was Kimo's blood."

"Which could mean one of several things," Dag said. "It could be quite old and have occurred from an earlier injury, or it could be from the night of the murder, which opens up a brand-new can of worms."

"Right. Let's ponder on it," Cary said.

"We're at the Monkeypod if you want to join us," Dag said.

Within twenty minutes, Cary was having a drink with the crew at the Monkeypod, and there was a kind of camaraderie that was sensed among each person in the group. Dag was sorry that DJ was gone, but aside from that, he was part of an ever-growing group of souls, each with his or her own story, and hearing those stories through the thoughts, words, and actions of these, his closest friends, was a true joy for Dag.

Cary commented, "It is the consensus of forensics that the blood in Kimo's place is not only his, but it is recent as well."

"So what we need to do is consider that the blood is connected to the night of the murder," Dag said.

"And what we need to also assume now is that the murder occurred there and not in Dag's place," Gates said.

"Why is that?" Annie said.

Gates responded, "Because there is no other plausible reason why there would be blood over here if the murder occurred somewhere else."

"Well," Cary added, "it is possible that the murder occurred over there, but if trying to hide evidence from the actual murder scene, one sure way to do that is to make it appear that the murder occurred somewhere else to take the attention away from the true scene of the crime. This drop of blood we found was a true screw-up on the part of the killer if, and that's a big if, we are on the right track."

For the entire group, this seemed like the first true sign of progress in solving the case.

"Okay, so the blood is in Kimo's bungalow and he was killed there. What info is there to be taken from that scene? Have the police already been over there to check out Kimo's home as well?" Dag asked.

"Yes, they have," Cary offered.

"So what could we possibly find that they couldn't," Annie said.

"Well, they didn't find the drop of blood we found," Jack said. "Maybe there is something else that they didn't find as well."

"Good point," Annie said quite seriously and without sarcasm, which took Jack and the rest of the group by surprise.

"I still think we need to concentrate on the paint under his fingernails," Dag said rather pointedly.

"Well, to be honest, it is actually the only thing we have to go on right now," Gates added.

"Now back to the paint then," Dag said. "We know that sometimes Kimo did some painting on his lanai." Each bungalow had a very small lanai, or back porch, that jutted out from the bedroom.

"Okay, then, let's get out there and see what we can find," Jack said.

The lanai, or back porch, of the small bungalow was hardly big enough for five people, so they agreed that initially they would allow Gates and Cary to go out there and have a look around with keener eyes, since they were trained in this type of work. Dag, Annie, and Jack watched from inside by the doorway that led out to the lanai. It took no more than two minutes before they noticed Gates walk over to Cary and ask him a question. Cary then pointed to a box hidden behind the small easel that Kimo had used to paint.

"Hey, guys," Gates said, "squeeze out here if you can."

The trio walked out to where Cary and Gates were and peered down at a box. When Gates opened the box, he saw six paintings, clearly autographed by Kimo Akamai, and they were in six slots that were upright in the box. There was room for a seventh painting in the box in the center of the slots and in a seventh slot, but it was missing.

"What do you make of this?" Dag asked as he removed the paintings one by one and handed them to his friends.

"They are Kimo's," Jack offered.

"Sure," Annie said, "but where is the seventh painting?"

"Wait," Cary said. "These paintings are in succession, as if they are telling a story."

CHAPTER 31

Onto Something

"They all seem to be events that have happened in the Kapolei area," Dag said, engrossed in what all this could mean.

"Yes," Gates said, "it appears to be a succession of events. On the paintings themselves are the actual dates of completion, which means it should be pretty easy to determine which event and as a result which painting is missing…that is, assuming there was some connection among the events."

Cary added, "Well look, the first one appears to be a farmer's market."

"Yeah," Jack said, "and the second looks like a dedication of the land across from the high school."

"Okay, not seeing a connection yet," Annie said, "but there has to be some way to figure this out."

"Well, let's keep going," Cary said. "What is the third painting about?" He turned to Gates, who had the third painting.

"It is a carnival," Gates said. "Wait, there is something attached to the back of this painting." Gates pulled what appeared to be some sort of program from behind the painting. Annie took the program from his hand and began to scour its contents.

"Look!" she said with glee. "It is a list of seven events occurring in seven days two years ago, and it has included the seven events that appear to be the subjects of Kimo's paintings."

"Wow," Jack said, "which one of the events is missing?"

"Let's see," Gates said, taking the list from Annie with a tug and a smile. "It appears to be the addition of a new wing to the police station."

"Now, why would that be the painting that is missing?" Annie said.

"Well, it could just be a coincidence, but I sure would like to find out where that painting is," Jack said.

"Me too," Gates added.

"Is that painting on the wall anywhere, or maybe in a closet or something?" Cary asked.

"Well, let's look around," Gates said.

The group felt a bit uneasy about searching the home of this kind man, but Dag figured that perhaps if Kimo trusted anyone with his things, it would be him. At that, the group scoured the home to see what they could find. In the living room, in an obscure and strangely constructed nook in that living area was a small desk, a collage of pictures, and in the center of the collage was the painting. Gates found the painting and removed it from the wall slowly, noting that the wall was discolored where the painting had been, of course leaving Gates to surmise that the painting had been there for some time.

Unlike the other paintings that were found in the box, this one was hanging on the wall. On the wall, yet a bit lower and to the left of the painting was a small plaque. The inscription read as follows:

Presented to Kimo Akamai for his contributions
to the new Sloan Ender Wing of the West Oahu
Police Department

"Okay, now this is a stretch, my friends, but why would Kimo make a contribution to a police station wing that was being built in the name of a Sloan Ender, and who is Sloan Ender?" Gates asked, clearly trying to figure out a connection.

"I think he's some kind of developer who has also had aspirations of public office," Cary said, "but look at this."

The group huddled around Cary and the painting. On the painting were seen faint scratches, clearly parallel and clearly made by fingernails.

"Wow," Annie said. "This is where some of the paint from Kimo's fingernails came from. Now why would he deliberately scratch this painting?"

"That is the sixty-four-thousand-dollar question," Jack said, grinning. "Is there anything missing from the part of the painting that he scratched?"

"Hard to tell," Gates said.

"I guess there's no way to determine that," Jack said softly.

"Unless we go down to the police station and compare the painting to what is actually there," Gates replied.

"Now see there. That is why he had the job he did. John Gates always thinks a step ahead," Dag said with a nod to Gates.

Gates, not one to relish the limelight, proceeded to ask another question. "Okay, so when do you guys want to drive down to the police station?"

"Now," Jack responded. Then he grabbed Dag's keys, pitched them to Dag, and said, "Let's do this."

It took the group of five about ten minutes to be standing in front of the Kapolei Police Station with painting in hand. As Gates held the painting of the scene up against a background of the scene itself, it was clear what was missing. There were two small ferns that were missing from the photo, which easily could have grown up since the painting was done, and then there was a sign that the ferns surrounded. The sign read "Sloan Ender Forensic Lab."

There were so many ifs now. If the sign was indeed a clue, and if Kimo had actually scratched the sign in his dying move to provide that clue, and if they searched all the other possible clues and none panned out, they could be onto something.

CHAPTER 32

Moving Ahead When the Trail Gets Cold

"Are we on a wild goose chase or what?" Annie asked in her unabashed way.

"No idea, my friend," Dag said, "but it's all we have so far, so I guess we should go with it."

"Makes sense, but I wish this mystery were easier to solve," she responded.

"Well, then, it wouldn't be much of a mystery, would it?" Jack interjected.

"Are you trying to take over Kimo's place as the wisest man around?" Annie quipped.

"Nah," Jack replied. "Way too much work." The entire group laughed.

Dag marveled at who Jack really was. He appeared to be a laid-back, fun-loving, and low-key guy who enjoyed letting others take the limelight. He more often than not played the amiable sidekick who at times even played the buffoon, and yet Dag saw that, through all this jovial exterior was a man of intelligence, class, and charm, who also had the goodness of heart to build others up and leave his mark as a kind, generous, and unassuming man who led a simple life. Without saying so, Dag had Jack's number. He knew who Jack was. Jack was about as bright as they come. His was a spirit of goodness.

"Okay, then, what's the next step?" Dag asked.

"Well," Cary said, "if we are going to follow this train of thought, and I must tell you that it is something of a longshot, then we are making an assumption that the scratches on the painting were made intentionally, that Kimo in fact made them, and that he was trying to give us some kind of message."

"Right now," Gates added, "we really have nothing else to go on, so I say we follow this trail to see where it either provides some solid info or hits a dead end."

"I'm in," Annie said. "I for one am going to pretend it is the way we want to go, that it is a great clue and that it will provide the answer."

"That is the best mindset for a case such as this," Gates responded, "but do not force an answer when you have a question. Let the evidence speak for itself."

"Makes sense, John," Annie replied, smiling a half smile.

"So again I ask," Dag said, "what's the next step?"

"The next step is to find out all we can about Sloan Ender, what he does, what his background is, and how he could possibly be connected in a negative way to Kimo Akamai," Gates said resolutely.

CHAPTER 33

The Benevolent Mr. Sloan Ender

That evening, the five friends sat around a table at the Monkeypod Kitchen and pondered next moves. The music was good that evening, with Hawaiian music in the air, with the bright orange blooms of the monkeypod trees swaying in the wind, and with five adults who were responsible and passionate, but still carefree enough to be laid back, even in the most intense of circumstances. At one point, Jack commented that he felt so young and cannot imagine being as old as they all were, to which Dag replied, "Hey, getting to this age is a privilege denied to many." This group was nothing if not grateful for the lives they were living.

They looked up at one point in the conversation to find Cary deep in thought and seeking something on his phone.

"You still with us?" Gates asked Cary with a snicker.

"Uh, sure guys," Cary said remotely, then continued. "Sorry, I was lost in thought about who Sloan Ender actually is, and I was searching to see what I could find on the Internet."

"No big deal," Dag offered. "We find ourselves tuning each other out all the time." The group laughed. "One thing I do know, and that is that I have heard the name about a million times during my time here on island, but I have never paid attention to who he is or what he does."

"Well, he is a wealthy developer from the mainland, apparently responsible for much of the construction out here on the west side of the island," Cary said, still glancing at his phone.

"And when some of the developers come to the islands, they are interested in one thing," Dag said.

"And that is?" Jack asked.

"Expansion at any cost," Dag responded.

"Okay, then," Jack interrupted, "why would Kimo support something that Ender was doing if Ender was a bad guy? I mean, I think we have heard nothing but good things about Kimo, and he was apparently okay with this new addition at the police station since he painted a pic of it."

"Now that is a good question, Jack," Gates said. "There are quite a few possibilities, but something to focus on is that someone was angry enough at Kimo to kill him. What we can do is to focus on Kimo's life and what he supported and what he didn't. Then we can see what corresponds with Ender and what does not."

"Sort of like piecing together a puzzle to see what fits," Annie offered, fully engaged.

"Absolutely," Cary said, "I wish we had something to write on and some markers. We could set up a makeshift investigation center in Dag's place and add details as they become available. Sorry, Dag, I should not have offered up your place. Oh, and on a side note, Ender apparently also does have political aspirations. He came to the islands, clearly loved it here, and has since decided to dabble in politics. That info is just for what it's worth."

"Are you kidding?" Dag said. "I am excited by this, and I have all the teaching and presentation materials you need. Let's do this."

The ever-growing group adjourned to Dag's place for coffee and a preliminary discussion concerning Kimo and his association with Sloan Ender. Dag brought out his easel with huge sheets of paper attached and some markers to create visuals for everyone. Many would likely laugh at the primitive nature of the meeting, but the group found it useful as well as entertaining. The topic quickly turned to Ender's connection to Kimo.

"Ender has been in politics for a long time," Cary began. "He has a long history of supporting development across the islands, particularly on the ewa side."

"Anything else so far?" Gates asked, seeing that Cary had his focus on Dag's computer screen.

"Well, yes," Cary said. "He was also connected to the police department and, in fact, worked for the police department for several years before going into politics."

"So there's the connection with the police department," Annie offered.

"Yes, that's true," Dag said, "if in fact there is a legitimate connection."

"As we have said before," Gates said, "I guess that's the only lead we have. Let's keep going with this until we hit a roadblock."

"Makes very good sense to me," Dag said.

"Okay," Jack said, "we know that Sloan Ender had his connections and that he was a political man as well as a developer. Still, even though those are things that it appears that Kimo Akamai would have been dead set against, Kimo seems to have supported the police department wing, even though it had Ender's name on it."

"Well, that doesn't surprise me," Dag responded. "Kimo wouldn't have really cared whose name was affixed to a project if it supported something he believed in. I even recall complimenting Kimo at one time about all the good he has done with animals in the area and that he should be given some kind of award for his efforts. He said that none of that mattered to him and that if you really are passionate about something, you won't care who gets the credit."

"But you know, this could be a real dead end," Annie said. "I mean, if all you guys are saying is true about Kimo being a simple and kind man and all. Maybe the guy was just killed by a random individual with a dark outlook. I mean, do we have any evidence that it wouldn't be something random?"

Gates interrupted, "Well, why the scratches on a painting that was still on the wall? That sounds as if a message were being sent by Kimo. At least I think it's possible."

"Yes," Dag added, "and have we talked about why there was that scratch on the painting, the paint was under Kimo's fingernails suggesting it was recent, and why the painting was back on the wall, not even hanging askew? I mean, does that seem odd to anyone?"

Heads were nodding, when Cary said, "Okay, think about this. Kimo is shot, the assailant leaves, Kimo is still alive and scratches the painting to leave a clue before he dies, the perpetrator returns to get Kimo moved to Dag's place not knowing Kimo had scratched the painting, he places everything back in order, to include the painting on the wall, and cleans the place up not knowing that Kimo's place would be noticed at all."

"Hang onto that scenario, my friend," Gates said. "There are many ifs there, but it could have happened, and that would explain why the painting was straight. The assailant would have had to come back to clean the place up, and that is an explanation as to why the killer would not have a clue as to the scratch."

"Fine," Jack said, "but what about the other paint under his fingernail? Where could that have come from?"

"Another good question," Gates said. "If we are under the assumption that the paint under his fingernails from the painting was recent, then it would stand to reason that the yellow paint would be that way as well."

"Do we have a fix on what kind of paint that was?" Annie asked.

"Waiting for the results from the lab," Cary responded. "We should know soon…probably tomorrow."

"I sure am glad you have an in at the lab," Annie said.

"Yes, and it is not really standard procedure for me to get this information, but I do have access," Cary said smiling.

The next day, as Annie, Jack, Gates, and Dag were having coffee and enjoying the view, which at this particular time was not obscured by fog, Gates's phone rang.

"Hello," Gates said in his usual polite yet no-nonsense fashion. "Oh, hey," he continued on the phone, "umhmm, umhmm, wow, interesting." He just as quickly hung up the phone. "Well, the paint is a specialized paint used for many things, but among the uses is for coding and marking pieces of evidence that come into the police station."

"Now how would Kimo have happened across that kind of paint? What else is it used for?" Dag asked.

"Well, several things," Gates responded, "but I think we need to do this. Let's see who on island carries this type of paint, and they could tell us other potential uses."

"That's a great idea," Jack said, always ready to move forward. "Who do we call?"

"Every place that sells paint. I know that sounds daunting, but on the island, there won't be as many places, and they can tell us who their paint suppliers are," Gates said.

"Okay," Annie added, "I am looking here online to find out paint suppliers, and there are about forty different places. What kind of paint do we ask about?"

"Here you go," Gates said, and handed Annie a slip of paper with the specialized type of paint. "It is different from other types of paint because there is an added rubberized compound that makes it not as useful for standard paint applications. It will not be used for houses, etc."

"Okay," Annie said, "there are four of us. Let's divide up these numbers and find out who supplies this type of paint and where they get their supply."

"Wait. Does this sound like a long shot to anyone else but me?" Jack whispered yet loud enough for all to hear.

"Sure," said Gates, "but investigations go on long shots all the time. I think that if things were a slam dunk, we wouldn't need investigators. One thing is likely. However the yellow paint got under Kimo's fingernails, it came from paint that was purchased and used on this island, and if we can pinpoint who uses this type of paint and narrow down the ways that Kimo would have come in contact with it, we might just happen upon a short list of people who might have done this."

"Well, when you put it that way…" Jack said smiling, which caused Gates and the rest to laugh.

The calls went on for a few hours, with Dag's bungalow appearing to be ground central while each of them sat in different corners of the room talking with paint suppliers on island. By the end of the two hours, thirty-six of the forty-plus numbers had been dialed.

At one point, Gates pulled Dag aside and asked, "How am I doing?"

"What do you mean?" Dag asked.

"Dag," Gates said nervously, "almost every contribution I make in the conversations I am having to think and rethink what was just said to make sure I am not off on some kind of tangent or something. I am having to consider and reconsider every comment to make sure I am not misremembering. It's maddening."

"Why don't you try this?" Dag said. "Allow yourself to relax and just say exactly what's on your mind. If there is a slip up, I will give you a sign through eye contact that will tell you to stop for a moment and reflect. To be honest with you, I have not noticed any kind of mishaps in your speech or action today, and since our conversation, I have been watching. I promise to not leave you high and dry."

"Thanks, my friend," Gates said.

"Sure," Dag replied. "Now let's gather everyone to see what info has been uncovered."

Dag was the first to bring the group together. "Okay, then," he began. "I for one have narrowed down the major uses of this paint to three things—marking spots for measurement in construction projects, labeling items with this permanent yellow seal to mark it as inventoried, and then for random artwork when a rubber textured paint is needed."

"Didn't have the artwork one," Jack added, "but I had the other two, and that's about it."

"Anybody else?" Dag said.

"No, that about sums it up, but still not sure how this helps us," Annie offered, "unless…the one who killed Kimo worked in construction or had something with him that required being inventoried."

"Wow, it seems like we are shooting arrows into the wind and trying to hit something," Dag said, seeming perplexed and dissatisfied.

"Yes, Dag," Gates said, "and there are about a thousand possibilities out there, but at the very least we might be eliminating something from consideration, which opens up opportunities to focus on something else. It is very interesting to me that this yellow paint has such limited uses."

"Why is this paint used for just those purposes?" Jack asked.

"Likely not of the right consistency for painting houses and such, probably peels off easily," Cary suggested.

"Well, okay then," Gates said after a brief silence, "we are making an assumption that the paint that came from the painting was under Kimo's fingernails as a result of the killing and that he was trying to leave some kind of message, or at least it occurred during the commission of the crime, which means it can provide us a clue. If—and that's a big if—that is the case, then the yellow paint would likely be part of the scenario as well."

"And why is that?" Annie asked.

"Because we can't find new evidence of anything else in the place that has that kind of paint on it, it is apparently not a paint regularly used by the average consumer, and like the other paint from the painting, if it were under one's fingernails in the general course of a day, one would want to wash it off, especially since we see that Kimo was into a fair degree of cleanliness."

"This all rings true," Dag said.

"Yeah," Annie agreed, "so we just have to find out how Kimo came in contact with that type of paint."

"Right," Gates said.

"You know," Cary said, "maybe someone down at the police station could give us some info. I mean, they don't know everything, but there are some real sharp cookies down there who might have some idea about more detailed uses of the paint."

"Yes," Gates said, "and we might also check with some of the major carriers of this paint to see if they can give us an idea of some specific customers who purchased the paint."

"I have an idea, guys," Dag offered. "Why don't Cary and John go to the police station since that is their area of expertise, and Annie and Jack and I can drive to a couple of these businesses we have called earlier to see if we can get some info about specific users of this paint? Normally, I think it is best if we all stick together, but I think in this instance, we can cover more tracks if we split up."

"That works," Gates said. "Meet back here later today?"

"Perfect," Dag said, and they all exited to the parking lot to hop into their respective cars. Jack and Annie got into Dag's Subaru, and they headed down to the local hardware dealer in Kapolei.

As they were walking out, Dag turned to Gates and said, "Don't be concerned while you and Cary are at the station. Just let Cary do the talking and comment when you have positive info that is pertinent. You've got this."

"Will do," Gates replied.

CHAPTER 34

Gathering Information

As they arrived at the Koka Paint and Hardware Store, Jack commented that it was so good to have the crew together, and he was very happy to have made friends with Gates and Cary as well. Annie agreed, but said it would be great if they could get another female in the group. Dag and Jack laughed.

Upon entering the store, they were approached by an affable older gentleman who, simply by appearance, seemed to know everything about the store. Dag imagined that he likely knew all the code numbers of each bolt and screw in the place.

"Hey, there, what can I do for you? Name's Nick, and you can ask me about anything in the store," Nick said jovially.

"Well," Dag replied, "we know of a specific type of paint that is not used in houses and such but is actually used in small doses to perhaps temporarily mark construction measurements or to mark items for inventory…that kind of thing. Any idea what type of paint that might be?"

"Sure do, bud," Nick said. "Follow me. We usually just special order this for big construction companies when they have a major project that will require temporarily marking a lot of places for measurements. They just came to pick up the lot for that new rail coming to the ewa side here, but we keep a couple of containers on hand for anyone else who might use it."

"Mind if I look at it?" Dag queried.

"Not at all," Nick said, handing him the tube-like container.

"Very interesting paint," Dag said. "Very interesting that it has such specialized uses."

"Well, sure," Nick replied. "In construction, building roads, etc., they can use it to build new projects and provide good markings, yet it is not permanent so it doesn't remain after the project is completed. It is also environmentally sound so it doesn't hurt the environment when it is washed away or fades away on its own."

"We also heard it was used in inventories. Why is that? Wouldn't you want something that lasts in those instances?" Annie asked.

"Sure you would, but that is the beauty of this paint. It is very stable and will last forever in an inventory as long as that inventory is in a stable, ideally climate-controlled, environment. This means that inventoried items can have the paint applied directly to them and then removed when no longer required to be in that inventory," Nick added. "Of course, the inventoried items I speak of would likely be hardware."

"Are you at liberty to tell us specifically what customers you have who utilized this type of paint?" Jack asked.

"Well, again, construction sites, police inventory, our hardware place and some others like it," Nick said quite freely.

The trio thanked Nick, who was more than happy to help, and they left to return to Dag's bungalow. On the way home, they stopped by a restaurant to pick up an order of Chinese food for the group of five. Not knowing what each individual might want, they picked up enough of a variety of food for everyone. On the way home, Annie shared an opinion.

"I wonder if we are any closer to solving this," she said.

"Well, yes and no," Dag said, "but the problem is that we have so many places that still come into play, and that is if the yellow paint under Kimo's fingernails is actually a hot lead at all."

"I know it seems bewildering," Jack added, "but remember the case in San Francisco? A quick glance from Dag in 1979 at a woman walking away from a fire with a boy solved a case for us."

"Yeah, but we don't have forty years to solve this," Annie said, smiling.

"Right, but that case was taken care of in a few weeks. There was just a forty-year hiatus in the middle of it," Jack said.

"True, true. I hate it when you are right," Annie said, laughing.

Dag interjected, "I think our next step is to get with Cary and Gates and go to the police station in the morning and ask some questions about how the yellow paint is used in inventorying evidence."

"Good plan, paperweight," Annie said, smiling. Dag remembered Annie calling him that once in 1979, and he glanced at her. She was looking at him and smiling with a softness that made each of them realize how dear they were to one another.

CHAPTER 35

Onto Something—Maybe

After enjoying a fine meal of broccoli beef, Kung Pao Chicken, chow mein, orange chicken, and more varieties of Chinese food than one can name, the group of five called it a night. Cary slipped off to his cabin on Sand Island but did not leave without making plans to meet at the police station the next morning. Meanwhile, the four remaining at Dag's cabin called it a night. Annie had Dag's room, Gates had his room, and Dag and Jack slept on the living room floor.

"Wow, buddy, just like old times. Things haven't changed much in forty years, huh? I mean, if we roll back the clock that long to this very day in 1979, I expect we would be at your place in San Francisco on Lost Mission Street, talking the night away," Jack began.

"Yeah, but this time, please don't suggest a nightcap at the bar down the street," Dag said, laughing. When Jack had done that in 1979, they returned home to a fire next door that led to a forty-year mystery.

"That's a promise I intend to keep!" Jack said. "And sorry, but I am not as wide-eyed as I used to be either, and with that, Jack was in deep slumber. Smiling to himself, Dag fell asleep as well, recalling the young Jack that he'd met at Harry's Diner in 1979. He knew then that they would be friends for life.

The next morning came early, it seemed, and the group of four had a very restful sleep. They all jokingly decided that it was the

Chinese food that made their slumber so sweet and therefore deemed it part of the menu henceforth.

Within twenty minutes of their rising, Cary stopped by and joined the group for coffee before they headed down to the police station. Cary said he had lined up for them to speak to a Lieutenant Jane McCord, who was in charge of inventory down there.

Having finished the morning coffee, the five friends made their way in Dag's car to the police station down the hill. As they entered the building, Lieutenant McCord was waiting for them. Cary found this surprising since he had not set a definite time for their arrival.

"Hello, all," she said in a friendly yet still matter-of-fact manner. "How can I help you? Hear you have some questions about the inventory system." She sounded very interested in showing the group the system.

Annie liked the lieutenant right away. "Excellent!" She started walking ahead of the group with the lieutenant. "We hear you have an inventory system that uses a specific type of paint to mark evidence into inventory. Mind if I call you Jane?" Annie was good at getting information.

"Oh, well, not anymore. In fact, we haven't done that for some time," Jane said, immediately dashing the hopes of the group.

"Really?" Annie asked, trying not to sound dejected.

"That's right," the lieutenant said most joyfully. "We have this amazing electronic coding system that allows us to maintain a perpetual inventory with items in evidence. It is so state-of-the-art that when a piece of evidence is removed from the room the system catches the coding on the item and removes it from the inventory, telling us exactly what was removed and when. As long as the system is engaged, we have to do nothing to keep track of the inventory except bar code it and assign the code to that item in the system."

"Sounds incredibly high-tech," Gates said. "I worked for the police department in the Bay Area for decades and did not have access to that type of system."

"Well, it does make sense that you would have it before we would, except that we were given a grant to use this as a test site for the system," Jane said. "Isn't that great?"

"Sure is," Cary added as they reached the evidence room. "So can you show us how this all works?"

"You bet," Jane replied, clearly eager to instruct the group on the system, which appeared to be her pride and joy.

CHAPTER 36

The Miracles of Technology and Old Techniques

"You have heard of those grocery stores popping up around the country where you place something in your basket and then walk out and it charges the coded item to your account?" Jane asked enthusiastically.

"Sure," Annie replied. "They are amazing."

"Well, same principle here. There is a code assigned and attached to each item submitted into this evidence room, and if anyone so much as walks out of here with an item, the scanners catch the item and immediately remove it from inventory and log the transaction. You can see here," the lieutenant said, scrolling through the items, "that an evidence bag containing some old documents, which are each specified right here, was taken this morning at 6:00 a.m." She pointed to the screen.

"Yes," Gates said, "and is it the same process in reverse?"

"Sure," she replied. "When the items are returned, the system-wide scanner picks up exactly what was returned and when. It even tells me where in the room they can be found. Fascinating?"

"Sure is," Dag said. "We can complain about technology all we want, but you have to admit that this is pretty useful." Dag loved technology.

After exchanging some other pleasantries and thanking the lieutenant for her very informative and interesting session concerning the inventory system, the group stopped at a local fish taco stand to take some items home for lunch. As a whole, the group was a bit dejected considering the fact that they had really learned nothing that would move the case forward.

"Everyone in for fish tacos?" Gates said as they stood in front of the roadside stand. "It's on me."

"In that case, yes, and I would like an order of six," Cary said. Cary had easily become a member of the group with his affable personality and clear desire to be part of the team.

"You got it," Gates replied. Everyone else wanted the same thing, so the order was easy. "Five orders of six tacos each," he told the old man behind the counter.

"Mahalo, my friend," said the old man, as he quickly got the items together and handed a huge bag to Gates.

The group made its way back to Dag's place and sat around the table, beside the counter, and on the floor, devouring the fish tacos and drinking sweet tea. Polite conversation was the order of the day, until finally, Jack spoke up.

"Look," he said, sounding a bit bewildered, "I have been agonizing over this case in my mind, and I am wondering if we are truly starting out from square one, or were we ever even on the board?"

"We have eliminated some very important aspects, Jack, and that is always a good thing," Gates assured him. "We know that the paint under Kimo's fingernails did not come from anything at the police station since they do not use that type of inventorying anymore, which would have been far-fetched anyway. I think the important thing to do now is to focus on the other ways that Kimo might have come in contact with that specific kind of yellow paint."

"Wait," said Annie. "Of the two types of paint under his fingernails, does it appear that he came in contact with the yellow paint first or the paint from the painting first?"

"Now *that* is a great question," Cary said. "The paint from the painting appears to be the most recent, since it was at the very tips of his fingernails. The yellow paint was deeper, and it is interesting to note that they are prominent under the very same two fingernails on his right hand—the index finger and the ring finger."

"Why not the middle finger in between?" Dag asked.

"Well, there are traces there, but most of it is under the other two fingers I mentioned, and it makes good sense. I mean, pretend you are scratching something," Gates said to Dag. Dag lifted up his hand and made a scratching motion. "See," Gates continued, "it is possible and even in some cases probable that the middle finger would not have as much under it, especially if it is retracted in some way when all the fingers are bent."

"Sure does," Dag said.

"So let's say the paints are both connected to the crime," Annie submitted. "Kimo comes in contact with the yellow paint while being killed and tries to leave a clue by scratching the painting."

"All plausible," Gates said, "but why would he have come in contact with the yellow paint?"

"Didn't some of these vendors we contacted say that it can be used in artwork?" Jack said. "And if so, the yellow paint would not have to be connected to the crime at all. Let's look around at Kimo's place to see if there is any trace of the yellow paint at all. I mean, the man dabbled in painting. It's reasonable to assume he got it under his fingernails in passing or in working on a painting."

"Could be," Annie offered, "but is the yellow paint only under the same fingernails as the paint from his painting of the new police station addition? If so, it stands to reason that they are both from scratching something."

"In all seriousness, that is true detective work," Cary said and nodded to Annie.

"Finally, someone who doesn't think I am a total windbag," Annie said, nodding back to Cary.

"Well, I never thought that you were a *total* windbag," Jack said, smiling.

Annie grabbed a throw pillow and did just that in the direction of Jack.

The group quickly gathered their eyeglasses and the keys to Kimo's place and scurried over to look at the place once again. After several hours of searching every nook and cranny, no yellow paint was to be found.

"Okay, then," Annie said. "Maybe the yellow paint *was* connected to the crime. If there is nothing to be found here, then perhaps it was somehow with the person who committed the crime."

"Yes," Jack followed, "and maybe we are spinning our wheels."

"Maybe," Cary added. "Say, he was shot with a .380, correct?"

"Yeah," Gates said.

"Well," Cary said, "this is an island for Pete's sake. Let's check out the different places where one can acquire a .380 on this island."

"Yes!" Dag said, uncharacteristically excited. "Also, let's go back to what we thought about doing the day of the memorial and focus on some of the people who attended the service."

"Now that's a great idea, Dag," Annie said. "How did we get off track?"

"No clue," said Dag, "but I wonder if someone in some of those photos might be connected to someone else who could easily gain access to a .380."

"Well, I think most of the city police department attended, which surprised us all," Gates said.

"Yes, so let's get the photos blown up and look at them," Dag said.

"Well, if it helps," Cary said, "I also videoed the whole thing. We could use Dag's screen over at his place to pull up the entire video and watch it over and over if need be."

The group was beginning to like Cary more and more by the minute.

"That is amazing!" Annie said. "You just might work out." She glanced at Cary and gave the thumbs up sign.

Dag snickered and looked over at Cary and said, "She's the hardest one to win over. The guys and I considered you part of the group the day after the memorial service."

They all laughed and retreated to Dag's place, hooked up the projector, and viewed Cary's video for the first time. They watched intently as they relived the memorial service for Kimo. They sat in silence for a moment to absorb the sadness. It was an awkward moment, as the feelings of loss caught them unaware.

CHAPTER 37

A Connection?

The group scoured the video time and time again, seeking something that might stand out. Considering all the people who attended the service, if there were a connection between one of these attendees and the crime, it truly was like finding a needle in a haystack.

"Glance at the crowd," Gates said, as if he were giving a lecture. The group complied, and for ten minutes they viewed and reviewed the people at the service.

When they pretty much agreed that they saw nothing, Cary then added, "Okay, now view it again and consider who in the crowd might have a need for or access to a small gun like a .380."

Dag was fascinated. He thought, *We are actually going through the process of elimination to seek out specific points of focus.* It was easy for Dag to cull out people who he thought would not have a need for that kind of weapon. *Let's see, an elderly person might want to use it for protection. It is more manageable than some larger guns.* This process was fun for Dag. Before the process ended, he had eliminated quite a few attendees, which did make him feel good about narrowing down the suspect list, even though it was still quite extensive by the look of things.

"That's interesting," Annie said as the conversation was winding down. "There's Lieutenant McCord at Kimo's service, and she has a couple of people with her."

As they looked closely at the screen, they could see Jane McCord, and the two people on either side of her.

"Who are they?" Cary asked. "Anyone know?"

Dag responded, "Yes, believe it or not, I know one of them. Well, I don't know him, but I have seen him at various events, usually events I attended with Kimo."

"Really?" Gates said, his interest piqued.

"Yeah, he is Clay Sharp, an employee of the Sloan Ender campaign," Dag said. "but we cannot really tell if he is with Jane McCord. They just appear to be seated next to one another."

"True," Jack said, "but look at them now. For people who just met at this service, they certainly seem to be talkative."

"Good point," Gates said.

"Yeah," added Cary. "I did some training in facial expressions, eye movement, and body proximity. They know one another, and I would be willing to say that they know one another pretty well."

"Sounds good," Dag said, "but it's really neither here nor there, right? I mean, this island is small. I am not really surprised that they know one another."

"Could be," Cary added, "but they are sitting beside one another at a memorial service, talking instead of focusing on the ceremony, and that can be a bit of an issue. If you look closely, they are not really paying attention to what is being said at all. I would be willing to state that they were not close to Kimo at all."

"That is quite an assumption," Annie said.

"Yes, but in this business, you learn to walk that fine line between making assumptions and making judgments. You don't want to make judgments, but assumptions are what can move the ball forward," Cary said, half smiling.

Gates nodded in agreement.

"Anybody see any other connections on the video that seem relevant?" Dag said.

"Well, no," Annie replied. "It seems we have looked over this video for eons now. I guess I knew it before, but it just seems that when you are really tired of collecting evidence is when you have to dig deeper to find even more evidence. Not sure I was cut out to be a detective."

"Oh, but you were," Gates said. "During the case in San Francisco, you asked pointed and relevant questions that frankly even I would not have asked. I have to tell you I was fairly impressed."

"Oh yeah?" Annie said.

"Well," Jack added, "Annie was never one to mince words." The group laughed.

"Okay, now why is that funny?" Annie said in a defensive manner, yet she was smiling just the same.

"Well, my friend," Jack said, "you can be a bit of a bulldozer." He laughed, and Annie threw another pillow at him.

"Hey, cool it!" Jack said, still snickering.

"Well, they are not called throw pillows for nothing," Annie said.

Cary put out two fingers and swept them toward his eyes as he stated, "Okay, back to the case."

Dag said, "Okay, we have found a tidbit of info here, but do you think this assumed connection between Lieutenant McCord and this Clay Sharp is worth pursuing?"

"I do, Dag, and let me tell you why," Cary said. "You have to remove first any idea of a personal connection between the people you are investigating, and for a moment consider them according to their work. Then ask yourself, in this particular instance, why a police officer in charge of evidence from hundreds of cases would have a connection with someone intimately involved in a political campaign?"

The entire group sprang to life with additional assumptions.

"Well," Annie said, as if she were a student in a classroom, "each of them has something that the other one needs professionally."

"Very good," Cary replied, "and what could that be?"

"Hmmm," Annie sighed. "I make a great comment and then come up with nothing to follow it up."

"Let me interject, Annie," Gates said in his calm yet deliberate way. "McCord could have connections at the police station that could get the police officers behind Sloan Ender if Clay Sharp says and does just the right things."

"Also," Dag said, "we can ask ourselves if the two of them have a common enemy. Sounds strange, but if we are thinking solely in the professional realm, that could still be the case."

"You and John are making excellent points," Cary said. "Now who might be a common enemy of those two professionals?"

"A politician and a police officer? Anybody! You know how some malcontents out there seem to vilify police when it is the malcontents themselves who refuse to obey the law," Annie said so strongly that it almost seemed personal.

"Yeah," Jack said, "and we can't narrow down the list any with politicians, either. These days you have to ask yourself who actually likes politicians. That's a much shorter list than who doesn't like them."

"You know who might have been an enemy of both?" Gates said softly.

"Who?" they all said at close to the same time.

Then Gates almost whispered, "Kimo Akamai."

"Now how did you reach that conclusion, John?" Dag asked.

"Okay, hear me out," Gates replied. "While he wouldn't say it, Kimo was not a fan of many politicians, and he likely was not liked by some police officers either, as he often protested issues that he thought were harming the environment or not respecting the small town atmosphere we have out here in the hills."

"Could be," Cary said, "and I am tracking what you are saying, but Kimo donated to the recent building of the new wing at the police station, so it doesn't make sense."

"But it does," Gates responded. "If he and others were engaged in endowing the police station and other parts of town with building improvements, etc., it doesn't mean they all saw eye-to-eye on how to get it accomplished. Besides, you've heard the old saying that it is not pleasant to watch sausage being made and laws being created? Well, it is also not fun to watch contributors to a cause interact. They each think that his or her idea is the best. They also have a specific way for how they want it accomplished."

"Okay then," Annie said, "what is the next step now?"

"We need to find out exactly how Sloan Ender is connected to the police department," Cary said. "You know, I am a consultant for the police training series, and I feel as if I am also going behind their backs to solve a crime with which I really have no connection."

"And you love it," Annie said, patting Cary on the back. The group, including Cary, erupted in laughter.

"Well, one thing I can do is to do some fishing to see how Ender is connected down there at the station," Cary replied. "Hope I don't open a can of worms."

"I hope you do," Jack said. "I am ready for some concrete action on this case."

The group dispersed. Annie wanted to do some shopping, so she and Jack headed for the new shopping center, Ka Makana Ali'i, on the ewa plain. Cary headed down to the police station to see if he could uncover some new info concerning Sloan Ender, and Dag and Gates opened a bottle of wine and sat in the breezeway between Dag's and Kimo's bungalows talking shop.

The conversation carried on for about a minute, when Dag raised the innocent question, "So I wonder who's going to buy Kimo's place."

Dag had never seen Gates jump out of his chair so quickly. "Why in the name of reason hadn't I thought about that! How would I go about figuring out how to buy this place?"

"Well," Dag offered, "I had a buddy who taught real estate at the university. I could call him and—"

Gates picked up Dag's phone, handed it to him, and said rather forcefully, "Call him. Now."

"But now, John, I must remind you that when you moved out here you told me in no uncertain terms that you did not want to own again. You said you wanted to be unencumbered, free." Dag said these things as if he were afraid to say them, as they could bring to mind Gates's memory issues in a very pointed way. Still Gates seemed unaffected and anxious to move forward.

Dag smiled and dialed, and soon there was an answer. He asked the question, and the person on the other end of the line must have talked incessantly for about ten minutes, as Dag was limited to an occasional *umhmm,* and that was about the extent of it.

"He's going to do some checking, but I tell you now, the places here sell in a matter of days, and the real estate people sometimes have connections on the Mainland or in Japan, with people already set to buy whatever becomes available. Just wanted you to not get your hopes up. My guy in real estate said he'd call me back right away," Dag said, happy to help Gates.

"Okay, perfect," Gates said. "So I guess we can just sit here and wait for the phone to ring."

"Well, it's not like there's anything else to do," Dag said, smiling.

The phone did ring. It was Cary, who told Dag, "I'm still here at the police station. Very interesting info to share. You guys still hanging around?"

"Yes, come on back up the hill. We might even save you a glass of wine," Dag said. Cary didn't even say goodbye as he hung up the phone, and in ten minutes, he was sitting with Dag and Gates.

"Okay, guy, what's the story?" Gates said, very anxious to hear what Cary had to say. Cary was new to the group, but he was already known as one who didn't hold back his words nor create unnecessary drama.

"Well," Cary began, "it seems that Lieutenant McCord is very friendly with the Sloan Ender campaign, and according to my new source down there, Jane McCord is the one who had been pushing for all these years to have the new wing at the police station named after Ender."

"That's not necessarily a bad thing, but it is intriguing," Dag said. "I guess I am just wondering why the two of them would be appearing at Kimo's memorial service. One thing in their favor is that they don't seem to have a problem with the world knowing they are tight. I mean, they were sitting at the service together and were talking and interacting in plain sight."

"But..." Cary added, "that is exactly what someone would do who is not above board. They would essentially hide in plain sight, especially on an island."

"Well, that makes good sense too," Dag replied.

"Here's the question of the day, yet again," Cary said. "Where is the murder weapon?"

"Yep, good question," Gates said. He snickered and added, "It is probably hiding in plain sight too."

"Well, then," Cary said, "why don't we start the way anyone starts when something is lost? Seek it at Lost and Found, which for us is the police station. I can check to see if a .380 has been turned in recently."

"Highly unlikely, I would think, my friend, but it's a good place to start," Gates said with a half-smile.

CHAPTER 38

The Things We
Learn by Chance

Cary, Gates, and Dag went down the hill to a roadside stand that was famous for grilling blackened opakapaka, which is also called Hawaiian pink snapper. Dag filled in his friends that opakapaka is a fish native to the Indian Ocean as well as the Pacific Ocean as far east as Hawaii and Tahiti. The fish smelled so good on the grill that Dag ordered a huge bag of fish tacos. The kind local man who owned the stand said it would take a bit to grill that much fish, and his son had to run to get some more locally made taco shells as well, so the trio decided to drop by the police station just to see if Cary's new information source was there by chance.

She was there. Her name was Sandra Conner, and she was a wealth of information. For some reason, she had no issue telling Cary everything going on in the department, which was technically above board since Cary was hired by the department and was privy to most information the police department held anyway. Cary was a man of honor, and Dag and Gates knew that Cary would not betray the department by sharing information that he was not supposed to share. Still, Sandra was a valuable ally, as she worked with Lieutenant McCord in the evidence room. In fact, Sandra was in the evidence room when the guys appeared at the station.

Cary walked up to her and said, "Say, Sandra, I would like to introduce you to my two friends here. This is Dag Peyton, and this is John Gates."

"A pleasure," Sandra said. Gates and Dag nodded politely.

"So my friend," Cary said softly to Sandra, "my friend Dag here lived right next door to the fellow who was shot up in Makakilo recently. He is very interested in helping find out who the killer is, but he doesn't want to do anything that is not on the up-and-up."

"Well, that's a good thing," Sandra said.

"Anyway," Cary said as if he were walking on eggshells, "we were at Dag's place talking, and we know that Kimo Akamai was killed with a .380, and we were just wondering if you'd had any .380s checked into the evidence room lately. I mean, maybe the killer ditched it and someone found it and turned it in?"

"Let me check," Sandra said softly. "Nope...but wait...this is strange." Her voice trailed off.

"What is it?" Cary asked.

"Well, I searched for .380s, and when I did, I noticed something weird about the inventory," she said, perplexed.

"Oh?" Cary said.

"Yeah," she replied. Turning to Gates and Dag, she said, "Would you guys excuse us for a moment?"

"No problem," Dag and Gates said almost simultaneously. They then turned and exited the room.

After they left, Sandra turned to Cary and said, even more softly than before, "I think we have a problem."

Gates and Dag wondered around outside the evidence room for what seemed to be an eternity, and in fact, it was about thirty minutes. Finally, Cary walked out, motioned for the two to follow him, and left the building, headed toward Dag's car.

"Wait, what are we doing?" Gates asked. "I mean, were we through talking to Sandra Conner?"

"Let's get the fish tacos and get back to Dag's place," Cary offered mysteriously.

Gates knew enough from his own experience to not utter another word about Cary's strange behavior, but rather to play along.

Gates could tell that Dag was about to ask pointed questions several times during the trip back to Dag's place, but Gates would either gently poke him and shake his head or give him a faint look of disapproval. When they got home, Jack and Annie had returned, and so they all sat down. Annie and Jack were chiming in innocently about the fish tacos and how tasty they looked, when Gates finally said calmly, "Okay, Cary, you found out something, but you cannot tell us, right?"

"You want tartar sauce on your taco?" Cary asked out of thin air, which made Gates firmly believe that he had hit the nail on the head.

"So spill it," Annie said to Cary in her usual direct but invested manner.

"No can do," Gates said to Annie. "Here's the deal, and I only know this because I was in the business. Cary works for the police department. Even if it is a contract position, he cannot divulge police department information that could in some way jeopardize the department without talking to the Chief of Police first. If he were to state something that he shouldn't and people were negatively affected, he could be in serious trouble, and as importantly, lives could be potentially jeopardized as well. So ask all you want, he won't tell."

"So that's it?" Jack said. "We have good info but cannot find out what it is?"

"Not exactly," Gates said. "If we can find something out on our own, we are fine. Remember the case in San Francisco? You guys were working on your own. It could have been dangerous, but as long as you were not doing anything illegal or that interfered with our investigation, we really can't stop you."

"So," Dag said, "what is happening here is that we need to discover what Cary already knows, and here's the good part: there's something, and it's connected to the police department. That's closer than we were this morning. Of course, what this means is that the PD has a lead that we do not, and they are so experienced that they might just find out the answer before we can."

Cary smiled as he bit into his fish taco. The group had the scenario down pat. He wanted to help them, but he couldn't.

"Well, this all began to get mysterious when we went into the evidence room and Sandra Conner began speaking with Cary. She saw something on her screen and then asked if she could speak with Cary alone," Gates said. "So this means that there is something going on with a piece of evidence that startled Sandra Conner, and at the time, she was looking to see if a .380 pistol had been recently found and turned in at the police department."

Cary smiled as he listened to Gates detail exactly what was happening.

Gates continued, "Now the only thing I can think of is that there was a .380 turned in recently, but if that's true, Sandra Conner could have told us that because it would mean that they had the weapon and could conduct their investigation. So that is likely not it, but it still has something to do with something in evidence, and it has to do with a .380 pistol."

Cary picked up his phone and called Sandra Conner. "Sandra," he said, "I need to talk to someone to get clearance for John Gates, former Bay Area detective, because I think he can help with the Kimo Akamai case, and he has several people he can interview who can likely give valuable information. I am calling because I want this all to be on the up and up." After saying this, Cary said *umhmm* a couple of times and hung up the phone.

"Wow," Gates said, "this would be amazing."

"She's checking right now, and she will get me an answer immediately. Trust me," Cary added.

Within ten minutes, the phone rang, and Sandra Conner asked Cary to bring Gates down to the police station for the clearance process. They hopped into Gates's car and sped down Makakilo Drive.

Gates and Cary wasted no time getting the clearance, verifying Gates's work with the Bay Area police, and registering him as a consultant for the local police. Technology made the process much quicker than it had been in the past.

"Wow," Gates said, "if there is anyone out there who thinks that this island doesn't have the latest technology and quite efficient processes, they need to think again. That was the fastest clearance I have ever seen, but don't get me wrong. They were thorough."

Given this clearance, Gates and Cary were able to discuss the case with anyone who could bring closure, as long as what they were doing was legal and adhered to the police department policies. Now Gates broached the subject of the .380 pistol yet again on the drive back to Dag's place.

"Okay, what gives?" he asked Cary quite pointedly.

"Okay, then," Cary said. "When Sandra looked at the computer screen when she searched for the possibility of a .380 being found and turned in to the police, she quite by accident discovered something that only a scanning system that complex might reveal."

"And?" Gates asked impatiently.

"There was a .380 in the evidence room inventory on April 20," Cary responded.

"So?" Gates said. "Do you think it was special in any way other than the fact that it was a .380 and we are looking for a .380?"

"Well, yes, I do," Cary offered. "That same .380 was missing from the inventory the next day and then mysteriously appeared again on April 22."

"Glitch in the system?" Gates proposed halfheartedly, knowing where Cary was headed with his thinking process.

"No, my friend," Cary said, knowing that Gates was following him completely. "The .380 was missing on April 21, and Kimo Akamai was murdered on April 21."

"So," Gates said, "is there any chance that this gun is *not* the gun used to kill Kimo?"

"Yes, there is a chance that it is not the murder weapon, but it would have to be a strange coincidence," Cary responded.

"Agreed," Gates said. "So are we thinking that the murderer is imbedded in the police department?"

"Perhaps, but it could also be that this is an aspect that is a coincidence," Cary said. "I think what we need to do now is to try to find out who has access to the evidence room and find and run any video we have of the room on April 21 and April 22. If we do not see who the murderer is, I expect we will see someone who is connected to the murderer."

"Or at least we will see someone who is connected to someone who is connected to someone," Gates offered, laughing.

"Well, exactly," Cary said.

The informed pair arrived at Dag's place, and of course the entire living room was abuzz with the potentially exciting information that could drive the case forward. Since Gates and Cary had the authority to pursue more evidence, they were allowed to give any information to Dag, Annie, and Jack that might make the case come alive for them.

Annie met them at the door. "Okay, guys, what's the scoop?" she asked pointedly.

"I think we have a very good lead," Gates said, barely able to contain his excitement.

"Well?" Jack said with intense excitement.

"Okay," Gates began, "Cary got me clearance, and we can talk about the case."

"That's it?" Annie queried.

"Your middle name isn't Patience, is it?" Gates said smiling. Annie lovingly shoved him lightly.

"So there's more," Dag said.

"Oh, yeah," Cary added. "There was a .380 in the evidence room on April 20 and on April 22, but it was missing on April 21."

"Are you kidding me?" Dag said. "This means it is likely that the murder weapon that killed Kimo is actually in the evidence room now?"

"Yep," Gates threw in, "and all we need to do is find out who put it back, which will hopefully lead us to the mastermind behind the entire thing."

"This is gonna be easy," Jack said.

"Likely not," Gates replied. "If someone was sharp enough to take it out and put it back, then he or she was likely aware of security cameras and set up a trail that could be hard to track."

CHAPTER 39

Momentum

The next morning, the group of five decided that it would appear much too "moblike" for all of them to go down to the police station to ask about video recordings of the people who entered the evidence room, so they appointed the logical choices of Gates and Cary to do that part of the work. Dag, Jack, and Annie stayed behind at Dag's place to make a list of people who appeared to be on the bad side of Kimo Akamai.

There were several people who fit that description. Of just the ones whom Dag knew, there was Kimo's wife, a few police officers who at times seemed to be at odds with Kimo, the extraneous neighbor here and there who appeared to be hesitant to engage him in a friendly manner, the man at the farmer's market the day Dag gave Kimo a ride, and then there were a few who were unhappy with Kimo for trying to protect the parks and feed the feral cats who lived there. They prioritized the list based upon who appeared to have the most intense issue with Dag, and without question, the man at the farmers' market had the most irate exchange with Kimo. Dag did clarify that Kimo appeared to totally keep his cool while the man in question had verbally assaulted Kimo.

The original trio decided that they should seek to discover who this gentleman was and then to inform Gates and Cary so they could determine how to approach him. Dag immediately called the coordinator of the farmer's market, whose name and phone number was plastered all over telephone poles and electric poles across the west side of the island. Her name was Hoku.

"Aloha, how may I help you?" said the pleasant voice on the other end of the line.

"Yes, aloha," Dag replied in a friendly way. "I have what might seem to be a strange question for you. At your farmer's market in Kapolei, there is a gentleman who attends regularly, yet if I recall he doesn't seem to purchase much, and he and a young woman were interested in getting my friend and me to sign a form for further industrialization of the area. Would you happen to know how I can reach him?"

Hoku replied, "No, I am sorry I do not know how to reach him, but his name is Jim Weathers, and he is a developer who has moved to the islands. From what I hear, his job is to convince land-owners to provide land so that it can be developed for commercial use. He appears at the farmer's market because that is where most of his opponents appear in one place, and he approaches them there to try to make his case."

"Ah, I see," Dag replied, "but he seemed particularly interested in Kimo Akamai on several occasions, and I have no idea why. Kimo led quite an unassuming and simple life."

"Yes, but Mr. Akamai was quite wealthy, as you know," Hoku said confidently.

"What did you say?" Dag said, unable to hide his surprise.

Failing to catch Dag's response of surprise, Hoku continued, "I think Mr. Weathers had been after Mr. Akamai for some time to give some of his land or other resources for development of the ewa side of the island, but Mr. Akamai was more interested in keeping the land the way it was, and of course, that did not set well with Mr. Weathers. It appeared that over time their relationship became rather contentious, with most if not all of the ill will coming from Mr. Weathers. I suppose Mr. Weathers saw Mr. Akamai as a barrier to Mr. Weathers's success, but I cannot say for sure."

"But, ma'am, you said 'other resources.' What other resources of Mr. Akamai's were available?" Dag queried.

"Well, as you know, Mr. Akamai had to be one of the wealthiest men in the state. He gave money to orphanages, to schools, to causes that dealt with the preservation of lands for animals and nature. He was a quite powerful man, but he never ran in the circles of the rich and famous, and I guess over time, he was just left alone because he chose to follow his own simple path," Hoku continued, "and while his philanthropy was anonymous, it was still widely known and generous."

Dag sat in disbelief for a moment, so long in fact that Hoku said, "Hello, did we get cut off?"

"Uh, no, I am sorry," Dag said, still surprised. "I was a neighbor of Kimo Akamai, and I had no idea he was so well-connected, or so blessed as well."

"Oh, yes," Hoku replied, "and it is so interesting because I met him when he would come to the farmer's market, and he was a 'salt-of-the-earth' kind of man. I didn't know him well, yet I sensed a kind of rare goodness about him. I always felt as if I could learn so much from him."

"Well, Hoku, if I may be so bold, I will say that I think you have him nailed down exactly," Dag said rather directly. "I lived beside him here in Makakilo, and this man was a pleasure to know, full of wisdom, and he had a quiet goodness that made him seem to be from another world. It's often foggy here in Makakilo, and our bungalows are covered by that fog, so I called him the Wise Man in the Clouds. People like that are so rare."

"They certainly are," Hoku said. "Well, I want to give you my best, Dag. You were blessed to know Mr. Akamai, and I am quite sure he would've said the same about you."

Dag hung up the phone with a lump in his throat.

When the gang of five was together that evening, Dag filled them in on the new information concerning Kimo Akamai and his great wealth. As Dag thought about it, he realized that it did make sense now that Kimo was able to hold his own with influential people, and those people always seemed to approach him. Dag finally felt as if he understood. Kimo was a magnet for all the people who wanted to change the island, and while he was a quiet and unassuming man, he was also a man of bravery and power. How strange it seemed to Dag that the more he learned about Kimo, even after his death, the more he respected him.

Annie was the first to chime in when Dag gave them the news. "So you are telling me that this man who lived right next door was one of the richest men on the island?" she said in disbelief. "You do know what this means, don't you? I bet he made the wrong person in power angry and that person had him killed. I mean, if Kimo had that power and that wealth, he could likely make some other powerful people quite angry."

"Makes good sense," Jack said, "but just who did he upset, and why? What's the next step?"

"The next step, I think," said Gates, looking over to Cary for support, "is to find out just what projects Kimo was involved in recently and try to pare down who might have been his adversaries in connection with those projects."

After a lengthy conversation about next steps, Cary left and the group of four settled in for the evening.

Dag's phone rang at about ten o'clock that evening, which startled the entire group. While it awakened them all, Annie stayed in her room, and the other guys didn't move from their spots on the floor. Dag spoke in a muffled tone for a moment and then came in quietly and awakened John Gates.

"Hey, guy," Dag whispered. When he had Gates's attention, Gates got up and walked out to the breezeway with Dag.

"Yeah?" Gates said half asleep.

"Sorry to wake you, but that was the realtor," Dag said. "I know it seems strange for her to call so late, but I told her to call at any time, and the truth is that these bungalows go fast, and also there is a major shortage of homes here on the island. Anyway, Kimo's place is yours if you want it, but if you want it, I need to call her now to confirm. I know it sounds melodramatic, but it could easily be gone if you wait until morning."

"Understood," Gates said, now fully awake. "What's the asking price?"

"Four hundred fifty thousand dollars, which is a steal for a two-bedroom condo," Dag said.

"I'm in," Gates said. "Let's make that call now."

And with a phone call, Gates became Dag's permanent neighbor.

The next morning, Dag filled in Annie and Jack concerning Gates's new condo purchase, and they were all excited together it seemed. The eclectic group of four, and five now with the rapid addition of Cary into the fold, became even more cohesive than ever, continually making comments reminiscent of the old days, and then they brought Cary into the conversation to see what he was doing during whatever time period they were discussing.

CHAPTER 40

The Joy of Common Ground

As it all turned out, the five of them were about the same age. Dag and Jack were three months apart in age, Annie was one month older than Dag, Gates was one year older than Dag, and Cary was the same age as Gates. They laughed one evening about being so close-knit because they were all born within one calendar year. This made for pleasant, jovial, and sometimes hilarious conversation since they had the same frames of reference yet had grown up in very different parts of the country.

As Dag, Jack, Annie, and Gates were eating breakfast, Cary knocked on the screen door and walked in without an invitation. "Hey, guys," he said, "I have some interesting news. It might not be earth shattering, but it is another piece of the puzzle."

"Shoot," Gates and Dag said at the same time, smiling briefly at the occurrence.

"The gun that was absent from the evidence room for a day had been checked into the evidence room long before it went missing," Cary said.

"Well, that's easy enough to know based on the new tech system they have in place," Jack replied.

"Yes, but that is not why it is interesting," Cary said.

"Oh?" Dag said as he leaned in.

"Yes," Cary replied. "The .380 had originally been tagged using the old yellow paint system, and there were scratches on the paint."

The room was silent.

"Is that so?" Gates said, with his eyes fixed upon Cary.

"Yep," Cary replied, "and they should be able to connect the paint scrapings from Kimo's fingernails to the gun, if in fact that is the gun used to kill Kimo."

"Well," Annie said, "is there anyone here who has any doubt that it is in fact the gun that killed Kimo?"

"No," Jack said, "not as far as I am concerned, but I bet you these police connected guys here will say something about remaining objective." Jack looked at Gates and Cary with a grin.

"You are right, my friend," Gates said, "but it is not because it is some extraneous policy that we hard-nosed officers of the law must keep. It is because when we lean in one direction, we lose objectivity, and then we begin to miss details that could lead us in another direction and perhaps toward a different and better outcome."

Dag patted Jack on the back and then turned to Gates and Cary and said, "We get it." Jack nodded as well.

Cary changed focus by saying, "Anyway, they should have some information for us at any time. They really work quickly when new evidence this strong presents itself."

Of course, Cary was right. He received a call from the police department stating that the scratches coming from the paint on the gun matched what was under Kimo's fingernails. So someone stole the gun from the evidence room, committed the crime, and then somehow replaced the gun.

Dag was not surprised when Cary called him early the next morning and gave him that news. Gates had gone down to the title company to get the papers settled for his purchase of the condo next to Dag's, but as soon as he returned, Dag, Annie, and Jack filled him in on what Cary was told. Gates was, of course, not surprised, either. The entire group agreed to meet for a drink at the Monkeypod Kitchen at Ko Olina to discuss next moves.

When they arrived, Cary was already waiting for them. "Man, you guys move slowly sometimes," he said with a smile on his face.

"Well, we were just waiting for Annie as usual," Jack said. Annie poked him because nothing could be further from the truth. Annie was always dressed and ready to go.

"I am guessing," Cary began, "that we need to get a list together of who the potential suspects are who could have taken the gun from the evidence room in the first place, and then make another list of how many of those people we know."

"Sounds like a plan," Gates said in agreement.

"Based on the video you shot of the memorial service, we know the lieutenant, and we also know Kimo's wife. By the way, does she stand to inherit any of Kimo's estate? I mean, she could be in for a real fortune based on what I have recently learned," Dag said.

"It all depends on whether or not the divorce was final, I guess," Jack said.

"It's final," Dag interjected. "Kimo was not one to dwell on his private life, but he did tell me that one day. It was interesting the way he told me. He had a wistful look as he shared the information, but not because it was sad. It was more that he was reflecting about the fascinating turns that life can take. Can a man be a dreamer and a realist at the same time? That's the way Kimo seemed to me."

"Wonder where all his fortune is going," Annie said.

"No clue, but I bet he didn't give it to an organization," Dag said.

"And why not?" Annie replied.

"Well," Dag added, "because he would want to use his fortune to keep Oahu the way it is and to protect its lands and natural resources, and I don't think he would rely upon any specific organization, however well intentioned, to do that. He would leave it to a trusted advocate to ensure that his approach would be honored. That's just my view."

Dag was right, but he had no idea how right he was. Dag received a phone call from the executor of Kimo's will, and there was a meeting to be held in two weeks concerning a reading of the will. The executor asked Dag to be present for the reading, which concerned Dag, and he shared that concern with his friends the following evening when they gathered at Dag's place for a glass of wine.

"I am not sure why you are worried, buddy," Jack said. "It is likely that Kimo has a couple of things he needs you to do as far as his final wishes are concerned, and this executor just wants to share those things with you."

"Yeah, I am sure that is it," Gates said, "and you are someone he trusted to make things happen. That speaks well of you, my friend." Gates was not the sappy type, and when he gave a compliment, he meant it. Dag smiled.

"There is also a side benefit to this meeting you are having concerning the will," Cary said, "but I don't want to sound too manipulative."

"Cary, we know you, and we know you are on our side. We also know you are working for the greater good, and I think I speak for all of us when I say you have our trust and respect," Dag added.

Cary blushed a bit and nodded appreciatively. He then went on, "If you are at that reading of the will, you can perhaps get us some more info about this case, such as who attends the reading, what their actions and dispositions are, and what they say that could perhaps implicate them."

Dag responded, "You know, I had not thought of that. As far as we knew, there were very few if any people close to Kimo. I never saw anyone enter his place except for Gates and me. The attendees at the reading of the will could be a real eye opener."

"That is a good point," Annie added, "but in the meantime, we need to get back to who attended the memorial service and who among them might be suspicious."

"Right," Gates said, "and I recall many police officers there, right?" The group looked at Gates with a befuddled look, as Gates would have certainly known that there were many police officers there. Perhaps this was a slip of the memory where Dag needed to interject something.

"You bet, and I expect you're asking that because you want us to make an estimate, right?" Dag said.

"Exactly," Gates said, looking at Dag with much appreciation for covering his slight yet noticeable memory lapse.

"Yeah, but I couldn't make a good estimate. I don't know why all the police officers were there," Jack said, "and they could have been there just because it was a murder, but it could be because the police department saw all Kimo did to get the new wing for the department and they encouraged officers who were available to attend."

"Another good point I hadn't considered," Dag said.

Dag's phone rang, and after a brief period, he exited the room, spoke in a muffled tone for a moment, and then returned to the group after the call.

"What's up?" Annie asked.

"Well," Dag said, "that was my sister. She is staying with my mother, and she has a farm and so many other things to take care of, and she needed me to come for a couple of weeks to help out. She never asks, so when she does ask, I know I need to go. May I make a suggestion?"

"Sure," Gates said, and the rest nodded.

"Okay," Dag said. "While I am gone, why don't you guys help Gates get situated in Kimo's place, or now Gates's place I guess, and then Gates and Cary can stay there if Cary would rather be closer to the action, and Annie and Jack can stay here. Then you are all here to research the case some more, and I can make it back in a couple weeks in time for the reading of the will."

"Sounds like a plan," Gates said, "and I would sure appreciate the help." Gates knew that Dag was having Cary stay over at his place in the event of a major slip-up with Gates's memory that would put Gates in danger. Dag knew that if the disease were progressing as rapidly as Gates contends, it would be better if he were not alone.

All were in agreement, and early the following morning, Dag was on his way to Texas.

CHAPTER 41

A Welcomed Interlude

Landing at the Dallas/Fort Worth Airport was something Dag had done many, many times, and when the doors were opened for everyone to deplane, a scent always wafted into the plane that was uniquely Texas, or at least it seemed that way to Dag. He loved that scent and that feeling of being home again.

While his family had spread to all corners of the state, his sister in the Metroplex was always there to pick him up early in the morning. It never took more than thirty seconds for the laughter to ensue, usually because Dag was used to having some kind of foible occur at the airport itself or en route to or from the airport. Upon his previous visit, his sister had called to say she was rounding the corner where she was supposed to pick him up, and she described her car to him. When the car arrived, Dag opened the back of the vehicle to drop his suitcase into the back, and when he did so, talking a blue streak as he usually did, he noticed a woman of Asian descent and realized he was in the wrong car. This episode alone left him with a reputation for "taking a ride from the first driver who would offer."

This time, however, Dag found the correct vehicle, deposited his bag, and hopped in the passenger seat.

"And how was the flight?" his sister asked.

"Not bad," Dag said, trying to rediscover the joy in flying that he once had. In a past life, Dag had a position in which he was in a plane pretty much every week. This made him homesick as well as a bit apprehensive about the tedium that sometimes presents itself at airports. Dag enjoyed being lighthearted with airport personnel, as he didn't envy them their jobs. "How's Mom doing?"

"She's doing well," his sister replied. "Still a ball of energy but frustrated that she cannot move quite as fast as she used to."

"Understandable," Dag replied.

Without a word, his sister pulled into a Sonic Drive-In, and without asking, ordered two large cherry vanilla Dr. Peppers, at which point, Dag felt completely at home. Both of Dag's sisters had a way of knowing what he wanted, and though he really as a rule didn't drink soda anymore, he was never going to pass up this delightful treat.

The two-hour drive to Dag's mother's home was uneventful yet fun as usual. It was full of tales of the past. And Dag relished them.

Arriving at his mother's home, Dag stepped out of the vehicle quite happy. Dag was always fascinated at how the past came rushing back when he arrived at his mother's place, with the huge porch that sat near a country road that seemed to escape into field after field, at the end of which was always a guarantee of a beautiful sunset.

"Hi, Mom," was the usual greeting, and his mother was always there with open arms. His mother was a fascinating woman. As a child of the Depression, she never threw anything away, and as a result there were sheds and closets full of memorabilia and unrepaired appliances and dated clothes that, according to Mom, could always be repurposed in some way. The house was as neat as a pin, yet Mom was not able to do as much as she used to do. Siblings of Dag pitched in to make the house a home, and they took turns taking care of their mother. Their mother was so pleased that her home remained ground central for reunions and quiet evenings gazing at the stars.

It took no time for the house to come alive with relatives. It was something that Dag looked forward to with every trip. At first, during each trip, Dag would notice subtle changes in the surroundings, and then within a half hour, he was so engaged in delightful memories that thoughts of change went out the window.

There are those who would think that Dag, his parents, and four siblings living together in a small home would be chaotic, yet the noise and the laughter and the debates and the hours upon hours of listening made growing up in this environment a treasure that Dag would not trade for the world. As a young man, Dag would visit his friends and often notice peace and quiet, yet it almost seemed at times as if the heart of the house was not beating, as if the home had yet to have life interjected into it, and Dag felt sorry for them. In later years, Dag realized that his family did not have many material possessions, yet he would never describe his family as poor. In Dag's mind, how rich they were to have experienced the joy that came from a large family. It was a wonderful family, with busy days, family meals that were a time for sharing the events of the days, and nights that usually ended in laughter. Every time Dag made the trip home, the only appropriate word to describe Dag during the homecoming was *grateful.*

At the end of the first day back, he found himself alone on the back porch. He knew that at any moment someone would come outside to join him, yet he took the moment of solitude to reflect upon the past and his path in life, for which he again was grateful.

He remembered with fondness the girl in his high school class who had long blond hair that was straight and thick and beautiful. Jeanne was a lover of horses, and she could even draw the equine form with such detail that he envisioned that if she had the desire, she could become a renowned western artist. She had a gift for art and an even greater gift for working with horses. Beyond that still, Jeanne was a sweet and kind girl, and Dag suspected that if he were to see her again, time would prove her to be a sweet and kind woman as well.

Also, Dag recalled a boy in his class with fondness as well. Alan was the only one in the class who was taller than Dag, and Alan, along with Jeanne, also had a gentle spirit. Dag heard that he'd joined the military long ago and, after being stationed in Germany, decided to stay there. There was no question in Dag's mind that this man would be a person of quality, a salt-of-the-earth kind of individual. Dag's memories of him playing basketball were fresh on his mind that evening.

He also recalled Trudy, whom he met later on in high school. Though she was a bit younger, perhaps by a year, they became fast friends. They couldn't decide if they were so connected because they both had May birthdays or if it was because they both loved to dance, but the memories of their young life as friends were something Dag cherished to this day.

It was a wonderful thing to Dag that memories of the past most often turn out good. These were the people Dag missed, and he had a sense of loss in not having kept up with them over the years. He resolved to spend some time to seek them out when he returned to the islands.

And then there was Kay.

Kay was the All-American girl-next-door type, who was full of fun, tenacity, down home wisdom, and the girl for whom sweetness was an ever-present quality. Dag said at one time that he felt as if he'd known her "since the womb," since they were the same age, went to nursery at church together, were confirmed in the same Lutheran church, and were in the same class together all through school. Dag recalled with fondness the note Kay gave to him in the third grade stating that she wanted to be his girlfriend. Dag emphatically stated that he could not be her boyfriend because she was older than he was (by six months) and that as a result the relationship would never work. Kay responded with a wisdom beyond that of an eight-year-old and said, "Age makes no difference!"

Even Dag's parents and Kay's parents were in sync. They didn't interact much, but Kay's father built the cabinets in Dag's family home, and even to the day fifty years later when Dag's mother was moving out for a more efficient place to live, Dag took a picture of the cabinets and sent them to Kay, exclaiming, "They are as sturdy as ever and one of the few things in the house that still needs no repair." Dag was convinced that if one day the house simply fell to the ground, the cabinets built by Kay's dad would still be standing. This was a testament to his work and was a mirror of his character as well. When Dag's parents spoke of Kay's parents, the common thread was that they were "good people," and the sentiments were returned by her parents as well.

Yes, Dag's fondness for Kay was real, was stable, and was unchanged through the years.

But as way leads on to way, Kay moved on after school, as did Dag, yet they still kept in touch every year on their respective birthdays through what became lovingly known as "the Mom Line." One of the moms was continually having to call the other, at the behest of Dag or Kay, to get an updated address. Dag thought for a moment about how tough it was to keep in touch before technology. When Kay's mother passed in 1998, she called Dag to tell him that they must say goodbye to "the Mom Line." Technology had rendered the line unnecessary in recent years, but never in the hearts of Kay and Dag.

Kay married a man who for all practical purposes appeared to be a very good man of wisdom, character, and class, which stands to reason after the fine model set for her by her own father. Dag was sincerely pleased that Kay's life was such a success story, and he was also proud that the bond had never been broken. *As we get older,* Dag thought to himself, *we often begin to realize how important it is to keep in touch with those special people who knew us when we were young.*

The next morning, Dag arose to find his mother's house empty, except for his mom, who was sitting in the kitchen looking out the window. As he entered the kitchen, he said, "Coffee?"

She replied, "Sure."

As Dag made the coffee, the conversation ensued.

"So," Katie said, "what's happening in paradise these days?"

"Well, work seems to be pretty much the same. I still enjoy teaching, and teaching online is a pleasure to do," Dag offered.

"Anything else going on?" Katie asked.

"Yes, as a matter of fact," Dag said, trying to determine how to piece together a very long story into one that was interesting and brief. "There was a very kind man who lived next door to me, a real genuine kind of fellow, whom over time I grew to discover to be very wise. I enjoyed our interaction. He was much like you, Mom."

"What do you mean *was?*" his mother stated, quickly noticing the past tense Dag had used to describe Kimo.

"Well, he was murdered," Dag said quickly.

"Really? Right there next door to you?" his mother said just as quickly.

"Well, yes," Dag offered, "but I was not there at the time. I was in the Bay Area with Jack, Annie, Gates, and Cary. I got the call while I was there."

"Do you know who did it?" she followed.

"No," Dag said, not wanting to be curt, but there really was no other answer upon which to expound.

"Well, look first at the person you suspect the least," Katie said knowingly.

"And why is that?" Dag asked interestedly.

"Because if this man is as wise as you state, he likely was interacting with many who were wise as well, and I doubt anyone who was frustrated with him enough to kill him would fail to come up with a pretty elaborate scheme," she replied.

Dag was struck by the simplicity of the conversation as well as by the wisdom of it.

"Thanks. This helps," Dag said, smiling on one side of his mouth.

"See," Katie replied, "you received all this valuable information, and it didn't cost you a dime."

They both laughed and drank their coffee.

During Dag's stay, he was struck by how much he enjoyed just being there with family. His brothers could be serious one moment and comical the next, which Dag thoroughly enjoyed, and the same applied to his mother and sisters as well. All the family in-laws added to the fun, and his nephew, who'd been in law enforcement for nearly thirty years, provided excellent insights to Dag's case. Through the years, there was certainly laughter as well as tears, yet more of the former. Dag enjoyed the "busyness" of his family get-togethers, the "all talking at once" moments, the oneness.

The lazy days wore on, full of laughter, great food, and more great memories that Dag was convinced could never be captured with any family but his, and too soon, he found himself back at the airport ready to fly home to the island. As Dag played on his phone and waited patiently for his flight, he pondered his mother's words.

Something she said about Kimo's murderer perhaps being wise and coming up with an elaborate scheme rang so true. He thought again about their finding the gun in the inventory at the police station and how strange that was, and he realized that it was likely that the only way that this could have occurred was if there was someone in the police station who allowed it to occur. It is very obvious that the evidence room in a police station must be closely monitored, and if the act itself were not committed by someone in law enforcement, then there had to be someone very closely tied to the police who could make his or her way into the evidence room.

Yes, it seems that the advice of his wise mother was indeed in itself wise. Someone off the street does not have enough clout to have these circumstances occur. Dag called Gates as his flight was about to board.

CHAPTER 42

Beware the Island Breezes

Just before boarding his flight to head back to the islands, Dag was able to reach Gates to discuss something Dag's mother said that had given him pause.

"Hey, John," Dag said, realizing for a fleeting moment that he rarely called Gates by his first name, "I was thinking about something dealing with this case."

"Shoot," Gates replied in a seemingly cavalier manner, yet Dag knew he was listening intently.

"The murderer may or may not have known that getting the murder weapon back into the police station would be discovered, but what if the murderer suspected that it might be discovered, and he or she did this just to throw us off and made us focus on connections in the police department itself. The killer knew it would take some time to scour the police department and records to try to find a clue, and all that killer would have to do is sit back and enjoy the show," Dag proposed.

"Sounds elaborate, yet it is something a wise person might do," Gates responded. "I mean, think about how smart it would be to throw off so many law enforcement officers and the time it would waste investigating internally."

"Well, exactly," Dag stated.

"But who would have this access to the evidence room except for someone who was connected to the police station?" Gates queried.

"Well, excellent question," Dag replied, "but let's think about it reasonably. There must be *someone* who has access who could pull this off."

"It seems to me," Gates added, "that the only way this wouldn't be connected to the police is if the perpetrator had a connection to a police officer, and the officer was not aware of what was happening."

"Okay, here's what we need…" Dag's voice trailed off as Gates interrupted.

"We need to find out who besides police department officials has access to the evidence room, and I am assuming that if anyone does there is a police officer on duty observing when this occurs," Gates offered proudly.

"Right you are," Dag followed. "Maybe Cary can handle this for us and come up with a list."

"You are reading my mind," Gates said. "I will get with him, and maybe we can even have a preliminary list before you return."

"By the way, how have you been?" Dag asked, knowing that Gates would understand that he was talking about his memory issues.

"Not bad this week," Gates replied. "I have good weeks and bad. So far all is well since you have been gone."

"Let me ask you something, John," Dag said a bit tentatively. "Do you think the time would come when you think we should talk to the group about this? Let me state first that I am not for or against it. I know you would have total support from the group, but I do not have an opinion either way. I am just thinking if there would be a better environment for you if others were aware. But rest assured, I have no intention of saying a word without your okay."

"I appreciate that, Dag, and let me ponder it and get back with you," Gates said with a serious tone that led Dag to believe he would truly think it through in all seriousness.

"Works for me, my friend," Dag said. "Okay, then you will get with Cary, and I will see you in about eight hours." With that, the conversation ended.

It took Gates no time to make contact with Cary, who was at the station doing some training. It also took him no time to convince the police chief to give him access to all who themselves had access to the evidence room. Yet by the time Gates accomplished this, Dag had returned, and Gates was there to pick him up at the airport. In no time, they were talking about next steps.

First, Dag and Gates wanted to review the non-police individuals who had any access, and then they would go about finding out who was connected to them.

"You know," Gates told Dag quite directly, "we might just be taking ourselves on a wild goose chase."

"Right you are, my friend," Dag said, "but it will be one less trail to follow if it doesn't pan out."

Since all entries into and out of the evidence room were recorded and videoed, all Cary had to do was talk to Detective James Augafa, the officer who questioned Dag immediately after the murder had occurred. Detective Augafa, with the police chief's approval, took the list of entrants into the evidence room since Kimo Akamai's murder, cross-referenced them with the videos in the archives, and in a matter of two days, had a comprehensive list available for Cary. Cary called Gates with the news, and they made plans to meet with the entire group of friends at Gates's place the next morning. The group really felt as if they were moving forward.

Cary called Dag the next morning before he drove up the hill. Dag, Annie, and Jack were already at Gates's place across the breezeway from Dag's bungalow when he called. He wanted to know if anyone wanted him to bring something for breakfast, and he was unprepared for the response. A half hour later, he appeared at Gates's door with pastries, muffins, egg and cheese biscuits, and all manner of fresh fruit for the crew.

"Wow," Cary said as he walked through the front door, "this group has a good appetite." Everyone laughed.

"Well, my friend," Annie said in response, "if you're going to run with us, you need to pitch in, and I think you have done well here. Before long I might even begin to like you." Cary smiled because, even though he hadn't known Annie for long, he knew that her comment was a big move toward acceptance. Little did he know that Annie had accepted him when everyone else did, but Annie was not one to cut anyone any slack.

As they opened the food Cary brought, Gates turned to Cary and said, "So, you have some info for us?"

"Sure do," Cary said, "and I have even done some follow-up to make your process easier."

Cary had not even been seated before he began to talk business. Cary was an interesting individual. He was very kind and fun, but when it was time for business, he was very business minded. This meeting was no exception.

"Okay," Cary offered first, "there are only nine people who have access to the evidence room: the Chief of Police, the lieutenant who showed us around several weeks back, Detective Augafa who came here to interview you guys recently, Sandra Conner whom we spoke to earlier, and the five security guards who guard the door. I know that five security guards sound like quite a few, but really they have to work in shifts, and when you think about it, it makes sense that there would be at least that many. According to the Chief, they work to limit those who have access for the very reasons you might imagine. They want a trail in case something goes wrong, and the fewer people on the list the better. Heads around the room were nodding.

"I think we need to focus on the security guards first," Gates offered.

"Why is that?" Jack asked.

"Well, the other positions are pretty high profile and vetted pretty well. The security guards, while screened, do come and go more often," Gates replied.

"Makes sense," Annie said. "So should we break up the list and do some background checks?"

"Well, my friends, I have done some preliminary checking," said Cary, which surprised no one.

"Oh?" said Gates.

"Yeah, and they all check out so far, but there is an interesting connection in there that was learned quite incidentally," Cary followed. "When all these DNA tests started coming out commercially, all the security staff did DNA tests just for fun. It wasn't a requirement or anything. Anyway, they all got together and had a party to talk about who was related to whom, etc., and there were many surprises. Turns out that Milton Cross, one of the lead deputies of the guards, is a close relative of Sloan Ender."

"The politician and developer?" Annie said loudly.

"You got it," Cary followed.

"Hmmmm, interesting," Jack said, "but why do we care?"

"Because if Milton Cross has that connection, then perhaps Ender is in on getting the gun and killing Kimo," Gates said. Jack nodded in understanding.

"I get it, but why, if they are connected through this DNA test and conspired to kill Kimo, would they announce it to everyone at a security party?" Jack said.

"Because," Dag said, "as a wise old woman recently told me, you need to look at the people whom you suspect the least."

"What?" Annie asked quizzically.

"Well," Dag offered, "I think sometimes it is important to look at who is trying to be too transparent. Sometimes we do not look at the evidence that is in plain sight, and these individuals, who by the way are no strangers to law enforcement, might know that."

"Makes sense," Jack said.

"Sure does," Gates added. "Looks like we're going to have to make Dag an investigator after all." The group laughed.

"Okay," Annie queried, "but why would they have anything to do with Kimo's murder?"

Cary jumped in by saying, "Ender was a major proponent of expansion in both his roles as a politician and as a developer. Kimo was clearly opposed to expansion that he perceived to be harmful or disrespectful to our environment. Now I'm not saying Ender is a bad guy, but this could be a plausible reason for some discord between the two."

Gates jumped in, saying, "As a former detective, I have to say that this case seems to be getting easier all the time."

Dag was a bit surprised to hear this from Gates, who usually weighed all the options and was slow to make a judgment. Of course, Gates was more adept at this than Dag. Still, Dag was glad that they were moving in a direction that could potentially lead somewhere.

At any rate, taking this approach would mean they all had some investigating to do.

Cary took the lead from there and made informal assignments. Of course, anything formal would need to go through the police department, but since this was so closely tied to the department, Cary had been given permission to proceed as he saw fit. While this was not a routine approach, Cary was on contract with the police department, and it wasn't that much of a reach. Giving Cary carte blanche to take the lead was a bit out of character for the police, but it happened, and nobody wanted to ask questions to stir up the pot and lose control. It seemed that the whole group, and especially Cary and Gates, were happy to have this opportunity to showcase their talents.

Cary asked Annie and Jack to find out everything they could about Sloan Ender—his likes and dislikes, his involvement with major projects, his political leanings, his temperament, and any negative press that might have occurred. Gates specifically asked Cary if he could tag along with him to do any police business connected with the case. Cary was happy to oblige. Dag asked if he could be a floater between the two camps and keep a journal of all the happenings. Everyone seemed happy and excited about the assignments and the fact that they were moving the ball forward.

It didn't take Jack and Annie very long to dig up quite a bit of information concerning Sloan Ender. He had been in politics for many years, running for City Council and winning at every turn. Of course, Ender was a major proponent of industrializing the island, which, as everyone knew, was not the direction that Kimo Akamai was headed. Kimo was a man of the earth, respecting land, animals, and others. He stated more than once that of all the creatures on earth, man was the one he could reason with, and yet he still had the most trouble with them.

Sloan Ender was said to have his eye on the governorship within the next few years, but he knew he would face quite a battle with environmentalists. Jack and Annie commented that while he seemed to be directly opposed to Kimo and his agenda, if in fact that kind man could have even had an agenda, Ender was not a bad man in the broad sense of the word. He was in the middle of many homeless initiatives, he donated much to the development of social and legal services, and he also had a foundation in his name that awarded scholarships to promising youth for college.

"This perplexes me," Dag said, "but I don't know why it should. There is good and bad in everyone. Still, this Ender guy seems to be focused on either clearly good and altruistic things, or on things that displace people and animals and destroys the natural beauty of the island. I cannot get a handle on his motivation."

CHAPTER 43

The Mystery That
Is Sloan Ender

The evening continued with Dag, Annie, Jack, Gates, and Cary, and the discussion of Sloan Ender seemed to dominate that evening discussion. John Gates seemed to be convinced that they were on the right track, and all were in agreement that so far, he appeared to be the suspect with the most to lose when it came to the initiatives that Kimo Akamai held dear.

When the group of friends adjourned for the evening and went their separate ways, Dag retreated to his room with a glass of wine and a book. It had been a long time since he'd read for enjoyment, and he wanted to spend some time *not thinking* for a while. It took no time for the book to fall into his lap as he nodded off to sleep in the chair in his room.

He was awakened abruptly by a limb from the eucalyptus tree in front of his bungalow striking the roof. Quite a windstorm had arisen in a short period. He turned down the louvered windows, went out to make sure all other windows were secure, and then returned to his room to climb into bed and fall asleep with the sound of the wind whistling through the small spaces in between the closed louvered glass.

All this wind that came out of nowhere made Dag think about what it is in the lives of people that makes them do the things they do.

He wondered what would make someone like Sloan Ender develop an interest in building up and commercializing an island while having political aspirations as well. To Dag, it made no sense. If you are wanting to win the support of citizens when running for public office, how can you connect that to the citizens you might enrage by changing their peaceful island homes?

Another limb fell from the eucalyptus tree and hit Dag's roof, jolting him out of his present mindset. He arose for a moment to ensure that there was no immediate damage, and then he climbed back into bed and stared at the ceiling, thinking about the weather outside.

Wow, thought Dag to himself, *it takes no time at all for a gentle island breeze to turn into a dangerous force of nature.* This truth made him connect the symbolism of the weather to the greater storm brewing in the murder case. He also had an uneasy feeling that this case concerning Kimo Akamai would be solved, yet he knew it would never ease the pain and sense of loss he felt at having lost such a wonderful friend.

CHAPTER 44

On the Trail of a Killer

The next day, Cary called to let the group know that the relative of Sloan Ender who was also a security guard at the police station was a distant relative at best and appeared to have no true connection to Ender. In fact, after questioning several of his colleagues at the police station, they all had the same story that he was in fact surprised about the connection when the group did the DNA tests.

"Yes, but this doesn't necessarily mean he is innocent or that Sloan Ender didn't have some motivation and could still be guilty," Gates said after Dag told him the story. Cary's call to Dag gave Gates the cue he wanted to get back down to the station and follow Cary around to see what other information they could find. Since Gates left to go to the station, that left the old trio of Dag, Jack, and Annie to ponder the case.

"Based on what you guys have told me about Kimo," Annie began, "it is simply unconscionable to me that someone would have a motivation for killing him. I mean, if someone was upset about Kimo's political leanings or his activism about the environment, why not just talk things out with him? It sounds as if he was very approachable."

"Yeah, it seems that way to us," Dag responded, "but this guy seemed to have quite a few enemies. I was shocked when I first moved here at how he was treated by neighbors, by people at the farmer's market, and by his own wife, yet I never ever heard the man raise his voice. If he had a dark side, I cannot conceive of his being able to hide it from me through the entire time we knew one another."

Jack jumped into the conversation. "Still, everyone has a dark side, don't you think? I mean, not us, but pretty much everyone else." Annie and Dag laughed.

"What I mean is," Jack continued, "that people have things they want to hide or that they'd rather no one else would know, right? I would imagine that would apply to Kimo as well, huh?"

"Well, we did find out purely by accident that he was quite rich," Dag offered, "but is that his dark side? Seems to me he used his money wisely, philanthropically, and without any sign of greed or expectation of reward."

"All I know," Annie added, "is that I am getting super frustrated at not finding anything that seems like a clue. Anybody know anywhere else we can search besides Sloan Ender and his security guard long lost cousin?"

"Well," Dag said, "we can go back to the video Cary took of the memorial service and see if we can pick out any other strange connections. I think we exhausted that avenue, but you never know. I have a copy of it here. Cary transferred it so we could watch it on the television."

"Nothing else to do," Annie confessed. "Let's do it."

"Sounds good," Jack said, "but I want some popcorn and lemonade before we do this. Anyone else?"

"Do you think this is a matinee or something?" Annie queried. "We're on a case here." She glanced at Dag and smiled as Jack walked into the kitchen.

"The way I look at it, we have two reasons to get some popcorn and lemonade," Jack said. "First, most people enjoy watching something and are more attentive if they are eating."

"Okay," Annie said, "and what's the second reason, genius?"

"It's very simple and something we can all agree upon," Jack offered. "If you're eating popcorn, your mouth isn't being used to talk."

Dag leaned over and whispered to Annie, "He wins this round. Just accept it and move on to your next quest." Annie smiled and conceded.

Jack soon emerged from this kitchen, quite proud of himself.

The trio reviewed the video of the memorial service at least four times. Sloan Ender was there, and on the fourth pass through the video, Jack noticed back in the background a couple of gentlemen in uniforms, and for a brief moment, they were speaking with Ender. None of the three knew who they were, so if nothing else, perhaps finding out who they were would be worthwhile. They decided to ask Cary and Gates, next time the group was together, if they could be identified. Since Gates and Cary were picking up some food for the group for dinner, they would not have long to wait.

That evening, as they sat around eating Chinese food from the food truck at the bottom of the hill, the case finally came up. Dag began by asking if Gates and Cary found out anything new.

"Not really," Cary said. "Earlier, I was trying to open up some new possibilities of potential suspects, but Gates here wisely suggested that we play out the Sloan Ender angle first and then we can eliminate him if it doesn't work out."

"Yeah," Gates added, "we need to really focus on Ender to see if we are missing something."

CHAPTER 45

The Trail Gets Warmer

After Gates and Cary arrived and brought the Chinese food and all were satisfied, the focus on Sloan Ender as a suspect continued. Dag suggested that they focus on specific reasons why Ender would have a need to kill Kimo Akamai. That is when the group began to talk non-stop.

"Well," Annie began. "He could have felt that Kimo was standing in the way of his development business on the ewa side of the island."

"Yes," Jack added, "and he also could have the idea that a failure in his development business might tarnish his reputation as a good businessman, prompting people to make a connection to his political aspirations, suggesting that if he couldn't run a good business that he might not be a good civic leader as well."

"Very good point," Gates responded. "Also, Kimo might have had something Ender wanted."

"Like what?" Cary said.

"Well," Gates replied, "like money, influence, and a wisdom that made Kimo feel quite secure in his own skin."

"You know, that's true," Dag offered. "From a psychological standpoint, I think many controlling individuals like Sloan Ender are actually quite insecure, and I would imagine it would frustrate him to no end to see Kimo Akamai so centered, so happy with his life, so sure of who he was. Ender could have been one of those people who had such control issues because there was so much chaos within. Many who are that way get frustrated by people who are at peace or who have a measure of joy in their lives."

"Okay, I think we can all agree that it's a possibility," Annie said, "but people who run in the circles that Ender was a part of know full well the consequences of murder. If he truly had so much chaos within, wouldn't this only add to the chaos?"

"It could," Gates replied, "but it could also make him feel as if he had controlled something that was a true deterrent to his advancement in business as well as politically."

"That makes sense too," Cary contributed, "but we know that someone with Ender's connections and smarts would likely be very sure to make the trail quite complicated and untraceable. We seem to have honed in on him quite easily and quite quickly." This comment made Dag reflect upon what his mother stated in a recent visit about the killer likely having a good idea of how to complicate things.

"And you know what that means," Gates added. "If he is that wise, he knows how to make the trail cold again, and he could do that by hiding in plain sight. I would be willing to bet that if we were to contact him about this that he would be willing to talk to us with no problem at all."

"And why is that, John?" Dag asked.

"Well," Gates responded, "he has to demonstrate the ease with which he interacts with everyone. It's part of the politician persona… to be cool…to not get ruffled."

"Then what is keeping us from contacting him?" Jack queried.

"Nothing," Gates said, "but we will have to be quite sure of what we ask and how we react to him. If he knows we are onto him, he will size us up as a threat and has possibly already considered how he will react to someone who suspects him. We need to be as sly as he is. We have to decide what our tack will be. Are we going to go in, seemingly transparent, and relay to him that we suspect him, or are we going to go in seeming to assume innocence on his part and ask questions to test his reaction?"

"This is way too complicated for me," Jack said.

"And me," Dag chimed in. "I say we let Cary and Gates talk to him. They can decide on the approach."

"Works for me," Gates said. "How 'bout you, Cary?"

"Let's do this," Cary responded.

With that process set into place, the time had come for Dag's meeting for the reading of the will. With very few people present except for representatives of Kimo's ex-wife and several charities in town, and with no suspicion aroused at all on the part of Dag, he was all set for the encounter to be a bit boring and unproductive as far as the case was concerned, except for one minor detail: In his will, Kimo Akamai left Dag Peyton a sum of two million dollars, to do with "as he saw fit." Dag was beside himself.

After the half-hour reading of the will, the attorney of record arranged with Dag to have the funds transferred to him. Dag left the meeting in a state of mild shock, as if he'd just awakened from a hard slumber and was trying to reorient himself to the world. He drove back home, where his friends were waiting. He told them the story, and in one voice, they all said this was no surprise. To them, Kimo knew that Dag knew how the money could be well utilized. The conversation ended surprisingly rapidly, and the conversation turned to Sloan Ender, ending with a confirmation that Gates and Cary would be meeting with Ender soon.

CHAPTER 46

Getting to Know Sloan Ender

Gates was right about having no problem making contact with Sloan Ender. Still, even knowing this, he and Cary were somewhat surprised at the ease with which they secured an appointment with him. In addition, they decided to take the more congenial route with Ender and act as if they were seeking information about the death of Kimo Akamai and that they were interviewing his friends and acquaintances to see if they knew of any reason why Kimo would be murdered.

Gates came up with the approach, and Cary thought it was brilliant because Ender might think that Gates and Cary perceived him as a friend of Kimo's and therefore he could take that in any direction he wanted to take it. Still Cary knew that if Ender poured on the charm too intensely as a result of this approach, he might very well have something to hide.

The pair seemed a bit nervous when they entered Ender's office building. Being such an influential figure as well as a political candidate with high future aspirations, his name and image appeared to be plastered everywhere within the city block where his office was located. He just seemed to have a presence that was more intense than anyone else. Cary was nervous because he wanted to get his role in the process correct. Cary couldn't figure out why Gates was nervous. Gates had done this kind of thing with prominent public figures all his life, yet he seemed preoccupied and less prepared than his experience would have suggested. Cary did not know of Gates's memory issues nor of the worry that went along with it, thinking he might be discovered at any moment to be losing his faculties.

"Hello," Gates offered almost timidly. "My name is John Gates, and I am here to see Sloan Ender, please. This is Cary," Gates said, pointing to Cary. "We called for an appointment earlier."

"Sure, guys," said the young assistant at the front desk. "Let me just tell him you are here."

"Great," said Gates, and the two of them took a seat in the waiting room. They had not been seated for more than two minutes, when Sloan Ender came through the door.

Ender was a large and stocky man, quite tall and to some people quite foreboding, yet when he was in good spirits, he was kind and amiable, almost gentle. "Hello, guys," Ender began, as if they had all known one another for many years. "What can I do for you today?"

"Well," Cary began, "we were doing some investigating to see if there are any friends or relatives who knew Kimo Akamai who could give us any leads into why and how his death occurred."

Ender briefly sat in what appeared to be stone-cold silence, but then his demeanor changed for the better.

With a smile, Sloan Ender said, "I am afraid I did not know him well, and I haven't spoken to him but once or twice in connection with some of the projects my organization has going around the island. Is this a formal police investigation?"

"Well, no," Cary responded, "but I am a consultant for the police department. I do need to make it clear that I am not asking these questions in conjunction with any requested police investigation." While Cary was thinking that this would give Ender a good reason to discontinue the conversation, he felt compelled to tell the truth. He certainly didn't want there to be any charges of false representation of the police department on the part of Sloan Ender.

"I understand. So this is really an informal investigation, and what we discuss is off the record, right?" Ender said. This question puzzled Gates and Cary. It appeared that he asked this question because he was planning on providing some important information that he might not otherwise feel comfortable divulging. Cary as well as Gates subconsciously leaned forward.

"Absolutely," Gates said.

"Well, then, I have a bit of information that I could give you," Ender stated and then leaned in as well.

CHAPTER 47

A Surprise

"Kimo Akamai was well respected," Ender said. "He was respected by me, by my colleagues, and by most of the people I knew."

"But how is that possible?" Cary said, clearly puzzled. "I mean, from the looks of it, I can see what you mean. He was admired and even adored by those who knew him well, but he had quite a few people in the community who appeared to be at odds with him, and from what we can gather, the people who appeared to like him the least were those who were trying to get community initiatives off the ground—business people, political figures, etc. It seems as if they perceived that he was standing in the way of progress, when I believe his actual intentions centered around preservation of land and culture."

"Absolutely, that was Kimo," Ender added, "but those very people understood where he was coming from and admired him for his ideals. Look, I know you guys likely know this about business as well as politics. You can have someone seemingly fighting against you every step of the way on some project that you are trying to advance, but at the heart of it, you and your opponent both know that you are each doing individually what you believe is best for the community, state, nation, or at whatever level you find yourself. You can round up every single person whom you perceive to have an issue with Kimo Akamai, and I guarantee you that you will also see an admiration and an appreciation for who he was."

Gates and Cary sat there, a bit deflated. This was not going where they thought it would. Then Gates said, "Sir, were you aware that Kimo Akamai was quite wealthy?"

"I had an idea," Ender responded. "I mean, he had the political clout that comes with wealth. He was a quiet man, a gentleman, but also a resolute man and a man on a mission to preserve the land and culture. But here's the deal, guys. With the mindset and the goodness in that man, isn't he the kind of man you would *want* to have a good stash of funds? I will also add that I am a bit surprised that he had wealth. People with his mindset of philanthropy usually give all their money away."

"Well, from what we learned," Gates added, "he was slowly doing just that, and he had no measure of extravagance in his personal life."

"Again, no surprise," Ender said. "His wisdom carried over into his financial affairs apparently. He likely was able to invest wisely and keep a steady flow of funding available for those in need. His method of distribution was one that would be ongoing and more fruitful for many more people. May I make a suggestion? Question the people who stood to inherit his money."

"Good point," Cary said. "I know one person who inherited from him."

"Good. Start with him," Ender suggested.

Gates laughed out loud, which was rare for him. "There is no way that man is needing to be questioned, and besides, he was off island in the Bay Area with me when it occurred." Of course, Gates was referring to Dag, who had received a substantial amount from Kimo. Dag, as expected, was going to donate it to charity.

"Well, okay then, but don't count anyone out. Sometimes murderers, thieves, and those who conspire with them are hiding in plain sight," Ender said eerily.

"We have taken enough of your time, Mr. Ender," Gates said abruptly. "Many thanks for your time." Cary was surprised at the quick ending to the meeting but arose as Gates and Ender did.

CHAPTER 48

Choosing a Path for Moving Forward

Cary and Gates no sooner plopped into the car to leave Sloan Ender's building than Gates piped in, "I am not giving up on Ender as a suspect."

Cary gave his full attention to this surprising train of thought from Gates, "Why, John? I mean, this guy and his comments seem rock solid to me. None of the criteria are there for continuing to consider him as a suspect as far as I can see."

"Which is the exact reason why he needs to stay at the top of the list," Gates replied. "This guy is a politician and a high-level businessman. Wouldn't you imagine that he knew that eventually someone would come to talk to him about Kimo? And wouldn't you also think that he would have rehearsed a response to our questions? I mean, the guy is a politician, for the love of Pete!"

"Well, when you put it that way..." Cary said, surrendering to Gates's train of thought outwardly, yet otherwise seeing the continuing focus on Ender as a waste of time.

When the pair reached Dag's place, Jack and Annie were grilling opakapaka, and the seasoning hit the senses of Gates and Cary before they even got to the door.

"Oh maaaan...that smells good," Gates said as he strode through the door. Dag looked up and pointed to the breezeway, where Annie and Jack were laughing and bickering, which somehow made everything seem right with the world. Dag was happy that all his friends felt comfortable treating his home as if it were their own. It was the Hawaiian way. Take off your shoes before entering, go to the fridge for the beverage of your choosing, and kick back for the day. There were days when Dag would run errands and come home only to find his door wide open with a pile of shoes at the front door and sounds of laughter coming from his kitchen. This setting warmed his heart.

"Lucky you," Annie yelled to Gates from the breezeway, having heard Gates's comment. "We're having fish tacos, and against my better judgment, you are invited."

Gates just smiled and yelled back, "It's all about the fish. I'll worry about your attitude later." The group joined in laughter.

After the tacos and a chocolate haupia pie, the group's attention turned to the matter of Kimo Akamai and Cary's and Gates's meeting with Sloan Ender.

"Not much to report as far as I can see," Cary began. "He was very receptive to our discussion, and he laid a minor bombshell on us that will surprise most of us, I think. He said that Kimo was admired by all these people. He said that there are conflicts but that it is just part of business as well as politics, and he recommended that we address the people who inherited money from Kimo, which of course includes Dag." He turned to Dag and smiled.

"Well," Dag began, "I think everyone here knew that my inheritance from Kimo surprised me more than anyone else."

Dag was still shocked to discover that he had been left a sizeable amount of money, with a message from Kimo stating that Dag knew what to do with it, so Dag was searching some charities and some benevolent actions that he could take to adhere to Kimo's purpose for the funds.

Gates laughed. "Yes, his suggestion that we investigate your relationship with Kimo Akamai was the non-starter of all non-starters."

"But who are the others who inherited from him?" Jack asked.

"We can assume, but we probably need to dig deep to find this out. We can talk to that attorney who informed me of my inheritance," Dag said.

"He won't give us anything as far as info is concerned, but it can't hurt," Gates said. "They can't just offer that information."

"Right, but we can try," Jack concluded.

"We certainly can," Gates replied.

The next morning, it took no time for Dag to get on the phone with Reuben Goddard, the attorney who handled the last will and testament of Kimo Akamai. Now that all had been settled with the estate and with the inheritance of property and money, there were really no more secrets necessary. Mr. Goddard spoke quite freely concerning the whole inheritance and with a surprising specificity.

"Well gentlemen," Goddard began, "many were surprised that he left quite a bit of money to his ex-wife." This statement surprised Dag. "Yes, he was quite generous, in fact. He told me when he was making out his will that he never wanted to hurt his wife and that he thought that the funds would make her happy."

"That is quite generous of him," Dag said, wondering if the wife knew of this windfall before Kimo's death. Perhaps she did, which could easily make her a suspect.

"And then there is a substantial amount that he left to the mental health center on the windward side of the island," Goddard continued, "but that's no surprise at all."

"Why not?" Dag queried.

"Well, you know, because of his son and all," Goddard added.

"I did not know he had a son," Dag said. "Was the son the biological son of Kimo's wife?"

"Yes, but there is a strange story to that," Goddard stated mysteriously. "The son was challenged mentally and with a bit of dementia as well," Goddard said. "Apparently, he had difficulty with long-term memory. Really a sad situation. He was in the mental health facility, and the strange thing was that Kimo would go to visit him, but his wife would never go. Said it was too painful for her. Anyway, aside from you and his wife and numerous charities around town, he left a sizable sum to a man also on the windward side of the island by the name of Smart, Luke Smart. No one around here knew him, and he is an odd duck of sorts, or so the story goes."

"And no one knows why this Smart guy was given an inheritance," Dag said, puzzled.

"Nope, but that is your cast of characters. All the charities he awarded are quite reputable, which of course was no surprise considering the kind of man we knew Kimo to be," Goddard surmised.

"Yeah, makes perfect sense," Dag said. "Well, thanks so much for your time. I appreciate all this information."

"You bet, my friend," Goddard said, hanging up the phone.

CHAPTER 49

Motivations

Dag hung up the phone with a smile on his face, which was curious to Jack, who had just entered the room.

"What gives?" Jack said.

"Well, I have never met an attorney so forthcoming about information concerning a former client of his. He would have had to have Kimo's approval to state all this, surely," Dag said.

"Well, if Kimo was the kind of guy you claimed he was, he probably said something like, 'Tell anybody anything you want.' You know the man was an open book. In fact, to hear you talk, I can't conceive of him having any secrets," Jack said.

"You know, that could very well be true, my friend," Dag said, "but still I cannot figure that out. I'm calling him back."

Dag picked the phone up and dialed, and to his surprise, he spoke directly with Goddard. They chatted, and he hung up the phone.

"You were right, Jack," Dag said. "Goddard said that when he and Kimo discussed his will, he reminded Kimo that being an individual of means, there would likely be many people who would wonder where his money went. Of course, Goddard said Kimo was of the mind that it was no one's business, but Kimo was never one to hold back information. Goddard even had him sign a disclaimer that if Kimo were in fact deceased, there would be no issue disclosing his beneficiaries. Kimo even said that perhaps it would convince more people to donate to the charities of their choice."

"Wow," Jack said, "we even learn of his goodness after his death."

"And that, my friend, is no surprise at all," Dag replied.

"So what happens next?" Jack said curiously.

"Well, he left an inheritance to many charities around town. Let's assume they are legit. Let's begin with some research concerning his wife, and this individual on the windward side named Luke Smart," Dag suggested.

"Works for me, but what would be wrong with just tracking his wife down and talking to her?" Jack offered.

"I do not see a thing wrong with that," Dag said. "We just need to think about how to approach the whole thing. My experiences of overhearing Kimo and his wife interacting were not pleasant experiences. I know it might sound as if I am biased toward Kimo, but this is a fact. I never heard his voice when there was a disagreement. Only hers."

CHAPTER 50

The Real Angela Akamai

Dag heard from Kimo at one point that Kimo's wife had moved to Kahala. Kahala was a neighborhood in Honolulu that was considered upscale. Through friends, Dag learned that his wife frequented a coffee house near her home in Kahala. Dag was familiar with it because he had a friend who taught at the University of Hawaii whom he would meet there when she and Dag were either at semester's end or just needed to talk. It was a strange relationship that Dag had with her. They were kindred spirits in a way, but they didn't interact much. They were at a workshop together once, and they were placed together in a group to work on some teaching techniques in higher education. They clicked. The basis of their relationship appeared to be laughter and then the occasional serious talk. Jan was into philanthropy and was familiar with the causes and projects that Kimo followed. As a result, she had met him as well as Kimo's wife.

Dag called Jan, and she knew that Kimo's wife, Angela, had moved into her neighborhood in Kahala, and she also knew that Angela was regularly at the coffee shop on Friday mornings.

So that upcoming Friday morning, Dag made his way to Kahala, which meant traveling toward town about thirty miles from his home on the west side of the island. As Dag reached the coffee house and was moving toward the front door, he felt a bit anxious about meeting this woman face-to-face. He was quite surprised when he walked in, immediately saw Angela, and she saw him as well. It

194

hadn't crossed Dag's mind that she would remember him from the brief interaction they had when she lived next door. But remember him she did. Dag walked up to the counter to order, sat on a stool to wait for his coffee, and then moved to a booth. He sat down and then looked up, and there before him was Angela, waiting to speak to him.

"I know you, and I know how I know you," Angela said resolutely. Dag asked her if she'd like to sit down. He was surprised when she accepted.

"I am sorry to hear about your ex-husband," Dag said, deciding to approach her as the grieving widow. Dag had a simplicity about him that seemed to make him believable.

"Thank you," Angela said. "You know I am so sorry to hear about what happened to him."

"Of course," Dag responded. "I cannot understand how or why someone would want to do that to him."

"Agreed," stated Angela in a manner that was neither cool nor warm. "I will tell you something that I expect you would not have gleaned from my relationship with my husband. I loved him. I still love him."

"That doesn't surprise me," Dag offered. "I mean, who can truly describe a relationship other than the two people who are in it?"

"Wow," Angela posited, "I wish I'd known you were this understanding when I lived next door to you. I just assumed you were like most of the neighbors and 'didn't care for that sweet Kimo's horrid wife.'"

"Seems as if we are being candid with one another, so I owe you that candor as well," Dag said, offering respect before he was what he considered to be quite direct with her. "I will state that I didn't understand why you were so abrupt with him, and like most people, I thought he was a very good guy, a wise man, a kind man, an unassuming man."

"Fair enough," Angela stated. She smiled a bit and then added, "Want me to knock your socks off? The truth is that I felt exactly the same way."

"For real? Then why the yelling?" Dag replied.

"It is understandable that you would ask that question," Angela began, "but you'd have to know the whole story."

"That is understandable as well," Dag said. "Shoot. That is, if you would like to tell me anything." He was expecting for her to storm away. She remained seated.

"Kimo Akamai was a giver—a self-denying giver who made everyone a priority except for himself," Angela said.

"Except for you?" Dag said bluntly, "and that's why you yelled at him?"

"I'm getting there," she said. "Kimo wanted to help everyone— the downcast, the downtrodden, the poor, the disabled, animals— everyone and everything but himself. I simply told him that if he wanted to do that he needed to move to a better neighborhood, mix more with the elite, get his name out there. That kind of press could get his name recognized and his words would mean more, and as a result, many more would share in his noteworthy causes and he could make more of a difference. But that was not Kimo. You met him. You know that was not Kimo."

"Yeah, I know," Dag said. "Did you ever express those sentiments to anyone besides Kimo?" Dag decided that the best way to find out more was to appear to be on Angela's side. Interestingly enough, in a way he felt as if he were, now that she had expressed her love for him.

"No. Kimo wanted our business to stay our business, and believe it or not, I respected that and kept our issues close to the vest," Angela stated softly.

"Now do you want me to knock your socks off?" Dag said, repeating her earlier statement for effect.

"Why not?" Angela replied. "I mean, we are being brutally honest."

"Okay. The last day I saw Kimo before we left for the airport and went to the Bay Area, we were talking about his life, and the topic of your leaving came up. He said without hesitation that he loved you, and he wanted you to be happy. He said he thought that your greatest happiness was not with him, so he needed to be willing to let you go to find your happiness, and he was hoping that you had indeed found it. I don't know you well enough to work this hard to make you happy. These words are true," Dag said sincerely.

For the first time, he saw the glint of a tear in Angela's eye. "You know, you don't have to get along with someone or even agree with them in order to love them," she confessed.

"We are totally on the same page," Dag said quickly.

"I did love him. I did. I truly did," Angela said, seemingly trying to convince Dag.

"Ma'am," Dag began, "you are preaching to the choir. I know he loved you, and I totally believe you loved him. Two things are certain. He went to his grave loving you, and he never once said to me that he thought you didn't love him. He said he couldn't make you happy. He never said you didn't love him. That leads me to believe that he thought you did."

"I'm not sure why we met, or what the purpose was, but I do know that you have made me feel better," Angela offered, "and here's the deal. There are going to be people who are going to think I had my husband…er…ex-husband killed. I am here to tell you that I did not. I am an open book. At this stage, I am happy to have anyone search any corner of my life to try to prove me wrong. They will find nothing. Funny, now that he is gone and has left all this money to me, it doesn't mean anything to me anymore. I just keep thinking about him and our little bungalow up in the Makakilo hills. I can never get it back. I will never see him again."

"I am sorry, Mrs. Akamai," Dag said with heartfelt sorrow, as the pain of Kimo's death gripped him once more.

"I am sorry too," Angela replied, standing up and walking away into what appeared to be a very sad and lonely world.

CHAPTER 51

The Other Potential Suspect

Dag sat at the coffee house for a bit longer, reflecting upon his meeting with Angela Akamai and feeling confused and saddened about the different and sometimes lonely and destructive paths that love can take. He didn't understand why relationships become broken, but Dag never looked at those kinds of things longingly or emotionally. He looked at them clinically, as a scientist might look at a research project. He didn't know why he was so detached, and for some reason even he couldn't understand, he didn't care. One thing that made him happy, though. He recognized love when he saw it.

Dag wended his way back to Makakilo after stopping at a few shops in the Kahala neighborhood. Dag had actually lived there for a brief time after he'd moved to the island. He went into a small tea shop he'd frequented during his stint on this side of the island, and he sat there for a time, drinking a cup of oolong milk tea and reflecting yet again upon his conversation with Kimo Akamai's ex-wife. When he wanted to, Dag could be very perceptive, and he tried with all his might to determine the guilt or innocence of Angela Akamai. For the life of him, he could not see guilt in her, at least not for this. Was she a lousy wife? It seemed that way to him. Could she have approached her marriage differently? Probably, by her own admission. Yet still, Dag knew it was wrong to judge the marriage. He had only known Kimo a brief time, and as he knew too well, it takes two to tango.

That is, no one person is ever to blame for the end of a relationship, or at least it seemed that way to Dag.

When he arrived at his bungalow, he was met by Jack, who said excitedly, "Hey guy, found out a tidbit about Luke Smart."

"Oh?" Dag said, interested.

"Yeah," Jack continued. "He is an entertainer in Waikiki."

"Sweet!" Dag said, for he knew that this meant they were going to go into town at some point to see and hopefully meet the mysterious stranger. At any rate, Dag loved Waikiki, and he loved the evenings there, ducking into the many seldom visited out-of-the-way places that one would only find after years of living on the island. There was an air of mystery, of connection, in these haunts that made one feel a sense of adventure, a faraway feeling that makes one feel excitement, a feeling of truly living. Dag loved getting lost in the city, and he usually did this alone, yet this time he'd be getting lost in the city with four other people. Sounded fun. He would try his best to focus on the fact that they had work to do to solve the case.

Most of these places Jack and Annie and the rest of the crew had never seen, and that made Dag even more excited to introduce them to them. One in particular was the Sunset Grill. It was tucked behind an old grocery store on Kuhio Avenue, and it was a lazy old cave-like structure that appeared to be ready to collapse at any minute. But there was always soft rock playing, about two decibels below what you'd hear in a standard haunt in town, and it seemed that when the patrons walked in the door, they knew that the atmosphere was low-key. No one had the compunction to raise a voice or to talk above the music. It simply wasn't necessary. Dag would take his friends there. They would fit in quite well.

"So when do you want to go and find out more about this Luke Smart?" Dag asked, sounding to himself like a child at Christmas.

Jack picked up on his enthusiasm. "Man, we can go any old time you like. Just tell me when."

Just then, Annie walked in the door. She looked at both of them and immediately said, "Okay, one or both of you has something to say. Spill it."

"You know, I don't know about Dag, but I have a problem with how perceptive you are. It gives me an uncomfortable chill. Kind of like you're some kind of double agent or something," Jack said with a smile on the right side of his mouth.

"Oh yeah, you're a real tough one to figure out," Annie offered sarcastically. "Jack, you have your life story written on your forehead, and your feelings are right out there for all to see. You are the quintessential definition of an open book. So what's the story?"

Dag piped in, "Okay, long story short. I met with Kimo's wife. In my view, she turned out to be a real person. I can see why Kimo harbored no resentment toward her. She's not bad at all. I cannot conceive of her having anything to do with Kimo's death. She was too open, too comfortable telling me who she was, and it all rang true. Anyway, the only other person Kimo left money to was one Luke Smart. We found out he's an occasional entertainer in Waikiki, and we are going to track him down—not to attack but rather to sidle in and see what we can discover about his connection to Kimo. He seems to be the most mysterious connection thus far."

"Excellent. I am looking him up right now," Annie said.

"You'll never find him. Too unknown I bet," Jack said.

"And here he is," Annie retorted, glancing over to Jack so she wouldn't miss the joy of proving him wrong. "He's at a place called the Sidecar, and he is there only on every other Friday, and this Friday is one of those days. Okay, guys, that's tomorrow night. You in?"

"Are you kidding?" Dag said. "I love hanging out in the city. One of my favorite things."

"We are of one mind," Jack said, turning to Annie and bowing gracefully, which made Annie snicker.

"Cool," she said. "It's on."

It appeared over time that all members of the group were in sync concerning going into town the next evening and having an enjoyable evening while doing some good work at the same time. Still, in the back of the minds of each of the five "investigators," they were silently hoping for some kind of clue that would help them to realize that they were not on another wild goose chase. They were ready for a good lead that would make them feel good about the path they were taking to solve this crime.

CHAPTER 52

An Unusual Suspect?

Dag, Jack, and Annie updated Gates and Cary about the planned trip into town for the following evening, and before they all blinked twice, it was late Friday afternoon.

Dag's Subaru held the five of them comfortably as they made their way into town with the dusk settling in for the evening. Dag was in his element. He loved the early evenings in Hawaii. There was a peace that seemed to settle on the island that made the time a joyful one, a time of quiet comfort; and he was headed into town to enjoy the city. There was a happy mood in the air, with his friends in tow. While there were many unanswered questions that Dag held about the case, he was determined not to let the negative take hold. After all, how could he be in a bad mood? The people with him were a group of intelligent, down-to-earth, real people who made living fun.

Many people will look back on their youth as the best time of their lives, when their lives were full of untried adventure and their bodies were resilient and their minds were clear and set on absorbing every new experience. Dag could identify with that, yet his favorite time was now, arriving at the autumn of his life with a comfortable peace, work he loved, and friends whom he had met along the way and treasured dearly. He reflected on the fact that all these people, growing up and spending their lives in different worlds, had been destined to come together and spend these precious days as friends, all of them clearly understanding the value in every moment, happy to be contemporaries in a world that they realized too soon, due to the passage of time, would not belong to them anymore. It made for a longing to be in the moment, to capture an image of this time in their minds that a photo cannot grasp. A comment from Annie served to bring Dag back to the moment.

"Okay," Annie said, "who is this guy we are going to see? Does anyone know anything about him? How old is he? How is he connected to Kimo again?"

Cary jumped in. "Well, let me think. Ummm, yes, it's official. You have exhausted your questions for the evening." Laughter filled the small SUV.

"Well, aren't you a piece of work," Annie retorted. "Where'd you get that smart mouth?"

"Clearly not from you. Yours is obviously still intact," Cary quickly responded.

"I have waited for this for forty years, man," Jack said snickering. "Annie's met her match."

"Yeah, you have had to wait, because none of you other clowns could keep up," Annie snapped playfully.

"Quick, Cary," Jack said, "say something to get her back."

"Sorry, dude," Cary said. "You are totally on your own on this one."

As they entered the outskirts of Honolulu, Cary asked what they were going to do for dinner before going over to the Sidecar Lounge to find out more about this Luke Smart, one of the heirs of the Kimo Akamai fortune.

"Well, my friends," Dag offered, "I have always wanted to treat you guys to a favorite haunt of mine. It is within walking distance of the Sidecar, so we will only have to park once, and it is nestled behind an old banana plantation home that has remained undisturbed in the heart of the city. All the huge buildings in the city grew up around it, and in the heart of town, you will not find a more tranquil place. It is fun, inexpensive, and laid back, but can be very busy. They take reservations far in advance, and don't seat anyone without one. The place is called Indigo, and lucky for you, I made reservations for every Friday this month."

"Very nice," Annie said, "but why every Friday of this month?"

"Because," Dag replied, "I like to come into town at least once a month, and I like to eat here. I can just cancel the rest of the reservations later. They know me so well that they don't mind. When I lived here in town, I used to eat here quite often."

"This is pretty cool," remarked Cary, who from the back seat sounded a bit like a kid in a candy store. "I am kind of excited about this evening."

"Me too," Jack said. "This is a great city. Reminds me of the Bay Area in many ways."

The crowd parked the car along the Ala Wai Canal and made their way to Indigo. True to form, as told by Dag, the restaurant was a real treat. Old ficus trees that were several stories high had grown all around what appeared to be an open hut but was in fact the old banana plantation home Dag spoke of earlier. They were seated, had a drink, and enjoyed a level of comfort that was felt and appreciated by all.

The special of the day was fish tacos, and they were served with onion rings that melted just as they entered the mouth. The group applauded Dag time after time for sharing this getaway with them. Gates especially was effusive in his praise of Dag. The individuals in this group could possibly be good actors, but none of them could be good enough to fake the enjoyment they had that evening.

After dinner, the five of them sat at the table for another hour, looking up at the ficus and bamboo that surrounded them and feeling as if they had entered the city and fallen into some kind of vortex of peace, serenity, and mirth. Finally, they ordered three desserts, which they shared among them.

It was one of those occasions in life when they simply did not want to get up from what was becoming yet another memorable time in the lives of Dag and his friends. The discussion was always good, even when it was light, and when it was deep, it was profound and unforgettable. It seemed as if they each brought something unique to the table—different backgrounds, different educational experiences, different careers—yet they shared many things as well—similar tastes in food and the arts, and the most important was that it appeared that none of them had lost a sense of humor. There was not a curmudgeon among them, there was no one among them who liked drama, and there was not a duplicitous one among them.

Annie recalled a woman she knew in a former life who was sweet and funny and generally good, yet she was the kind of person who would say ten good things about a person and then slip in an insult in the middle of them. In Annie's words, this person was very "'small' and didn't even know it. They agreed that life was too short for that approach to life.

The final conversation at Indigo was centered around the case. It was an unplanned preparation for how they were going to approach Luke Smart. Up to that moment, none of the group had discussed this important aspect of the evening. They enjoyed their time together so much that they sometimes forgot to discuss the business at hand nor the reason they were actually in town in the first place. Jack was the first one to jump into the conversation with an idea that was truly indicative of Jack. Jack was a very bright man with a simple approach. He was the kind of person who would innocently announce the presence of the elephant in the room and ask questions that would bring a deep conversation back to ground zero and a common sense that left people speechless.

"I think we need to simply see first if we can talk to him at all," Jack said, "and while I am not the detective in the group, I don't think we need to team up on him."

"Very good point," Gates confirmed. "We have no idea what this guy is like. He could give us all the information we need to find the killer, or he might take off like a scared jackrabbit. I think we approach him, in a casual conversation tell him who we are, and then let him do the talking."

"Agreed," Cary said. "In this conversation, we should look for subtle signs as he is speaking, which means, as Gates said, that we need to let him do the talking. We look for subtle nuances in his mannerisms or changes in his demeanor as we discuss the case."

"And of course, all this sounds to me as if Gates and Cary need to approach him. We can hang back," Dag offered, sacrificing Jack and Annie as well as himself. They didn't mind and nodded in agreement.

With the modus operandi in place, the happy group left Indigo for what they all agreed would not be the last time. They felt a sense of happiness that evening, a lilt in the air that made the evening seem like a gem in the days of their lives. There was an unspoken appreciation of the opportunity to live it.

Dag was right. The walk to the Sidecar Lounge was brief and pleasant. The evening was perfect, seventy-five degrees, breezy trade winds, and a dusk that was breathtaking, even surreal. As they reached the door to the lounge, Dag entered first, having made the reservations.

"Table for five under the name of Peyton," Dag said.

"Great," said the young lady who escorted them. "This way, please."

As they were walking back to the table, Dag added, "I have been here before, and I requested a table in the back for reasons that you will soon understand." As they reached the back, and as others began to filter into the folksy but clean room, they noticed that the three tables in the back were a bit elevated, spacious, and comfortable. It was almost like reclining in one's own living room.

The seats from just in front of their table and all the way up to the VIP seats in the front of the room were crowded and appeared to be less comfortable. It also seemed as if the patrons had to crane their necks to look upward to the stage. Dag's friends immediately noticed this.

"I already appreciate your seat selection," Cary said. "If I were to sit any farther up, my neck would be sore for a week afterward."

"Yeah," Annie said. "How can a person sit that way for a couple hours? And we have a straight shot to the stage."

"I knew this because I had made the mistake before," Dag offered. "I mean, I even bought a VIP seat. It is right in front of the stage, but so is the bar, and people are literally standing right in front of you during the concert, ordering drinks. In addition to that, the VIP seats are actually just stools! They have no backs on them. It was rough."

"Yeah," Jack said, "but do they ever come back here to serve dri—"

"May I get you guys a drink?" came a soft voice from beside them. The group turned to Jack and laughed, as he was about to be concerned about being served.

"Sure," Dag said. He ordered drinks for everyone, they arrived immediately, and they kicked back, ready to hear the songs stylings of Luke Smart. They were all enthralled in the event, which was interesting, since none of them knew what he sang or if he was a good singer. They soon found out.

Just as they were closing the conversation that began at the restaurant, the lights dimmed, and the announcer came from behind the curtain. He was a chubby local man, and he had a voice that could be booming if he wanted it to be. Instead he was quite clear, articulate, and deliberate. He set the mood for the introduction quite well.

"Good evening, my friends," he began. "Tonight, we have a special treat for you here at the Sidecar. If you've ever heard a combo of blues, soft rock, 1960s folk, and jazz, and if you liked it, you are going to be thrilled this evening. We have the relaxing, mood elevating, peaceful sounds of Luke Smart. Let's hear it, folks!"

The crowd had apparently heard of him before, which surprised Dag and his friends, because they immediately turned on the applause. Perhaps it was because they frequented the place and had heard him before, but perhaps they'd heard of him and made plans to come because he was very good at what he did. Whatever the reasons, applaud they did. It was a muffled yet sustained applause that one would expect in this element, and it went on for an entire minute. Then out came Luke Smart.

Luke Smart was a man of average height, average weight, with a dark black beard that was trimmed close, and a friendly face that made it seem as if he would like to personally thank everyone for coming. Without a word, he walked over to the piano and began to play. The soft, lilting rhythm of the piano immediately put the audience in a quiet mood, and he softly sang a quite memorable lyric of his own making:

> The day you broke my heart, I wandered off to cry
> Instead I took a pen and pad and wrote the
> reasons why

I blamed myself a bit, I blamed you some
as well
    Then I put the music to the words and
promised not to dwell
    On anything…but this song
    I sang the song for friends, they gave it to
a man
    Who said I'd be a hit someday in a smooth
one-person band
    I toured the city o'er, some people came to
hear
    And it changed my life, brought me here
tonight, and I'll hold the memories near
    Close to my heart…like this song
    You're likely far away, in a town I'll never see
    Finding joy with those who share your love,
and that's just fine with me
    I'll take these written words, and sing them
now and then
    And the years will fade like a summer's day,
and these moments I will spend
    Where heartaches end…in a song.…

Luke Smart spent the rest of the evening singing songs he'd
written himself, and the evening was magnetic. There was something
about his music and his voice that made you feel comfortable, as if
you deserved to relax and be happy about your life.

He was clearly a happy man, a content man, a centered man. It
was interesting that as Dag's mind was coming to the same conclusion, Gates leaned over to him and said, "He reminds me of Kimo,
huh?" Dag had never before felt as if he had the exact same thought
at the exact same time as someone else, until that moment.

The session ended, and all were in agreement that it was a fine
one indeed. They had been so enrapt in the music and the soothing
demeanor of the artist that they for a moment forgot the reason why
they were there. As Luke Smart slowly made his way off stage, their

small group began to stir nervously due to the lack of preparation for this moment.

"Okay," Gates said, "we agreed that Cary and I were going to handle this part of the process, right?" The others nodded, and just as Cary and Gates were about to stand, Luke Smart walked directly by their table and to a group sitting in front of them. Dag and his friends listened in on the conversation, and he was having a pleasant conversation with the people, whom he had clearly never met before. They were effusive in their praise, and he seemed to be soft-spoken and humbled.

In a moment, Luke Smart turned to walk to another table, when Gates called out to him from where the group was sitting. "Excuse me, sir," Gates began. Gates raised his hand so he could be seen by the singer. The lights were still quite dim.

"Yeah, hey guys, what can I do for you?" Smart responded.

Since Smart was being so congenial, Gates looked at Cary, and they both decided to just stay at the table and discuss things with him from there. "We certainly enjoyed your music," Cary began.

"Absolutely," Gates added, with Dag, Annie, and Jack remaining silent out of respect for the process that had been discussed earlier.

"It was my pleasure to bring it to you," Smart said with a smile.

"How often do you play here?" Cary asked.

"Oh, now it's about once a month. I have a business on the North Shore, and that keeps me busy," he added.

"What kind of business?" Gates inquired.

"It's a not-for-profit. Trying to help some of the less fortunate in our community, I guess," Smart said almost shyly.

"Sounds fantastic," Gates replied.

"Yeah, and the proceeds from this session tonight go directly to the cause, so thanks for your contribution," Smart said, turning to walk away.

"Actually, Mr. Smart..." Gates began, but Smart cut him off.

"Call me Luke," came his reply.

"Sure...Luke," Gates began, "we have a dual purpose in coming here this evening."

"Oh?" said Luke.

"Yes, actually, we knew Kimo Akamai out in Makakilo. In fact, my friend Dag Peyton here lived across the breezeway from him, and I now own the bungalow where he lived."

"Really?" Luke said, acting neither surprised nor excitable. "Kimo Akamai was a fine man. I still have moments of extreme sadness when I think about how he died and what he must have been thinking."

"It has been a real sadness for us," Gates continued.

"Well, for me," Luke offered, "it is only sad when I think of how he died. Of course, I am sad he is gone, but I know he is at peace now, and so when it comes to his being gone, I am sad for me, but I know he is doing well in heaven. He belonged there."

"Understood," Cary said, sliding into the conversation quite fluidly. "He was a man I wish I had known."

"If you never knew him," Luke continued, "you will never know what a rare jewel of a man he was. A real force of goodness. I have never known before a person who was so centered and so good that evil would try to find him, but I think that is what happened. I think someone quite evil could not handle his positive influence, and I think whoever did it knew him and knew what kind of a man he was."

"Any ideas concerning who might have done this?" Cary asked.

"None, and I will tell you why," Luke responded. "Kimo Akamai was such a force for good that any number of people with evil intent could have wanted to see his end. You know what I would do? I would make a list of someone who might have known Kimo and who appears to be good natured and delve into their nature. I think the killer is someone we would never suspect. I can see why you might have come to me. I am sure you know that he left me money…much money, right?"

"Yes," Gates responded.

"And you think I might have been wanting to get my hands on the cash sooner than later, right?" Luke added.

The group sat silent.

"Well, Luke," Gates began, "I need to tell you a bit more of the story. I was a detective for three decades in the Bay Area. I moved out here after I came out to visit my friend Dag here. Cary here is a consultant for the Kapolei police. When this murder occurred, it aroused a natural interest in all of us, and having the connections with the police as we do, we decided to do some searching on our own. We are not here to point fingers."

Dag jumped into the conversation. "Luke, if you were under suspicion because of the money Kimo left to you, I would be as well, since he left some to me also. We thought you might have some information, that's all."

"Makes sense," Luke offered. "Look, guys, I hold no concerns about this, and I have no issue answering any questions you have about me, or my connection with Kimo, or anything else. In fact, I wish the entire island would show an interest and get on this case. If there is anything I can do to help, let me know. In fact, if you would like to see where Kimo's money went, I can show you if you want to come to the North Shore. It might even provide some insights for you concerning the kind of guy Kimo really was. I can share with you my history with Kimo. I would be happy to do that."

"Well, I have to say," Cary responded, "that I for one was not expecting this gracious reply to our questions. I would love to check out the North Shore."

Gates nodded and looked around the table. Everyone nodded. Gates decided to explain a bit about the group. "These two in the back there are Jack Gray and Annie Wright. They have been friends of Dag's since the world looked level, and they provide insights to us as well."

Luke replied, "It's all good, man. When would you like to come out?"

Again, Gates looked around the table. He said, "I am available tomorrow if all of you are game."

And again, heads around the table were nodding.

"I know this might sound informal, guys, but just show up any time. I am always there when I am not here. I am available all day tomorrow," Luke offered.

"It's a date," Cary said.

"Okay, well, I need to wonder around a bit and say hello to a couple more people. I will look forward to seeing you all tomorrow, then," Luke said as he waved and walked away.

"Wait!" Gates said. "How do we get to your place?"

"Freeway H2 north, follow the signs. You absolutely cannot miss it. It's called Akamai Farms," Luke said, grinning.

"Sounds excellent," Cary said.

Then to end the conversation in a quite interesting and mysterious way, Luke Smart said, "To get a jump on our time together tomorrow, why don't you look up Kimo's last name and see what it means."

"Akamai?" Dag said. "I already know that. It means *smart*." By then, Luke had wondered away to another table. "Wait a minute! Luke's name is Smart, which is what *Akamai* means. Do you know what this means? There is some kind of connection, and more than just admiration, between Kimo and Luke."

"But what could it be?" Jack queried.

"Yeah, and if they are related or something and admired one another so much, why would he go by Smart when Kimo went by Akamai?" Annie followed.

"Good question," Cary added. "Well, one thing for sure is that we know there is a name connection because he would not have told us this clue had he not known or felt some kind of connection. I appreciate the fact that he is making this interesting. Cannot wait to hear the story."

"Me too," Dag said, "but right now I am all about getting back to the bungalow. Anybody up for a nightcap back at my place?" They all said yes except for Gates.

"I am going to go ahead and turn in at my place when we get home guys," Gates said. "I have a ten-mile walk early in the morning before we go to the North Shore to see Luke's place. I am trying to get into the routine of doing the ten-mile walk every Sunday before the sunrise."

Annie jumped in, "But tomorrow is Saturday."

Gates was immediately apologetic. "I am sorry, guys. I don't know what's gotten into me lately. Still, I will just see you all tomorrow."

And with that, the group hopped into Dag's Subaru and journeyed west toward home. The ride was uneventful, with Annie falling asleep, an event to which Jack whispered to everyone, "Isn't it peaceful when you-know-who is out of the picture? You can actually hear other sounds."

The car again erupted in laughter, at which point Annie said, "This is about me, isn't it?" Again, and right on cue, the laughter ensued.

CHAPTER 53

The Real Luke Smart

The group awoke early on Saturday morning. It seems they were all anxious about getting to Luke Smart's place on the North Shore. They congregated around Dag's car, that is, all but Gates. Dag was surprised when he wasn't there.

"What's going on?" Cary asked.

"I think he wasn't feeling well when we drove home last night," Dag said.

"I get it," Jack said. "I'll drop by his place."

As Jack walked over and approached Gates's bungalow, Gates opened the door with a broad smile. "I am really sorry, man. Is everyone else ready? I was a bit under the weather last night and then overslept. This retirement thing is throwing me for a loop."

Jack just smiled, "Yeah, we're out at Dag's car. Let's go." Jack was concerned that Gates appeared to not be feeling well and was really not himself, but he did not let on at all.

They arrived at Dag's car, hopped in, and the trek to the North Shore, which would take all of forty-five minutes, began. Dag, having lived in Texas all his life before moving to the island, was at first surprised when he would hear someone talk about twenty miles being "so far to travel." He learned over time that he had become acclimated to the same mindset. After he moved to Makakilo, he found himself wanting to drive twenty-five miles into town and at the same time thinking about how far it was from his home. *It's all about perspective,* he thought to himself.

The trip to Luke Smart's place was enjoyable, as were all travels with his group of friends, and especially Annie and Jack never failed to entertain.

"Jack, do you think we should move out here to the island?" Annie asked.

"What made you think of that?" Jack responded quizzically.

"Well, I don't know. We don't know anyone in the city anymore, we could sell out and be around these three clowns all the time, and the cost of living is about the same. We could both retire. I have no idea what I am going on about. You are about as likely to leave San Francisco as I am," Annie concluded without further input from Jack or anyone else.

"Well, hold on, there. It sounded there for a minute like you were having a conversation with yourself," Jack commented. "Yes, the Bay Area has its hold on me, but I will say that it is loads of fun being here. And knowing how often we are likely to come here, it sure would save us some airfare."

"Now that is something I had not even considered!" Annie said, surprised. "You know, Jack, you are smarter than you think you are."

"Correction," Jack added. "I am exactly as smart as I think I am. I am actually smarter than *you* think I am." He smiled at her as if trying to get her to confess as to his wisdom.

"Maybe," Annie said. And with that the conversation moved forward to the reason for their drive to the windward side of the island.

As they approached Luke's place, they discovered that Luke was right. This place could not be missed. There were signs on telephone poles that were bright yellow with black print. Dag saw the signs and not only realized that Luke's business had something to do with being a refuge for animals. He also noticed that Luke was good at marketing. Most marketing experts would tell you that the colors of yellow and black were indeed the most eye-catching ones when marketing, and there was another rule of thumb about signs on the road: not more than five words, and at no more than a third-grade level. The signs were simple, attractive, and visible as billboards. Of course, the signs on the telephone poles were about all they could do, as billboards were not legally allowed in the state of Hawaii.

They drove through a large gateway with an arched covering that said *Akamai Refuge* on the center of it. It was like entering another world. While all of Oahu and Hawaii in general were beautiful, this was indeed a paradise that seemed to have been set aside for God's own purposes. They drove down the palm tree lined drive and up to a circular drive that revealed, rather than the expected mansion, a vast expanse of open land with animals wondering to and fro. It was something that none of Dag's group had witnessed before.

Dag was often surprised that during his time on island he seemed to find places that he'd never seen before that were not just beautiful but stunning. This was one of those times. The setting was unspoiled, wild, breathtaking.

The backdrop of the mountains was simply majestic, and the only sign of human habitation was a well-kept dormitory style structure on the right, tucked into a small hill. It was so skillfully constructed that it appeared to have been created when the landscape itself had been. Dag drove up to the entrance and parked in one of the three parking spaces that were available. He expected there to be more spaces for visitors and said so to his friends, to which Cary replied, "I'll bet you that there isn't much space designated because this isn't a tourist-oriented establishment. It appears to me to be a sanctuary for animals." As they exited Dag's car, the feeling of overwhelming nature and calm and peace was palpable.

"Man, I do not even know what I'm looking at," Jack said. "I have never been in this kind of setting before. This is amazing. I feel like if I touch something, I will spoil it." The group nodded in unison.

"For once we agree on something," Annie responded, looking around like a child in a candy store.

In about a minute, the large front doors of the building opened, and out walked Luke Smart, smiling and completely at ease, just as he had been at the Sidecar Lounge the night before. In his completely relaxed fashion, he said, "Hey, guys. Welcome to the home of thousands of God's creatures, with twenty-five of them being humans." He smiled at Gates and Cary and then looked at each of the other three visitors and nodded cordially.

The giant ficus trees were everywhere on the grounds, with just enough space in between for many beautiful monkeypod trees, and shaded under the trees were patches of orchids, having clearly searched for and found the perfect place to thrive. There were plumeria trees and pua keni keni trees that were so fragrant that one could close the eyes and imagine being in the middle of a perfumery.

The valley in between the two mountain ranges was lush and perpetually green, with animals roaming, free from fear, unconfined, in their natural habitat. In Dag's mind, it was what the Garden of Eden must have looked like. Once again, the voice of Annie brought Dag, and apparently others in the group, back to reality.

"Okay," Annie said, "I have got to know this story. I mean, this is amazing, but it would help if you could begin by telling us how you are connected to Kimo Akamai. It will help us to gain a perspective concerning why we are here."

"Sure," Luke said. "Last evening, I asked you to think about my name and Kimo's name. I am pretty confident that you knew then or know now that *Akamai* means *Smart*."

"Yes," Dag said.

"Okay, I was a young child in an orphanage. My parents were killed, and I had no other relatives. Kimo Akamai visited the orphanage regularly, and I learned in later years that he had been donating funds to the upkeep and education of the children in the orphanage. He took such an individualized interest in the children there. Then one day, we were informed that the orphanage where we were located was going to remain as is, but for those of us who were over eighteen years of age, there was a new structure that was being built where we could stay until we could get a start in life and on our feet. That structure is this building behind you. Kimo, being the wise individual you came to know, had purchased this refuge long ago, and he offered every person who was living here a job at the refuge if we wanted to work taking care of the animals. About seven of us stayed and have been here the entire time. Every cent of the money Kimo left me has been turned over to the foundation to provide upkeep for the refuge and the home here."

The group was visibly touched by Kimo's generosity. Annie said, "This all seemed so secretive. Why would Kimo not want others to know he owned this?"

"Kimo Akamai was a humble man," Luke said. "He believed that every gift a person received was from God and that each person had the responsibility to use what God gave him wisely and in service to others. Of the people who really knew him, they were aware of his vast resources, and while they might have been at odds with him, there was a respect there because they knew he was working for good in whatever he did. You want my advice for finding out who murdered him?"

"Of course," Cary said immediately.

"Look for someone who really didn't know him," Luke replied. "There was so much respect for him and his work that if one of these rich and powerful people on island did it, one of the others would find out and have them called to account immediately. Look for someone who didn't have a real connection—someone who knew of him perhaps but didn't have a grasp on who he really was." Luke's words were followed by a long silence from the group, as they clearly were contemplating the wisdom of this young man. Finally, Dag spoke.

"I think I know what I want to do with the money he left to me," Dag said.

"Want a suggestion? Don't donate it to the refuge. I think Kimo gave you money separately so you can use your own imagination for good. I think he must've had much respect for you," Luke offered.

"Just a question," Annie said. "He clearly didn't want notoriety, so why is the place called Akamai Refuge?"

"That one's easy," Luke responded. "It was called Smart Refuge until last week. He wanted no connection to his name. When I became of legal age and wanted to change my name to Akamai because of all he'd done for me, he said he was very proud of that, but by then, I was working out here and he didn't want the connection to the refuge, so I changed my name to Smart, he named the place after

me, and I have now changed it to Akamai Refuge to honor him."
One could not help but see the influence that Kimo Akamai had on
Luke Smart.

The group was visibly touched by all they had heard. Luke took
them on a tour of the place, which lasted over two hours. There was
so much land, and there were so many amazing animals. Luke Smart
did tell them that they allow limited field trips from schools to allow
children to witness this phenomenon that exists right here on the
island.

They were also quite touched by the fact that Kimo Akamai
lived such a minimalist life and yet had vast fortunes, and all this
money was in fact being resourced in such a thoughtful and stew-
ardly manner. The moment of enlightenment for Dag from the day
was the realization that Kimo thought enough of him to include him
in inheriting part of his fortune and left it to Dag to discern what
he should do with what was being left to him. Dag was resolute that
he would ponder this carefully and make Kimo proud of him in his
decision.

The continuing issue of the day, however, was that they were no
closer to discovering the who the killer was, and Luke Smart's suggestion that they focus on someone who didn't know Kimo that well was
wise, yet it widened the suspect list even further. In fact, there was
no way that Dag could see to pare down the list anymore. This was a
true frustrating dilemma for Dag and the entire group of five friends.

The small entourage of friends left the Akamai Refuge that day
with a renewed faith in the goodness of mankind, but still they had
to refocus on the evil side of mankind that would take a life that was
responsible for such goodness.

"Okay, what's the next step?" Annie asked as they drove out of
the refuge.

"I am trying to think of how we'd even start a list of suspects,"
Jack said, "especially after what Luke said about considering people
who didn't know him that well."

"True," Cary said, "but keep this in mind. There are ways to
narrow down a long list. We can start by naming every person we
can possibly think of whom Kimo would have come in contact with,

in his present life just before the murder. Then we can research the connections those people have with other people or events or positions that Kimo might have opposed. When you get discouraged, just think about the fact that every person you eliminate as a suspect gets us a step closer to focusing on the true killer."

"Yes, it's a long shot," Gates added, "but the killer is out there, and in every case, we are able to find some small fact that a killer missed that gives them away." Gates's confidence gave the entire group a can-do attitude.

"Great," Dag offered, "so, why don't those of us who knew Kimo begin lists independently of the people with whom Kimo might have come in contact in his present life just prior to the murder. Annie, Jack, and Cary, why don't you brainstorm others whom you suspect might have had some kind of a connection with Kimo? Then we can all come together as a group and see what we all have in common."

"Very good, my friend," Cary said happily. "How'd you come up with that idea?"

"It's all a part of a rounding technique I teach my students in research methods. It's not exactly the same, but the goal is to develop an area of focus," Dag replied.

"Okay, let's do this," Gates added.

CHAPTER 54

A Process of Elimination

Dag and Gates worked diligently, yet separately, to try to discern those with whom Kimo would have interacted in his life just prior to his death. The first and most obvious names were Dag and Gates themselves, and after that, there was Kimo's wife, Sloan Ender and some of his entourage, and then perhaps a few others at the farmers' market and anyone dealing with the feeding of the cats at the park. Other than that, Kimo Akamai was unencumbered with the cares of this present life. He appeared to have no axe to grind with anyone, which is why Luke Smart's recommendation to search for someone who might not have known him that well, or not at all, might have been a very good approach to consider.

Since listing random people who would kill Kimo would be an exhaustive list, as it would be for anyone, they decided it would be best to keep with the concept of listing people with whom Kimo had at least a passing acquaintance.

It seems that the brainstorming among Jack, Annie, and Cary yielded the same conclusions, and the only path they had not considered would be to go to the farmers' market when it next was occurring, have Dag point out people with whom he'd seen Kimo interact, and go from there. Since the farmers' market had a week-long event beginning on Monday, the group decided to make a day of it. Dag even found some vegetable recipes he'd wanted to try, so perhaps the group would be able to look around at the market, talk to some people, and take care of several things at once.

When Monday rolled around, the group was glad they simply had to go down the hill from Makakilo Heights to the large open field on Farrington Highway. It was only a two-mile drive at most.

"What's the game plan?" Annie asked first, though it was on the minds of Jack and Dag as well.

"Well," Gates said, "let's spread out and just ask any of the vendors in passing if they'd heard of Kimo. I think if we look at the produce and speak to the vendors individually, it will be less likely to appear to be a confrontation."

"Sure," Jack said, "but how do we bring up Kimo's name?"

"Good question," Cary replied. "The best way is just to comment on how good the vegetables look and tell the vendor that you heard of this place through Kimo and wondered if the vendor knew him."

"Perfect," Gates said. "Let's just meet back at that taro stand over there in about two hours."

"Excellent," Dag said, and with that he walked away, as did the others, all in different directions.

The market was fun for Dag. He enjoyed going from booth to booth and finding fresh vegetables to buy. The conversations were fun as well. Usually very kind people take the time to market their produce in this way. There was something natural about the process, something good.

Of the five individuals in the group, Dag was the only one who might have inwardly had to push himself to speak to the vendors. He usually enjoyed it when he did, but he was an introvert. Still, as always when he came to the market with Kimo, he had meaningful discussions that were pleasant as well. While the conversations were nice, Dag got next to no information that would be useful to their cause, which was finding someone who might have had a motive to kill Kimo Akamai. Thankfully, that wasn't true for all five of the group members.

As the group of friends gathered at the taro stand as promised, each of them sidled up claiming no success in finding out any information of value concerning a connection with Kimo. That is, except for one. John Gates reported a lengthy conversation with a woman who was packing up her stand. She knew Kimo, said Kimo loved the watercress she sold at her stand, and she recalled seeing a well-dressed man with a political button of some sort arguing with Kimo on the weekend before Kimo was killed.

With this newly discovered clue, the group decided that Gates and Cary would take the lead and decide where to go from here. It seemed as if there was consensus in the group that those who'd had long-term dealings in the profession would be better suited to guide the process. This did not mean that the others would not find complete excitement in joining in the investigation, but still it was wise to hand it over to the experts officially. Besides, Cary had it in his mind that if the man having a disagreement with Kimo indeed did have on a political button of some sort, perhaps he was connected to Sloan Ender after all. That would make Gates correct about the entire thing. One thing Cary was learning quickly was that Gates knew his way around an investigation.

The interesting thing about Cary's thoughts about Gates was that Gates was thinking the same thing about Cary. One does not become a trainer like Cary without being in the field and being able to assess the demeanor of a suspect quite well. Gates knew this, and for that reason alone, he respected Cary and his well-considered insights. There was nothing not to like about Cary.

In addition, the two of them worked well together. However unspoken, they both felt the mutual respect and were glad to be working on this case together.

"You know," Cary said to Gates as they stood together in Dag's breezeway, "the political button you saw the man wearing makes me think you were right about Sloan Ender having some kind of involvement in this. Could I be that much off my game? I have been credited with good reasoning skills for many years, and that skill has led me to accurately determine a suspect's motives or lack thereof many times. When you said you think he should stay on the suspect list, to be frank, I thought no way, but I am beginning to rethink it."

"Oh?" Gates responded. "Why didn't you say anything at the time?"

"Well, you are the one who has been out in the field for so long, and I certainly respect your views on this," Cary added. "I thought it couldn't hurt to leave him on the list to see how the investigation plays out."

"I could be totally wrong about all this, Cary," Gates said, "but the woman at the market telling me about the man prompted me to press the reset button on Ender myself."

"Understood," Cary said in agreement. "Let's see what other background information we can find on Sloan Ender."

With a hint of a direction resolved, Gates and Cary informed the rest of the group of their plans, and the other three were in agreement that this would be a good direction, especially since there was really no other specific direction to take at the time.

Dag suggested that a good starting point would be to find who the key parties were who worked in conjunction with Sloan Ender in his political aspirations as well as in his business ventures. This process was much easier to accomplish than any of the five thought it would be. When Cary called Ender's office, Sloan Ender instructed his executive assistant to provide any information Cary wanted. She produced a list of four individuals who worked directly for Ender, and they were as follows:

- Jason Barr, the executive who handled all Ender's schedules and attended all public events with Ender.
- Keoki Alii, the local events coordinator. Alii scouted out all the events occurring to see if they were worthwhile for Ender to attend.
- Janine Larsen, the woman who assisted Cary with his request. She worked directly with Ender but was mainly the office manager and attended few events.
- Ted Palmer, who coordinated logistics for travel and materials to take for marketing and promotion purposes.

Cary asked Janine Larsen for general descriptions of the three gentlemen and passed the information along to Gates and the rest of the group. Gates immediately stated that the woman at the market seemed to be describing Jason Barr to a tee. He was about fifty years old, dirty blond hair that was cut very short, and a very dark tan. Gates was so sure that this was the guy that they were seeking that he asked Cary to assist him in finding out some background information on Barr. Cary hopped into his car and headed down to the police station.

In about half an hour, Cary called Gates, who had gone over to his bungalow for a short time to clean up some odds and ends. After the call, Gates went across to Dag's place and met Dag, Annie, and Jack. He told them that Cary was on his way back up the hill and was bringing fish tacos for dinner, and then he began to describe his conversation with Cary.

"Okay," Gates began, "it seems that this Jason Barr is a real source of energy for the Ender enterprises as well as for Ender's political aspirations. That is not always a bad thing, but he has a reputation for being a bit overzealous at times. He has no problem running roughshod over people who seem to stand in the way of Ender's success. He's definitely worth checking out."

"So what do we do? What does this mean for us?" Jack said. Jack was not one for sitting around when there was a task to do.

"Well, for now, Jack," Gates replied, "we need to find out all we can about this guy, and that is going to involve Cary and myself going to meet this guy to see what he might have up his sleeve."

"Okay," Jack said, sounding a bit dejected.

"I'll tell you what the three of you can do that will make this process easier for all of us," Gates added.

"Yeah?" Annie said.

"Yes, you can do one of those mystery shopper calls to Ender's office. Since we know that Barr handles all these events that Ender attends, think of some kind of event, ask Janine Larsen at Ender's office if it is appropriate for Ender to attend, and then ask who would handle all that info. She will refer you to Jason Barr. Then you can ask questions about his background and what exactly he does," Gates said, happy to include his friends in the process.

While Gates and Cary were off finding out more information about Jason Barr, the original trio wasted no time in contacting Sloan Ender's office to see if they could find out some information as well. Without even addressing who was going to make the call, Annie seemed to be the logical choice for all three of them, since her "acting" served them all very well in the case in the Bay Area. She knew how to reach people and get to the heart of an issue before the other person even knew what had happened. After the three of them discussed what form their organization was going to take and all the information about the event was determined, the call commenced.

"Hello, my name is Angelica Wright, and I am helping to coordinate an event in West Oahu early next year. I knew that Mr. Ender would need plenty of time to get the event on his schedule if he is interested, and so I wanted to call as early as possible," Annie began.

"I see, dear," Janine Larsen replied, "and what kind of event is this?"

"Well," Annie continued, "it is a walk for juvenile diabetes. We were not sure if Mr. Ender would like to be part of the event, but we thought we'd ask."

"Thanks so much for considering him. Mr. Ender is very interested in any and all events that benefit others within the community and the island as a whole," Janine responded.

"You know," Annie added in a very engaged, almost gossipy, tone, "I heard he was going to run for State Senate, and I think an event such as this would be ideal for him to support."

"At the outset, so do I," Janine said. "Can you tell me the date of the event?"

"Yes, and it is actually coming up pretty early next year. It is February 1," Annie added.

"Oh my, it is certainly coming up quickly, but I do think he would be interested. Let me transfer you over to Jason Barr. He would handle the details of all this," Janine said quickly, and before Annie could respond, she heard the phone ring on the other end. It rang for some time, and Annie surmised that Janine was filling Jason Barr in on the details. She hoped so.

"This is Jason Barr. How may I help you?" came the voice from the other end of the line.

"Hi, I am Angelica Wright," Annie began again. Before she could go any further, Barr interrupted quickly yet politely.

"Yes, Janine filled me in," said Barr, quite professionally.

"Oh, that's wonderful," Annie responded.

"I do think it is something that would interest Mr. Ender," Barr continued, "but can you tell me some more about it?"

"Certainly. You know, sir," Annie began, "if you were to ask a group of people to raise their hands if they knew someone who had diabetes, you would likely see hands raised from almost everyone, and if this event is anything like I think it will be, it will be a superb opportunity for exposure to Mr. Sloan Ender. Ummm, but I do need to make sure I am talking to the right person. Forgive me."

"Okay, no problem," Jason Barr said. "I am directly responsible for Mr. Ender's schedule, and if you are at the event and if we decide to attend, you will likely be able to meet me there so we can talk about future events as well."

"Well, that sounds just amazing," Annie said, "but it must be incredibly tiring for you to have to interact with so many people."

"It's my job, ma'am," Barr said quickly.

"Sure," Annie replied, "but I simply must ask. Do you ever run into conflict with people while you are out there on the campaign trail or just doing business for Mr. Ender? I mean, there simply must be people who are opposed to Mr. Ender's agenda on several items."

"Uh, I guess so, but let's get back to the event," Barr said.

"Well, of course," Annie complied. "We do hope you can make it. I have this number. Is this where I need to call to reach you most directly?"

"Well, no," Barr said. "You can reach my cell at (808) 555-4920. If I do not answer, just leave a detailed message. I will get back to you."

"Excellent, sir, and many thanks," Annie stated as she ended the call. Jack and Dag were set to ask many questions.

"You know," Jack said, "he is going to do some research to find out if this event is legit. Then what are you going to do?"

"Nothing, because he will discover that it is legit," Annie replied. "I saw it in a diabetes magazine sitting on a table when I was waiting to get my hair cut last week."

"Well now, you are just prepared for everything, aren't you?" Jack said sarcastically in Annie's direction.

"Yes," Annie stated coolly, "I am."

In no time, the group of five reconvened at Dag's place, with the hope of a good direction in mind.

CHAPTER 55

The Forgettable Jason Barr

"I hope this attempt at finding the killer leads somewhere," Annie said, acting tired. "I mean, I don't want to wish ill will on our Mr. Jason Barr, but it sure would be good to find a nugget of evidence that could move us forward."

"Now see, my dear," Jack replied, "you simply do not have my patience. You need to remain calm."

"True. I have neither your patience nor your lack of wit," Annie quipped.

Jack nodded and then said, "Hey!" The group laughed.

"Oh well," Gates interjected. "Now we have a lead and potential for a strong one at that. So I think what we need to do is to find out the next event that Jason Barr will be attending and see how he interacts with others. And if necessary, we can accidentally run into him. He doesn't even know what Dag and Jack and Annie look like, which is a very good thing."

"I like it," Annie said, "but how do we find out his next event?"

"Duh," Jack said jokingly, "just look on Ender's website. I am sure it contains everything Ender is involved in on the island."

"Oh, that actually makes sense you clown," Annie retorted. Annie was once again impressed with Jack's intelligence and foresight, yet she would never allow Jack to know how much she respected him. Of course, he already knew.

"Done," Cary said, hearing the entire conversation while playing on his phone. "He will be at the Pokai Bay Fish Market tomorrow, apparently confirming his love for the sea as well as the fishing industry on the island."

"Nice," Dag said, "and when does this event begin?"

"Two o'clock tomorrow afternoon," Cary added. "You know this is a beach thing, so wear lots of sunscreen. The sun here can be totally brutal. It sneaks up on you."

"Good point," Dag said.

The next day, the group of five hopped once again into Dag's car and trekked out farther west to Pokai Bay, a popular yet low-key area, where fresh seafood was served. The atmosphere was one of laid-back peace in which everyone seemed to relax. They could immediately see why Sloan Ender would want to stage an event there, or perhaps this was all the doing of Jason Barr. Whatever the situation, it was a wise move.

They arrived at the event, and Gates and Cary quickly told Dag, Jack, and Annie to separate from them so that Barr and Ender would not make the connection. The trio dropped back from Gates and Cary yet trailed them to find an opportunity to see Barr and Ender in action if the situation presented itself. It did.

It took no time for Sloan Ender and Jason Barr to see Gates and Cary from a distance. Sloan Ender even called John Gates's name and waved. They met near a stand selling shaved ice, and since Ender had met Gates and Cary already, introduction of the two to Jason Barr was fluid and cordial. As they spoke, Dag and Annie and Jack went up to the man behind the shaved ice stand to buy some, and Annie hung back and listened to the conversation.

"This is a great event," Ender said. Of course, Annie was thinking, *What else would he say? He has to say those kinds of things.*

Still, through the course of the conversation, Annie, who was no doubt the most cynical, skeptical, and suspicious of the group, had trouble finding any plausible reason why Barr would be engaged in any type of nefarious activity involving Kimo. He appeared to Annie to be an upright individual—assertive to the point of being aggressive at times perhaps but upright just the same.

As they continued talking, Dag walked over to Annie, handing her a shaved ice. "Well," he stated nonchalantly, "anything?"

"Nope," Annie replied, "and to be honest I am more anxious to hear why Cary and Gates think this guy is guilty of anything."

"Hmm," Dag said, and walked away slowly.

Cary and Gates spoke to the gentlemen for a few more minutes, and then Ender, who had a brief presentation to give and a few more people to see, excused himself and walked up to a podium and in an impromptu manner began to speak.

"It is wonderful to see the turnout here today, and in my view, there are few causes that are as important as supporting our fishing industry in a responsible, sustainable way," Ender began.

"We have many people who do not fish responsibly, only trying to catch what will get them an award versus catching only what can be eaten and allowing the rest to be reintroduced to the water. Ladies and gentlemen, it is so important to use our resources wisely, and I am proud that we have a fishing industry in the islands that respects sea life as well as the people of this area."

There was almost continual applause during the time Sloan Ender spoke. It would start to die away, only to be overtaken by more applause. Clearly, Ender appeared to be a friend of the people of the area and on the ewa side of the island in general.

As the group decided that there was really no more to see at this particular time, they piled back into the car and headed back to Dag's place for a review and to see what the next steps should be. Overall, it was a pleasant day.

As they drove away from Pokai Bay, Jack introduced the topic, "So did you guys find anything out about the case that can move us forward?"

"Well," Cary offered, "I am more reluctant than Gates to continue on this path. Ender and Barr seem pretty upfront to me, yet John has his suspicions."

"What are those suspicions based upon?" Annie asked.

"A few things," Gates began. "First, the woman at the farmers' market saw Kimo talking to a guy that matches Jason Barr's description to a tee. I asked Barr in our conversation just now if he knew of

Kimo Akamai, and he said he did not, but what else is he going to say? Also, Barr stated that he had not been out to this west side of the island in a long time. First, why would he say that, and second, why wouldn't he have been out here? I mean this is his boss's district, for cryin' out loud! It sounded as if he was trying to disassociate himself with the area for some reason. Finally, if he is working for Ender, he knows who Ender knows. Believe me, Ender would require that. I think he knew Kimo, Kimo was more of a threat than Barr and Ender wanted to admit, and they were behind the murder."

With that, Cary jumped in, "So for those reasons I am going to stick with Gates on this and see if we can't follow this through to some conclusion."

The others nodded, and at that time they were just pulling up into Dag's parking space.

Dag said, "Okay, everyone who wants to can come in for sandwiches and whatever else you can find in the fridge."

Immediately, the other four travelers exited Dag's car and headed straight for his door.

CHAPTER 56

Discussing the Case

As the group sat around discussing the case, they realized that this case was just one of many life events that bonded them together, and that made the desire to solve the case even that more compelling. It seemed that they all loved the idea of being a group, a cadre of souls brought together at this point in eternity to be contemporaries, to light the way with joy and heartache, laughter and tears, until at some point it was time for them to leave this world to others who would undoubtedly do the same. Yes, there was a bond that created a wholeness, a feeling of being a part of something that was bigger than all of them.

"Okay, Dag, we're out of coffee. I told you to keep your eye on the coffee because you all like it and it's pretty much my lifeblood, but you didn't keep up, did you?" Annie said, smiling.

"Oops," Dag said. "I'll buy if you'll fly. I don't care much for leaving the house on weekends."

"Sounds a bit lazy on your part but okay. Jack, let's go," she responded.

"Aw, man, I was just getting comfortable," Jack said, rising to slip on his shoes.

"Dude, you've been comfortable all your life. Let's go, and Dag, give me your keys," Annie replied.

The two hopped into Dag's car and hurried down to the convenience store at the bottom of the hill. In fact, they went so hurriedly that Annie blew right past the turnoff to the store. "Never mind," Jack said. "There's another one a bit farther down."

It took longer for them to return than Dag expected. So long, in fact, that Dag began to be concerned. He called Jack's phone and then Annie's, but both phones rang in the kitchen, and Dag realized that neither had taken a phone with them. Finally, some time later, they returned.

"Did you pick the coffee beans yourself?" Cary asked jokingly. "We could've planted them ourselves here and grown a batch as long as it took the two of you."

"Oh, a real wise guy," Annie said. "Okay, I missed the first store, and the second store on the way to the airport is always closed on Saturday. There's a note on the door that says the owners are Seventh Day Adventists and do not open the store on Saturdays. So we had to go even farther to get the coffee, but here it is, valuable as gold!"

"You know," Dag offered while the small talk ensued, "I have been going to that convenience store ever since I came out to this side of the island, and I never knew the place to be closed on Saturdays. I guess I don't venture out much on Saturdays."

They were all glad to see the coffee, save Dag, who'd of late began drinking decaffeinated coffee. These afternoons filled with freshly brewed coffee and homemade desserts made him happy yet restless at night, so he settled on a cup of decaf tea and sat down with the group to talk about the case as well as other events that had touched their lives. Aside from the case at hand concerning Kimo Akamai, all else took a back seat.

"You know," Dag said, "there is one little fact out there—one little fact—that will solve this case for us. We just have to find it, and sometimes we happen upon those types of facts by chance."

"True," Gates offered, "but still we have to never take our eyes off the hard facts of the case."

"Can we review those facts?" Annie asked.

"Sure," Gates responded. "First Kimo Akamai was killed by a gun. That gun is now in police custody, and as far as we can tell, it was in police custody before as well as after the murder. That leads us to believe…" Gates was cut off by Annie.

"What you are about to say is not a fact," Annie said. "Let's stick with the facts."

"Okay, then," Gates continued. "Another fact is that Kimo was rich, in fact much richer than any of us imagined. He was resolute about preserving his culture. He also seemed to butt heads with quite a few influential people on island."

"Yes," Cary added, "but according to Sloan Ender, he was not as disliked as many would have us believe."

"Right," Gates said, "but that might not be a fact. In fact, Ender could be hiding something by suggesting that very thing."

"Hmm," Jack said, jumping in, "then let's talk about the suspect list. Has it changed any since we last discussed this?"

"Well, not really," Gates said. "We have Kimo's wife, Sloan Ender, potentially someone from the police department since the circumstances of the location of the gun is so strange, and those who inherited from Kimo, excluding Dag, of course."

"Isn't this fun?" Annie said.

"Where are you going with this?" Cary said.

"Nowhere," Annie replied, "but listen to the music and take in this night. We are going to figure this out, but in the meantime, there is no place I'd rather be."

The group of five, to a person a bit perplexed at Annie's rare yet poignant comments, remained silent as an old song by Elton John filled the breezeway between Dag's and Gates's bungalows:

> I hope the day will be a lighter highway
> For friends are found on every road
> Can you ever think of any better way
> For the lost and weary travelers to go
>
> Making friends for the world to see
> Let the people know you got what you need
> With a friend at hand you will see the light
> If your friends are there then everything's all right

A PERFECT MISTAKE

It seems to me a crime that we should age
These fragile times should never slip us by
A time you never can or shall erase
As friends together watch their childhood fly

Making friends for the world to see
Let the people know you got what you need
With a friend at hand you will see the light
If your friends are there then everything's all right

CHAPTER 57

The Unwelcomed Clue

The group sat around a while, not discussing the case at all but instead just soaking in the music and that wonderful Hawaiian twilight air. There were moments when there was no discussion at all, and then moments when everyone was talking at once, and still moments when there were side conversations that proved to be of no real significance.

The group retreated to their own places for the evening, taking a half hour to say their goodbyes.

"This is beginning to creep me out a little," Jack said.

"What?" Dag said, surprised by Jack's comment.

"Well," Jack began, "when I was a kid and my parents had friends come over to our place, I remember how strange it seemed that they would say they had to leave for the evening, and then they all took forever to say goodbye. As a kid I remember wanting to tell them all to either sit down and keep the evening going or leave already! Now I am doing the exact same thing."

"I hear you," Dag said. "I will say I need to leave someplace and then stay and chat at the door for longer than I was there in the first place. It's an old person thing."

"Except not for us," Jack responded. "For us it's just a trend."

"Rings true to me," Dag said, smiling.

With everyone leaving and the next day being Sunday, no one really knew what the next day would bring.

It was an uneventful Sunday for Dag and the rest of the group. Each of them was either off doing his or her own thing in town, going to church, running errands close by, or kicking back in the breezeway with a glass of wine. They were coming and going, each of them sticking a head in the door to ask Dag a question or just chatting for the fun of it.

Dag had been focused all day on the case and was beginning to sense a frustration that perhaps he and the gang were never going to solve the case. This realization was too painful to consider since, aside from his work at the university, this case was much of the focus of his life for months now.

The day came to a close, and at twilight, Dag told the crew that he was going to retire early. Of course, that didn't mean that the rest of the group planned on doing so at all. Annie stayed awake until about one o'clock watching a movie, Jack went over to Gates's place for a drink and to continue to shoot the breeze, and Cary had taken leave of the place hours before. Dag knew the place was vacated when, at about three o'clock, he noticed that he could hear the slightest of sounds…a bird chirping in the distance, a cry of a young child that came over the roof from a house down the street, and the whirr of the occasional car passing by on Makakilo Drive. At that moment, Dag realized that he was about to fall into a deep slumber, that deep REM sleep that often can happen just before you have to get up to go to work—except in this instance, Dag didn't have to do that, and he loved the feeling. And Dag indeed did fall asleep. It was that all-consuming slumber he'd hoped for, that kind of peaceful feeling that comes from having no cares.

Fifteen minutes later, Dag awakened with a start. Though remaining perfectly still, his eyes opened wide with a realization that he did not want to know, with a fear he did not want to consider, and with a newly discovered piece of knowledge that shook the foundation of his world. For a moment, the only thing keeping him sane, he thought, was remaining still. And remain still is exactly what he did, wishing he could go back to sleep and unlearn what he had pieced together.

This can't be, this can't be, this can't be true, Dag kept saying to himself in his mind. He said it to himself so many times that he worked himself into a frenzy of fear and nervousness that made him finally realize that it was the middle of the night, and the only escape from these thoughts was sleep. Dag gave his Echo the command, "Alexa, play thunderstorm sounds." It seemed so appropriate for the maelstrom of thoughts going through his mind, until somehow it was all too big for him, too much to take in, and he fell asleep.

Dag often awoke to the sound of his friends in the living room or in the breezeway talking in a low voice so as not to disturb him, but today, as he awoke, shaken, there were no sounds at all. There was dead silence. He arose without a sound and stumbled into the kitchen for some coffee. He took the coffee, staggered to his living room chair, turned it so it looked out toward Diamond Head and the ocean, and stared. Just when he was about to determine that if he remained still, he could escape his own thoughts, there was a creaking sound as his front door opened. It was Cary.

Dag glanced at Cary for a moment, and Cary glanced back. Without a word, Cary made himself a cup of coffee, strode over to Dag, pulled up a chair so he could face the same direction as Dag, and sat down. They both looked at each other with a sad look that appeared to make Cary physically cringe, and with that one look, they knew they were both thinking about the murder and were of one mind. Cary uttered one word that Dag dreaded hearing, but he knew Cary would say it, and he knew Cary was right. The word was...Gates.

"This cannot be happening," Dag said with a look in his eye that told Cary that he was not in disbelief. He was certain of what he knew now. So certain that Cary did not even respond. He knew that Cary knew. Cary knew that he knew. And they were both just as certain as they could be.

"What brought you to this conclusion?" Cary asked Dag, hoping to find something that would disprove what they were both thinking.

"Well, when Gates and I went to San Francisco and met up with Jack and Annie, we went to the airport on a Saturday. As we were nearly to the airport, Gates said that he'd forgotten his wallet at the convenience store, and he told me specifically which one it was. It was the one that Annie and Jack said they stopped at for coffee the other day, but they said it was closed," Dag hesitated before continuing, "but we went to the airport on a Saturday. Annie and Jack said it is never open on Saturday because the owners are Seventh Day Adventists. How could he have picked up his wallet if they were closed?"

"Anything else?" Cary asked.

"Yeah," Dag began. "We left for the airport to head to the Bay Area on April 21. Apparently, that was when the murder was committed. If Gates did not forget his wallet, what else was he doing? Add to that the fact that he would've had time to commit the crime, drop the weapon off at the police station for someone to notice at a later time and place back into inventory, and no one would be the wiser. He has an in with the police department and, if I know Gates, could have pretty easily gamed the system to get the gun back to the inventory. Besides, who would have suspected him? I mean, you yourself got him access to the department so we could all work on the case."

"Well, it could all be a coincidence," Cary offered.

"Could be, but it isn't," Dag added. "I also recalled when we were leaving for the airport. I walked into my living room to tell him I was ready. Gates was already packed and set to go. I now faintly recall his wallet being on the counter when I entered the living room, and then when he followed me out, I told him to remember to turn out the living room light. When I turned around to tell him that, the counter was clear. Nothing on it at all." Then Dag turned to Cary, asking, "What brings you to the conclusion that it was Gates?"

"Okay," Cary began, "when we were talking to Sloan Ender, Ender himself subtly gave us some very good reasons why he would not be implicated. Still, when we left Ender's office, Gates was still convinced that it might be him. With Gates's experience in this field, I acquiesced at the time and thought that maybe he had a hunch that I just was not getting, so I went along with him."

"Anyway, I made some calls and discovered that, so far, what Ender said makes sense. These people were frustrated with Kimo, but it was the frustration similar to when you are in a business meeting talking about budget. Vying for budget dollars, you can be at one another's throats throughout the meeting, and then you all break and go to lunch together and laugh and converse as colleagues. I have spoken to people at the police station, at the farmer's market, and around the complex here. Many of these people were frustrated with Kimo, but there were no axes to grind against him."

"Well," Dag interjected, "that doesn't necessarily implicate John Gates."

"No, it doesn't," Cary admitted, "but what clear headed detective continues to go down a path that is being proven again and again to be the wrong path? I provided all this information to Gates, and it seems that the more I disprove his angle, the more he adheres to it. I have been in law enforcement long enough to know that a seasoned professional does not waste time following a scenario that is rapidly unraveling. Also, he seemed to be all for pinning the guilt on one person here, another there. That is again not what a seasoned professional would do."

"Noted," Dag said. "Anything else substantial?"

"Just another hint," Cary said. "Lately, to me and from what I can gather only to me, Gates has been talking Kimo Akamai down for reasons I cannot understand. He keeps talking about that he wasn't perfect and that maybe Ender had good reason to be angry with him since he worked to impede progress in the community."

"Wow, he never said any of that to me," Dag said.

"He likely wouldn't. He knew how much you admired and respected Kimo. Perhaps he thought that, being the outsider, I wouldn't raise my eyebrows if someone were to find fault with Kimo. So what is our next step?" Cary asked almost innocently.

"Actually, my friend, I was going to ask you the same thing," Dag responded.

"Hmmm. Well, I think for now we need to keep this revelation between us," Cary said, "and I think we need to talk about this in private again soon after we've had a chance to calm down and think more clearly."

"Sure," Dag replied, "and can you give me any hints on how to act around Gates from here on out?"

"Dag," Cary offered, "when you were teaching in front of those students you had, you were speaking to professionals, to police officers with the HPD, with soldiers, with officers, and with many others, and you were one of the professionals in the room. Turn on that side of you, think about what you are stating, and be the person you have always been to Gates. If anyone can do this, you can."

CHAPTER 58

Getting Their Act Together

Dag and Cary spent the next week keeping a horrible truth a secret, while at the same time spending time each of those days with someone suspected to be a murderer. At one point, Dag addressed his intense uneasiness to Cary with such intensity that Cary said to Dag, "Look, my friend, I have been trying to come up with the best way to handle all this. I am not for keeping this between us any longer any more than you are, but the truth is that we need to act now anyway because we never know when Gates, as insightful as he can be, will be onto us and he might flee.

"Here's what we have to do. We have to talk to the authorities. They need to be the ones to arrest him, and neither we nor especially Jack and Annie need to be around for this. We need to coordinate this with the police, and then we need to make sure we are all absent when this arrest occurs. I do not know what Gates would do if he were to be arrested with us around. He could blame us as well, or he might get violent. I would like to think that he would not be capable of that, but look what we are dealing with here. I am not sure what he will do."

Dag interjected, "But don't we need to get to the station and explain why we are thinking what we are thinking?"

Cary responded, "Absolutely, and doing that ASAP would be ideal. But how are we going to get away with just the two of us without everyone else wondering where we are?"

Dag said, "Well, guy, it's just you and me now, so why don't we go now?"

"Let's do this," Cary said, almost before Dag finished his sentence, it seemed.

"Okay," Dag added, "and we can come up with an excuse later."

"We likely won't need to do that," Cary said. "We can come back here, tell Annie and Jack that they need to come with us, and then when we are away, we can tell them why we took them away from your house for a time. They will be in such shock that they will understand why we took the actions we did."

"Okay," Dag said, adding, "this could be one of the saddest days of my life."

CHAPTER 59

Informing the Police

Dag and Cary drove right down to the police station. They were met by the Chief of Police, as Cary had called on the way to inform them that they were coming.

Cary and Dag covered the issues and told the chief of their suspicions concerning Gates. The chief had one issue. There did not seem to be a motive. Without that, he saw no real point in entertaining the suspicions of Dag and Cary.

"Then what do you suggest?" Cary asked the chief.

"I think you need to let me call Gates and ask him to come down. Then you need to be gone from here by then and let me tell him that there was a tip and that someone had supplied evidence suggesting that he was responsible for the death of Kimo Akamai," the chief offered.

"Sure," Dag said, "but what happens when you let him go and he comes back up to his bungalow, which is actually attached to mine? Exactly how do I handle that?"

"Let me handle it," the chief said. "I was not made chief because I failed at interrogation."

For some reason unknown to Dag, he agreed to allow the chief to handle the situation. He and Cary stayed at his place with Annie and Jack that evening. They saw Gates leave his place, and Annie said, "Hey, where's that clown going without us?"

Cary and Dag looked at one another and then told Jack and Annie to prepare themselves for the surprise of their lives.

CHAPTER 60

Breaking Hearts

Dag began, "Do you guys remember yesterday when one of you wanted coffee and so the two of you took off to the convenience store to get coffee?"

Annie and Jack nodded, listening attentively.

"Well," Dag continued, "you discovered that the one store out there by the University of West Oahu was closed on weekends because the owners were Seventh Day Adventist, right?"

"Yeah, so?" Annie said.

"So when Gates and I were headed to the airport to come to visit you guys in San Francisco, we were nearly at the airport when he said he'd forgotten his wallet at the convenience store earlier in the day and needed to go back to get it," Dag continued. "I immediately wanted to turn around, but then I said that maybe he should drop me off with the luggage and I could go through that agriculture inspection that we have to do with the luggage each time. Then he could run in and get his wallet."

"And? I don't get it," Jack said quizzically.

"He said he went there on a Saturday to get his wallet," Dag said. "He even called them from the car to see if they were open."

"Wait, wait, wait!" Annie said loudly. "I *know* you are not about to tell me that you think Gates killed Kimo, are you?"

"I am," Dag said softly. Jack just looked at Dag with a sadness that he knew they were all feeling.

Cary jumped into the conversation. "There are other circumstances as well. He began to talk negatively about Kimo to me and to no one else, and as a former detective, he is holding onto unrealistic scenarios that would link others to the crime. I mean, even a mediocre detective would have moved off some of these suspects. I didn't say anything to him because I respected him, and yet as the investigation continued, I felt a pressing uneasiness. I think Dag and I came up with this conclusion at the same time yet in different places. When I went over to Dag's the next day, we sat in silence for a moment, each of us knowing what the other was thinking."

"I simply cannot believe this," Annie said. Jack nodded in agreement.

"And we are telling you now," Cary said, "because the four of us need to be ready to react depending upon what is about to happen. We went to the police station, and the chief is talking to Gates right now. I have no idea if Gates will come back here or if he will be held. Knowing that someone else knows, I have no idea what he will do. We need to be prepared."

"And how do we do that?" Jack asked.

Cary said, "I am hoping that the chief will call as soon as he finishes talking with Gates to tell us the outcome. If he lets him go, he will be back up here shortly and we will need to have a plan."

At that moment, there was a knock on Dag's door, and the group looked fearfully at the door and at one another.

CHAPTER 61

Bravery in the Face of Fear

Dag slowly walked to the door and was relieved yet puzzled to find the chief of police standing there.

"You startled us," Dag said. "We thought you might be John Gates. Of course, he never knocks at my door, so I should have known better."

"Just wanted you to know that he's being held," the chief explained, "but he has a strange request."

"Oh?" Dag followed.

"Yes, he wants to talk with you," the chief added. "Now, sir, you need not do this unless you want to do so. It is completely your decision."

"No, I want to talk to him," Dag said. "Maybe he can explain to me some reason why he would do this thing. Did he confess?"

"He asked for a lawyer, and that is all," the chief replied, "but he did not give one word otherwise—no regrets, no anger, and no questions about who reported him. Maybe he has his own answers or feels something I am not seeing, but to me he looks like a man who has been caught. If anything, he looked surprised at first and then immediately resigned to the fact that it was over."

"When does he want to see me, and is it okay if my friends tag along?" Dag asked.

"Well, why don't we do it this way—you bring everyone, and we will consult with him when we all get there?" the chief proposed.

"Works for me. So we are going now?" Dag asked again.

"Sure. Let's get this done," the chief said, immediately turning to go to his vehicle. The group, having heard the entire conversation, immediately left behind the chief.

Of course, the trip to the police station was short, but it was particularly brief today. Dag assumed this was because he didn't know if he was more fascinated or more pensive about meeting Gates. What Dag dreaded most was the moment of first contact. He was quite an empathetic individual, and so were Annie and Jack, and they were all uneasy. It was strange to all of them that they were about to see either a good friend or a complete stranger. Based upon current events, they had no idea which one.

CHAPTER 62

The Dear Friend We Never Knew

They entered the police station with trepidation. It isn't every day that you meet a friend whom you just discovered had murdered someone, and that friend lived next door. Dag in particular was hesitant and even considered leaving, as this event was painful to the point of physical illness.

The chief led them down the corridor that they had seen before to an interrogation room that was well lit and actually stark. There was no décor, which they expected, but it was cold, sterile, and soon to be filled with nothing but words, words that could not describe the intensity in the room nor the sadness that hung over the meeting like those clouds that often settled down on top of Dag's bungalow on foggy days. The difference was that on those days, Dag settled in with the clouds for hot tea and a day of work or relaxation. These imaginary clouds were different, ominous, symbolizing death, the death of many things.

Gates was seated at a large table with eight chairs, looking straight ahead and appearing to be totally inside himself. Then he looked to the floor, then again straight ahead. With the chief present, the guard in the room backed toward the wall behind Gates, never taking his eyes off him.

The chief began, "Mr. Gates has requested your presence here today. I do not fully know why or what his plans are concerning this conversation, yet I do know that there will be no untoward behavior from any party in this room. The moment this becomes anything other than a quiet conversation, it ends. My understanding is that it was fine with all parties to have Dr. Dag Peyton, Mr. Jack Gray, Ms. Annie Wright, and Mr. Cary Rogers in the room, correct?" Everyone in the room nodded except for Gates, who looked up at the chief and then back down as if to acquiesce.

The chief turned and motioned for Dag, Annie, Jack, and Cary to be seated across from Gates, and the chief moved to the side of the table where Gates was and sat down next to him. He turned to John Gates and said, "Do you have something you want to say?"

It took Gates a full two minutes to even acknowledge that anyone else was in the room. Finally, he fidgeted in his chair for a moment, still as if he were sitting in the room alone. It appeared that he felt as if he were uncomfortable not having control, and his delay in speaking was a way of gaining back some of that control. Still taking a moment to soak in the magnitude of these events, he squirmed once again in his chair. After a bit more delay, the chief said quietly but firmly, "We are ready."

CHAPTER 63

The Most Important Words We Hope We Never Hear

Gates's Confession

John Gates sat with a stone silence that was frightening to the group. There was a coldness in Gates' eyes as he stared to the floor. One might think it to be fear, and yet his face became resolute to the point of being crazed. Dag had personally never experienced seeing someone with a face that was saying so much while seemingly expressionless. Just as the mood in the room was becoming more and more morose, Gates spoke in a soft and raspy tone, his words, his expression, his entire demeanor showing no signs of remorse:

"From the time I was a kid, I loved cops and robbers. I was always the robber, and being the robber, it was incumbent upon me to find ways to escape, to free myself from the shackles of daily living, to try any way possible to circumvent the law and seek out the best way to escape, to find freedom in a way that no one was expecting.

"Later, as a teenager and then as a young adult, I became obsessed with novels in which a sinister character had perpetrated the perfect crime. These stories enthralled me, absorbed all my attention. In later years, I recall reading these books and thinking, *If they'd just made this move or that move, they'd have escaped. They'd have beaten the system. They'd have won.*

"There were lucid times when I would tell myself that this type of winning wasn't really winning. It was, in fact, losing in the worst way, because I'd heard so many times that we never really win when we take advantage of another. To me, it seems now that there is a black mark in the sky that I can never get out from under. I can never be me again. It has become a part of me. Now and forever the world will see me for one act of evil." Then he held his head down as if he were crying, and yet when his head arose, there was a grin on his face that exuded evil, that defied goodness, that marked him as a person Dag and his friends did not know.

Gates continued, "Over time, I began to sense that the part of me that felt a sense of guilt when I would concoct these ways of committing the perfect crime was slowly ebbing away, never again to be retrieved. And it all became more and more inescapable in my mind that this was my fate as I became a detective and pored over volumes and volumes of cases at the precinct in an effort not to solve the crimes but rather to discover how the perpetrator slipped up and what could have been done to make it the perfect crime."

Gates looked up at the police chief, then to others in the room, and finally toward Dag and the rest of the group that he'd lived with, become friends with, and trusted, as they trusted him. Dag was certain that Gates was going to express some kind of remorse, but no. His expression was one of reality setting in and facing that reality, as one does when he would see a horrific accident and know that he had to assist rather than back away.

Gates again continued, "When I came here and camped out on Dag's couch for a few weeks, I came to really enjoy the island and the lifestyle it afforded a newly retired guy like me. I could spend time in the great outdoors hiking, running, everything. Then Dag introduced me to Kimo Akamai, and I spent more time inside than I ever thought I would, listening to his words of wisdom, his gentle approach to life, his oneness with the universe." To Dag, Gates stated these words in a strange, almost sarcastic, way.

Dag couldn't tell when Gates made that comment if he was admiring Kimo or mocking him. Dag was perplexed, as he considered himself an observant person, and he'd never had a hint that there was a conflict between Kimo and Gates. Maybe there was not, which made Gates's actions seem that much more sinister.

Gates continued, "So here I had met a man who was unassuming, for all practical purposes a loner, and who appeared to have quite a few enemies. I recall the day when the thought entered my mind that I could commit the perfect crime. I would be having a beer alone at night and think, *I wouldn't be suspected if I play my cards right. I am a former detective. I have spent my life finding people who'd done this kind of thing. I am golden.*"

Annie was visibly shaken, and for the first time in all the years he'd known her, Dag felt as if he wanted to put his arm around her to comfort her. But Dag decided she'd never go for that. She was a tough one, her own person, independent, with no need for that type of support. Just as he'd fully decided against it, he felt her hand on his arm. If this were a different situation, and less serious, Dag could hear Jack saying, "Well what do you know? She *is* human." Dag just turned his attention back to Gates, as did Jack and Cary.

Gates remained stoic, dead in the eyes, as he said some of the coldest statements almost in a businesslike manner. "I told Dag I'd forgotten my wallet at the convenience store that I had gone to earlier in the day. It was in between the bungalows and the airport, so I thought I could easily get back to Kimo's place and do this. And everything was going my way. Dag thought I was going to get my wallet, no one else on island knew me, except for Kimo of course, Kimo would be alone, many people appeared to not care for Kimo Akamai, so no one would be looking for him for a while, and I would have the alibi of being far away, not even on island, and I could have Dag vouch for me if necessary."

Dag said quickly, "But you did not suggest my going to the airport while you took my car back for your wallet. I did. So how could this have all been part of the plan?"

Gates responded coldly, "If you hadn't suggested it before we reached the exit to turn around, I would have. This falling into place was just another thing that made the whole process seem like a ripe opportunity. Also, I had access to a gun that was already in police inventory, and I could replace it after the fact with ease. When I went down to get some things for the trip earlier in the day, I was actually just setting up my story about going to the convenience store, but I also went to the police station with my pass as a former detective and took the gun from the inventory."

Dag interjected, "I noticed some strange actions, not major ones but ones I attributed to your memory loss."

"There is no memory loss," Gates said with a smirk on his face, apparently happy that he fooled someone. "As soon as I had it in my head that I was going to do this, I began this story of being forgetful. You might recall that we'd take off for a movie or to eat, and I would forget this and that and have to run back to my place to get something. Not once did I actually forget anything. I concocted the whole episode so that you would subconsciously not suspect me and in fact explain away my occasional absences, and once I had it planned out how I would do it all, it fit in perfectly with my forgetting my wallet at the convenience store. You asked me when I dropped you off at the airport and went back to the convenience store to pick you up some Haribo Peaches. After I had done what I went to do, I stopped at the drug store and got them for you. Yes, I had my tracks covered."

Dag continued, as if he could figure out something that would somehow make Gates innocent, "But long before all this, on your first trip out with Annie and Jack, you had forgotten which day you were supposed to leave to fly out here. That could not have been a game."

"No," Gates said, "that just happened to occur. I only got the days confused because I was wrapping up loose ends at the precinct, giving instructions to the managers at the restaurant, etc. Just too busy, that's all. It was not part of the plan but ended up being something that corroborated my fake story about the memory issues."

"But there were suspects that we researched. All that was just part of the game?" Annie asked.

"Of course," Gates replied. "Remember when we all went to the farmers' market and broke up and talked to different individuals to see who might have interacted with Kimo Akamai? I came back and said that there was a woman packing up her car at the market who said she recalled Kimo having a fairly heated conversation with a man in a suit with a political button with short dirty blond hair? That was all a sham. I had already seen Jason Barr and known his connection with Sloan Ender and decided we could pin things on him for a time and no one would be the wiser."

"Wait," Cary said. "How did Kimo get the paint under his fingernails?"

"Well, when he saw me there about to shoot him, I moved into close range to muffle the sound," Gates said. "I was so close, in fact, that he grabbed the gun and apparently scraped some of the inventory paint off and under his fingernails. Then after I shot him, I walked outside to see if anyone was the wiser, and seeing no one, I went back into Kimo's place. He was still alive, and since I had shot him in that nook over by the corner, he had reached up to scrape the painting of the police department that was hanging on the wall, perhaps out of a loss of balance, or perhaps to give someone a clue that the perpetrator might be connected to the police somehow. After I made sure he was dead, I then took the painting and placed it back onto the wall."

"So all the info about the man at the farmers' market arguing with Kimo, all the info about Sloan Ender..." Jack began.

"You made it all up," Dag said.

"Sure did," Gates replied, almost proudly, "and it was fascinating to see everyone going through the research about the paint under Kimo's fingernails, the photos being taken, the whole thing. No one was on the right track, and it all came crashing down through one inadvertent mistake that had a great likelihood of never having been discovered. So many cases are solved by things simply not lining up. Every time I heard a suggestion for a lead to follow, I laughed inside because I knew it would come to nothing. I knew it would be a wild goose chase. I knew you wouldn't find out the truth going down that road. That is why I diligently guided you down those rabbit holes. There was nothing there, and I knew it would ultimately lead to frustration."

Jack then exclaimed loudly, "Gates! Why Kimo? Why?"

"Because all the signs pointed to the perfect crime, and Kimo was in the middle of it. There would be many suspects, and all I would have to do is watch the fireworks," Gates replied. He then looked up at the group with an evil look that no one would ever want to see on the face of another human being. It was a look of satisfaction, of almost getting away with it, of surprising and shocking his friends. Yet rapidly yet quite briefly, the evil look turned to one of regret—not that he had committed this terrible offense but that he'd, in fact, been caught. He briefly shook his head in disgust, at times almost appearing as if he didn't know how to feel about all the events. Then the evil appeared yet again, as if it were flashes of a wasting disease that was going to overtake the man they once knew and respected. Seeming to find some kind of joy in shocking his friends, he continued.

"When we left your place for the airport, you were looking for Kimo," Gates said, seeming to enjoy giving the play-by-play. "His place was dark, but I had noticed him go inside earlier. When I walked to the other side of the building to get your mail out of your box, I noticed that he was out on his lanai painting. You couldn't see that from where you were, looking inside his front door. It just looked dark and empty. It was as if all the pieces were falling into place. You would leave a note for him, thinking he wasn't at home, and I could come back to take action knowing that you would have it in your mind that he was gone when we left." Gates said the words building up to this detail with such passion. It was as if he were a narrator in a horror movie, chilling the audience, with himself becoming quite excited with each gruesome detail.

Annie, Jack, and Dag were speechless. Jack had actually reached the point of having a sick feeling in the pit of his stomach. It was so knotted and so painful that to him it felt like a cancer that would overtake him at any moment. There was such a feeling of incredulity that Annie and Jack and Dag wondered if it would truly affect their minds, damaging them in a way from this time forward, making them permanently cynical, eternally untrusting, forever bitter and disappointed.

Dag wanted to believe that John Gates had experienced an episode of temporary insanity and that these actions could in no way define the Gates they knew and had grown to love as a dear friend.

Yet there was no remorse, and the explanation of how he planned and premeditated the act of killing Kimo Akamai was too logically planned out, too much a part of what Gates had been all his life. It was part of who he actually was, and Dag was internally horrified that he had provided days and weeks of shelter to a man who was responsible for ending the life of a man whom Dag respected, trusted, and wanted to protect.

"Are you sorry that you were not able to piece this together more quickly?" Gates said, awaiting an answer as if he were testing Dag.

"No, I am sorry that Kimo Akamai doesn't get to live anymore," Dag replied.

Dag stood in disbelief, as if he should have been astute enough to sense that Gates had this side of him that was willing to kill an innocent man simply for the thrill of having committed the perfect crime. He wanted to run from the room, which to him would signify running away from this terrible truth that his mind kept rejecting. And just when he thought it couldn't get worse, Gates added, "I would have committed the ultimate crime if it hadn't been for Annie and Jack discovering that the convenience store that I used in my story was closed on Saturdays. The moment they came back from getting coffee and said that store was closed on Saturdays, I felt a crack in the armor, a glitch in my story. Dag, having heard that, obviously put two and two together, and the suspicion began."

Dag found the words to say, "This clue was certainly not something I was searching for. It actually found me and crept into my thoughts while I was going in and out of sleep. In fact, I tried to suppress the thought of it, but it was forcing itself upon me. I didn't want to think this. I didn't want to know it."

"Well, you do know it," Gates said softly, "and you can't unknow it." Then Gates just snickered, having been overcome by a sinister personality that Dag feared and despised. He was not fearful of the presence but rather more fearful of the possibility that anyone could have this inside them.

Annie and Jack left the room in sheer disbelief and disappointment, and Cary followed to try to comfort them. The only ones left in the interrogation room were the police chief, the guard, Dag, and Gates. Out of nowhere, Gates motioned for Dag to come closer across the table. Dag felt drawn in to hear what Gates had to say. To release some of the anger, fear, and sadness, Dag spoke first to Gates in a kind way, saying, "John, what can I do?"

Gates's demeanor changed abruptly from eerie to sad, and Dag noticed the slightest hint of a tear in Gates's eye. Gates's countenance immediately turned back to a cruel demeanor that Dag almost feared as he stated one final statement to Dag. With a voice of resolute evil, Gates stated, "I don't ever want to see any of you again."

Dag arose slowly from the table, straightened his shirt by pulling down on the tail of the shirt, and stated with confidence, "Done." And with that one word, Dag turned to make his way to the door.

"Is it really that easy for you?" Gates said, seemingly wanting for it to be more difficult for Dag for some reason.

Dag felt as if he should turn and deliver a final soliloquy to Gates, telling him how his arbitrary decision ended a life, shocked his friends, and changed the lives of countless others, but instead he continued walking, realizing that he was no longer dealing with John Gates. He was dealing with the presence of pure evil, and he refused to acknowledge its power.

As he was walking, Dag recalled Martin Luther, the famous church reformer from the 1500s. Luther was said to have such faith that, one evening, he was sleeping, when he was awakened by a noise, rolled over in bed, and there beside his bed was Satan standing before him. Luther simply looked at him, said "Oh, it's you," and turned over and went back to sleep. Dag decided to take a note of this wise move by not giving the evil in the room what it wants. It wanted fear, it wanted power, it wanted control. Dag would not allow for this to occur. As far as Dag Peyton was concerned, John Gates was no longer there.

While Dag had no way of knowing this at the time, his resolute one-word comment to Gates was something he'd regret for the rest of his life. In later years, he would recall the look of pain and sadness in Gates's eyes and wonder if John Gates could have been saved, if in fact Gates still occupied that body. It was as if Gates were Dr. Jekyll and Mr. Hyde, and even Gates himself had no idea when one would regress and the other would appear. As Dag entered the hallway and began to focus again on his surroundings, he was overtaken by Cary, who appeared to be the one in control in this entire scenario, perhaps because of his years as a police consultant, and perhaps because he had known Gates for the least amount of time and could therefore separate himself from Gates and any friendship that might have been forming.

"Dag, I need you to help me with Jack and Annie," Cary began.

It sounded like a misplaced sentence to Dag, as he never perceived either of his friends to be in need of help. Still, Dag mustered up the presence of mind to say, "What do you need me to do?"

Then Cary said something that did make sense. "Dag, these two have known Gates for a while, and they are putting up a strong front and acting as if they are unaffected by these events. You are their close friend. You need to somehow let them know it's okay to express how they are feeling about this. They too are suffering the loss of a friend."

Without a word to Cary, he motioned for Cary to join him and went over to Annie and Jack. "Okay, guys," Dag said matter-of-factly, "I know it's mid-afternoon and you haven't had lunch, but don't eat anything right now. I am in the mood for my mother's King Ranch Chicken, and I am going to whip up a batch of it for an early dinner." Then he turned to Cary and said, "And you're coming, too. You can stay over tonight with us. No need to head back to your place tonight. Here's what we are going to do. We are going to eat as much as we want, drink as much as we want, talk as much as we want, and be together. We all need it, and that's final. Let's go to the store. I have some things to pick up."

The group followed him out without a word, they got into Dag's car without a word, and they drove to the market without a word. In a matter of two hours, they were eating at Dag's place, trying to capture a sense of normalcy that had alluded their grasp of late.

The dinner was pleasant, notwithstanding the cloud that hung over the group caused by recent events. The one positive thing that occurred that evening was that all four of the friends realized that the wound was too raw, too fresh to discuss, and they all made the conversation light, simple, and meaningful. It was as if they each needed a kindness in their lives right now, a peacefulness that had been severely lacking in the past days, a reassurance that the world was okay and that they would all be ok.

"Guy, that food was amazing," Cary said to Dag as he leaned back in the rocking chair on the breezeway.

"Yes, it seems to solve so many of life's ills," Dag said. "Growing up, we could have the worst day ever, and all we had to see was a batch of this coming our way, and things just seemed brighter."

"Yeah, things might be brighter, but I know I am not any lighter," Annie joked. "I ate two huge helpings of it. If I'd have known you could cook like that, I'd have been nicer to you all these years." The group snickered quietly. Despite the pall of sadness over the group, they felt a collective support that helped them to realize that they would be okay. The name of John Gates was not mentioned that evening. It was too soon.

The only conversation that went anywhere near Gates that evening was when Annie said to Dag, "Why did you make this meal and avoid talking about the horrible events of the day? Don't get me wrong. We needed it, but what made you think of it?"

"The Kennedy Assassination," Dag said.

"The what?" Annie replied.

"Yep, in a day's time, the president had been killed and LBJ had been sworn in as the new president," Dag continued. "While the focus was on JFK and Jackie and the horror of it all, not many focused on LBJ and Lady Byrd, going to Washington that very evening to face a life change that might to them seem to be insurmountable. So you know what Lady Byrd did? She walked into the kitchen and made a whole mess of fried chicken. I think she did it to introduce normalcy into a situation that was rapidly spiraling out of control."

"Makes very good sense to me, Dag," Jack said.

"Yeah, and thanks for doing that," Annie followed.

CHAPTER 64

Crossroads

The conversation slowly shifted to "what's next" for the four, and Cary began the discussion. "Well, my friends, I have to get back to Clifton Forge, Virginia, for a while. I had a life there, and I suspect that my neighbors are getting tired of looking after the place. They would never say so, but I just don't want to inconvenience them forever. Plus, I do have a job waiting there. And I can always come back to my place here. Just need to get away, I think."

"What do you do?" Jack queried. "Same thing you did here?"

"Exactly, Jack," Cary replied. "It's on a smaller scale in terms of the size of the police departments I train, but there are actually many more of them. So it all kind of evens out. It might seem to you that my work was sidelined of late, but the truth is that this has given me so many good tips for training. Besides, the chief down here in Kapolei said I was at a stopping point. What about you guys?"

"I have to get back to the city," Annie said. "I usually do some part time nursing gigs. I am sure you all know how great the demand is for nurses these days. I could work forever if I wanted, but I would rather pick up a gig here and there and not work when I don't want to work."

Jack piped in, "Yeah, I'll probably accompany our soft-spoken friend here back to the Bay Area. She needs to be monitored." Annie jokingly gave him a look of frustration.

"You know, Dag," Annie said, "there is absolutely nothing keeping you on island for now. Why don't you hop on the plane and go back with us, and then you can come back whenever you feel like it and we might even come back with you. I mean, you're working online now. You can work from anywhere, and you can stay at my place."

All three, Jack, Annie, and Cary were shocked when Dag said, "I'm in."

After Annie collected herself from her look of surprise, she said, "Excellent. You can stay with me, and so can the sidekick here if he wants." Annie pointed to Jack, and Cary laughed.

"Okay, when are we going, and why can't Cary come with us?" Jack offered.

"No can do, guy," Cary explained. "I have to be at work in three days, and I have to get settled in at my mainland home before I get back to work. If I might impose, could I get someone to take me to the airport tomorrow?"

"We insist," Jack said, jumping in and offering up Dag's car. Dag laughed.

"Excellent. When will you guys head back to the city?" Cary asked.

"It depends. Guys, how long can you give me to get my act together?" Dag said.

"Tell you what," Annie offered. "Why don't we plan on leaving in three days? We're in no hurry, and you can take your time."

"Perfect," Dag said. "I think we have a plan."

CHAPTER 65

Too Many Goodbyes

The rest of the day flew, with the four friends talking until midnight. Then Cary insisted that he'd like to stay over but must go back to his place to pack, and then he took his leave, promising to be waiting for them at the appointed time.

Like everything else in life these days, the night and the next morning passed quickly, and they piled into Dag's Subaru and headed to Cary's place.

The trio drove up to Cary's modest but well-kept home, and as they drove up, they saw Cary waiting for them, bag in hand. As they approached, Annie said, "Why didn't he just stay with us while we were working on the case?"

"I don't know," Dag replied. "We didn't know him. We'd only met him on the plane when we were returning from San Francisco. We didn't know we'd have any kind of connection until he appeared at Kimo's memorial service. Come to find out, there are several reasons, I guess."

"I guess we are thinking that because he turned out to be such a quality guy," Jack said.

"Yeah, he certainly became one of us," Dag said. "And not only that. The night I woke up in the middle of my sleep with eyes wide open and realized that it was Gates who'd done this, I wondered if I'd get any of you to believe me. The next morning, Cary was at my door, and I could tell in his eyes before we said a word to one another that he'd figured it out too. It was that kind of moment where not a word is spoken and still you feel totally in sync. I mean, words were totally unnecessary. We just sat there…knowing something we didn't want to know. So scary. I mean it was actually frightening. Haven't felt that way since I was a kid."

The car pulled over, and Cary opened the door to the back seat and dropped his bag between himself and Jack. "What's up, guys?" he said casually, with a tone that affirmed the comfort level among them all.

"Oh, we were just talking about how we think you are possibly a halfway decent individual," Annie said.

"High praise coming from you," Cary shot back in his low-key manner. The group laughed.

"You now know Annie like we know Annie. Welcome. You'll never be the same," Jack said.

"You know, don't you, that I can reach back there and slap you silly, but that would be overkill," Annie retorted.

"If I had feelings that would hurt," Jack shot back.

The ride to the airport was pleasant indeed, with all the occupants of the car feeling somehow closer, as if all these events made them want to hold their friends close to them and never let go. They had all been attacked by the gnawing reality that someone from among them had been someone they in many ways didn't know. They were all still trying to shake themselves back to the calmer reality they'd known a short time ago.

As they reached the airport, Cary hopped out with his bag as soon as they had completely stopped. "Not much for long goodbyes, especially in this case," he said, his voice trailing off.

At once, Annie, Jack, and Dag jumped out of the car as well, and Annie said, "Understood, buster, but if you think you're leaving without a hug, you've got another thing coming." Cary resigned himself to Annie's resolute demeanor and opened his arms wide. Each of them hugged Cary, and as they let go, there was a tear in Cary's eye.

"Okay, enough," Cary said, smiling. "If you guys get to Roanoke, Virginia, give me a call. You never know what mess we can get into there."

"Well," Jack countered, "you never know what the future will bring. I mean, who'd have thought we'd end up in Hawaii solving murder cases. Clearly, catching up with you in the future is a distinct possibility."

"I would be pleased to host," Cary said, bowing with affected words as a Southern gentleman. Without another word, he walked away, raising his hand over his shoulder and not looking back.

"What a pleasure to know that guy," Annie said.

"Wow, Annie," Jack said, smiling, "you never said anything like that about us."

"Yeah," Dag said.

"There's a reason for that, you clowns," Annie said, hopping back into the car.

"She got us again, Dag," Jack said.

All Dag could muster was, "Yep."

The ride home was uneventful and mostly silent.

The trio, having made it back from taking Cary to the airport, seem to collectively not know what to do with themselves. Dag was at the end of the term with some time off, and Annie and Jack, who both were usually quite spontaneous about finding something to bring joy to their lives, felt and appeared to be resigned to quiet contemplation. Then Dag spoke up.

"Guys, I usually count on the two of you to lift me out of whatever I am doing and help me to engage with the world again," he said, "and you're not doing your job." Dag smiled briefly and sat down beside them.

"You know what?" Jack said, breaking the seemingly oppressive silence that was taking over the late afternoon. "I have watched planes take off from the airport, and I have always wondered if they can see us from up there."

"I guess it's possible," Dag added. "In fact, I know it is. I have been looking down from there on trips back here to the island, and when they take that swing west before heading straight to the airport, I can almost always make out my place and some people milling around, that is, unless it is cloudy."

At once the trio realized that Jack wanted to get up and do something. So the three of them wandered out to the breezeway edge and looked up into the sky. The entire activity had no point but to get them engaging in life again after such a horrific event that this same life can bring. Mindless as it was, they breathed in the sea breeze and while feeling a bit more refreshed, the very exhaling of the air made their efforts seem futile, not desiring to become more energized.

Then Dag decided that, just as Gates chose what he did, he too would decide to attempt to reengage in life.

CHAPTER 66

Moving On

Dag stood on the edge of the breezeway of his bungalow, looking out at the ocean, just in time to see a plane fly over his home and then turn sharply east. Based on the timing and the flight that he knew was taking Cary back to Roanoke, he inadvertently waved with his hand high in the air. He knew the odds of Cary seeing his goodbye were slim, but still he felt compelled to try anyway. With Annie and Jack on the breezeway edge beside him, he felt a continuing appreciation for his old friends, a new appreciation for their new friend Cary, and deep and lasting sadness at the circumstances that took John Gates away from them all.

What makes people do what they do? Dag thought, knowing that if he knew the answer to that he could make millions.

At just that moment, Annie broke her silence with an uncharacteristic softness. "Dag," she almost whispered, "what do you make of all this?"

Dag paused, knowing the trio was all of one mind in what they were thinking. Then he replied, "I have tried to come up with some wisdom that would help me out on this and maybe give me a modicum of peace, but the only thing I can come up with is…Judy Collins."

"Judy who?" Jack said, puzzled.

"You know," Annie said, "that folk rock singer from the sixties. That's whom you're talking about, right?" Annie had turned toward Dag.

"Yep," Dag responded. "She sang that song called 'Both Sides Now,' and in it she said, *But something's lost but something's gained in living every day.*

"The way I see it, we lost Gates and gained Cary, and there is a reason why that I will never understand. Whatever reason we discover is never going to make us happy about the outcome of losing Gates, so we need to appreciate what we have gained and stop trying to figure it out. We just need to remember that we lose some of life every day we live, but we gain something in friendship, wisdom, knowledge, and hopefully, peace of mind." Then there was a long period of silence.

"Anybody want coffee?" Jack finally said.

Annie and Dag nodded, and the trio slipped inside Dag's bungalow. Soon the scent of freshly brewed coffee and the mellow sounds of Judy Collins were wafting through Dag's kitchen window and into the twilight air.

It's life's illusions I recall,
I really don't know life…at all.…

EPILOGUE

Time went on for the amateur sleuths, and Dag followed his long-time friends to the Bay Area for some R & R. Dag worked from Annie's loft, which was formerly his loft in decades past, Annie took the occasional nursing assignment, and Jack filled in at Bart's occasionally and took a real estate assignment here and there.

Life seemed to be moving smoothly as they adjusted to the loss of John Gates. In time, Dag headed back to his home on island, and life progressed. The trips between coasts were frequent and welcomed.

The trio ultimately made their way to Clifton Forge, Virginia, to see Cary as well as to Davenport, Iowa, to visit DJ.

Many adventures awaited the group throughout the rest of their lives until it was time for them to find adventures in a better place. Dag found himself eternally grateful for all the joys and sorrows in life that led him to his path, for he would not have traded it for the world.

ABOUT THE AUTHOR

Dr. M. T. Outlaw is a professor, writer, and consultant living in the state of Hawaii.

CPSIA information can be obtained
at www.ICGtesting.com
Printed in the USA
LVHW051400250820
664155LV00003B/301

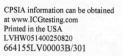

9 781662 404948